GW00792227

HUNGER

A Novel

HUNGER
A Novel

AMRITLAL NAGAR

Translated from the
Original Hindi by

SARALA JAG MOHAN

ASIA PUBLISHING HOUSE

(a division of Books From India UK Limited)
45 Museum Street
LONDON WCIA ILR

First published in UK 1990

© **Amritlal Nagar**

All rights reserved. No part of this book may be reproduced or transmitted in any form or by any means, electronic or mechanical, including photocopying or by any information storage and retrieval system, without permission in writing from the publishers.

ISBN 0-948724-16-1

Published by Shreeram Vidyarthi for
ASIA PUBLISHING HOUSE
(a division of Books From India UK Limited)
45 Museum Street, London WCIA ILR

In arrangement with ABHINAV PUBLICATIONS
E 37, Hauz Khas New Delhi-110 016 (INDIA)

Lasertypeset by
Shagun Composers
92-B, Krishna Nagar, Street No. 4
Safdarjung Enclave
New Delhi-110029

Printers
Pooja Offset Process Private Ltd
Okhla Industrial Area, Phase I
New Delhi-110020

As Panchu Gopal Mukherji, headmaster of the Anglo-Bengali School, Mohanpur, set his foot on the verandah of the school building, he was reminded of Ganesh, Hiru Bagdi's son, who had finally died that morning after having waged a ten-day battle against malaria.

News of this death was more shattering than the fact that Panchu had been starving for the last four days. It seemed as though death had come especially to reveal itself to him. Panchu felt an utter sense of loss. The relentless reach of the famine had sapped him of strength, both mental and physical. Even so, his basic faith in life had asserted itself and Panchu could not really see how bleak the future was. Ganesh's death, for the first time, brought him face to face with what awaited himself and his family.

Suddenly a darkness descended before his eyes and Panchu reeled. His hand reached to the pillar for support and he stood there, shaken and bereft, for a few moments. Ganesh had been his first student. Memories flashed past his mind. He had just passed the intermediate examinations. He wanted to study further. He would apply for a government scholarship. Then, a letter from his mother urging him to do his duty to his family. "If only I had studied further. What a bright career I had before me! Principal Jordan would have got me that scholarship... But would that have changed the situation?" Panchu was jolted out of his daydreams. And then he argued, " I would have been in England. There would have been no house, no property left. What happiness would an ICS degree have brought?"

He was glad he had not opted for the ICS. Too many ICS types had stomped their Dawson boots on the head of this unfortunate country. Servants of the people had turned masters, their origin and duty duly forgotten.

He too would have become a civil servant. He too would have inspected the starving people as an SDO. He too would have accepted the hospitality of zamindar Dayal Babu, imbibing Scotch whisky and polishing off plates of delectables. Monai the bania with the grinning face would have helped government officials bulge their pockets. And in no time, like a contagious disease, the greater part of those pockets would have passed into the pockets of SDO Panchu Gopal Mukherji, ICS!

Panchu was filled with repugnance. Turning his eyes away from the town of Mohanpur that sprawled beyond the school campus, he walked slowly towards a classroom. By the door a government poster exhorted: Grow More Food. "For whom?" asked Panchu, in disgust. And with one movement of the hand, he tore the poster off. The mood of triumph, however, did not last long. "I hope nobody saw me," Panchu worried. "Suppose someone saw? That policeman near Monai's shop... I'm doomed if he saw. He will promptly come and hold out his hand or else he will threaten to report me. But how can I give anything to the wretched fellow? Why would my family be starving then? But why should that rascal care about our plight? The whole village thinks I have amassed a fortune that lies buried in my house." With a furtive look this way and that, Panchu stepped into the classroom.

Silence hung in the air. Four long rows of desks and benches badly stained with ink and laid thick with dust; a chair, a table, three maps of Bengal, India and Europe on the walls; a globe atop a small stool in one corner; on the blackboard the words of an English poem. The peon had been on leave for a week and nobody had swept the school premises in his absence. Panchu had not done it either. Although there had been a time, those Saturdays not long past, when he and his boys together set about sprucing up the school. A pale smile flickered on Panchu's lips. The hubbub of those days, the excitement, the glory... Ah, sweet dream...

Panchu dropped into the dusty chair. He rested his arms on the table and lowered his head. "What if they close down the school?" This horrible thought sliced through the coat of illusions he had deceived himself with thus far. Ganesh's death had been no illusion and the question stared him grotesquely in the face.

The school, Panchu's only means of supporting a family comprising 11 members. What if this school closed down, what then? He had wanted to marry off his young sister Tulsi this year. Who imagined a famine such as this? Would it never end? Or was this the end of the universe? A blanket of darkness seemed to be dragging Panchu into its eddying vortex. "Am I dying?" wondered Panchu.

"No, how can I die," Panchu thought as he fought the strange sensation in his head. "Ganesh had malaria on top of his hunger, whereas I have only been starving. Mother and others too have been starving. As if it is so extrordinary to go hungry for four days ...After all we are Hindus and we observe many fasts during the four monsoon months. In any case, I should be able to get some rice by this evening... No, there's nothing to worry about."

Panchu mustered up courage and raised his head from the table. Then, as though to free himself from the grip of a deathlike stupefaction, he pushed himself up and walked up and down the room. He took one round, then another, but as he started on the third, he stopped short. "No, I'm not giddy, " he assured himself, "I'm just standing.... Oh Lord! Just look at the dust on this table," and with that, Panchu pulled out a handkerchief from his pocket and started cleaning the desk at which he sat. How nice and shiny these desks had looked when they were new. And now look at the ink stains! "But this is bound to happen" Panchu muttered. "After all, boys will be boys." Ganesh had been the brightest of all his boys... "Children will be careless. Were we not careless?... But I used to be so careful. And these rascals—they don't even bother to lock their desks!"

Panchu opened the drawer. There was a slate in it, with a pound-shilling-pence sum worked out. Through force of habit, Panchu checked the figures—at every step the 'answer' showed an extra two numbers. The teachers' instinct in Panchu was aroused. He muttered in exasperation and almost flung the slate aside. Had the owner of the slate been on the scene, he would have received a sound thrashing alright.

Panchu looked in the drawer again. This time he located a piece of paper, a cutout, the masterpiece of some unsung artist among the boys, created with thick and thin pens and colour pencils obviously for the entertainment of his class fellows. On top was drawn a circle with two ears that had been cut down; a tuft jutting out of the cap, at somebody's request, as it were, but falling withing the circle of the head, as also two eyes complete with spectacles and ear-rests; a long stroke for a nose topped off with a long moustache. The neck given the finishing touches with the help of his father's blade served as a primitive bridge to join the small circle to a large circle.

The labour that had gone into shaping two hands and legs perfectly from the large circle was evident. Below the legs ran the caption in English: This is Kanai Master.

Panchu burst out laughing. "These children are such devils," he said to himself. Greatly amused, he pulled out the drawer further wondering what more treasures lay in wait. There was a page torn out from an English textbook: Lesson 24, Humpty-Dumpty... "Rascals! Do they ever read? Simply fool around with their books!" On the other side of the paper was scribbled a leave application in Bengali, signed D.R. in English. Below this was written in English, 'Granted,' signed G.K.C., in bold characters and dated 27-1-43! "G.K.C.—Who the hell is GKC?" Panchu puzzled, trying to figure out which of his students was a great one that had granted leave. "Oh Gopal! I see! Aunt no. 8's nephew!" The retired sub-postmaster Ramtanu Babu was Panchu's uncle and neighbour. The ill-fated Ramtanu Babu had lost seven wives—death had smothered each one up. Only his eighth now threatened to survive even the terrible famine. Gopal was her brother's son.

Panchu's heart was filled with unexpected happiness. For a few moments he forgot his hunger, his family, Bengal, the famine. Expecting to find more treasures, Panchu pulled out the drawer fully. "What's this?" he cried in dismay. "Termites!" The joy of the moment gave way to intense pain. A sense of failure crushed him.

He turned out the drawer and examined the back. He peered under the desk. He checked other desks as well. There were clusters of termites busily eating into the furniture.

Now the school would definitely have to be closed down—all because of the termites. Some day the famine would end. And the school would be reopened. But now, even that hope seemed dim.

For the past several days, Panchu had worried about the future of his school. Attendance had started dwindling right from the last week of February. Out of one hundred and twenty-two boys, gradually twenty, twenty-five, fifty boys had left. And now, on March 19, there was not a single boy in the school. For one week now, he had been the only one at school. Sometimes, Monai's son Nyada would come to school, satchel under his arm. It was a week since Khidu, the peon, had left the town. Since then, three rooms had not been opened at all. Kanai Master had left Mohanpur for good and gone to Pachhauh in January itself. He had since been working as a craftsman.

Kanai Master was a good man. When the entire town had turned against Panchu and his school, only Kanai the blacksmith had stood by his side. Panchu vividly recalled the time when he and Kanai studied together at Debu Pandit's school. Kanai could not afford to study further. But by the time he had left Debu Pandit's school, he had learnt to read and write (in Bengali). Later, Kanai's father withdrew him from school and trained him so well that Kanai became an adept craftsman. He earned a good name in four or five villages around. Panchu had secured a first class in college and Kanai had even heard that he was going to England on a government scholarship. When Panchu arrived in this town, Kanai felt proud of having been his classmate. It was another matter that they met rarely, because his work kept him busy.

Kanai used to subscribe to the Bengali weekly *Desh*. He would read the magazine so thoroughly that he could even reel off the advertisements from memory. If Panchu provoked him about any poem, story, article, play or even advertisement, he would promptly recite it verbatim.

Once Panchu challenged Kanai to learn by heart Bankim Chandra's entire novel *Anandmath*. Kanai made no comment. He simply took the book and went home. He was back after four days and flaunting the book in front of Panchu, started spewing the contents of the book from the first page, not omitting even the punctuation and the misprints. He finished the book in three hours. Only after he had listed other publications of the publisher and comments of praise as well as the prices of soft-cover and hard-cover editions did he stop to drink water. This feat soon became a legend.

The entire town had opposed Panchu when he started his school. On the one hand, he had to keep the school going and on the other hand to pay frequent visits to the city for Principal Jordan's help and advice. At home only his mother stood by him. "Don't worry, my son," she said: "God tests our strength only in times of trouble. He will help on His own when He wishes to be generous."

One day, Kanai came to Panchu and announced theatrically, "Your courage has inspired my faith in you. You're our Napoleon Bonaparte!" Then, advancing towards Panchu, he whispered: "I've no savings, brother. But with whatever I have, I can help you run the school in whatever way you suggest."

Panchu was in real need of financial help. Kanai said confidently: "I shall teach the boys whatever I've learnt. You don't worry. Go to the city and get some help for the school. I shall manage things here. But master, you must make your school so good that even big sahebs are forced to come all the way to see it. Then alone the people of this town will realize that those who are devoted to learning are no ordinary creatures." And he patted Panchu on the back.

Suddenly Panchu's hopes ran high. In a flash he realized that his mother's God had come to him in the form of Kanai when he was totally disheartened. Then Kanai's voice broke into wonderment: "Panchu Babu, I wrongly called you Napoleon. Actually, I wanted to call you Shakespeare. Panchu Babu, when it comes to learning, you are no way behind Shakespeare. He educated people by writing poetry. You're doing so by opening the school."

He paused and then remarked with a touch of finality: "Yes, that's so. You're our Shakespeare. Napoleon used to fight."

"Ha, ha, ha!" replied Panchu.

Hearing the sound of his own loud laughter, Panchu came back to consciousness. He saw in front of him the drawer full of termites. Kanai had left. Govind Master had left in the first week of March. "I can't manage on twelve rupees, Panchu Babu! Let somebody go and ask zamindar Dayal Babu if one can live without breathing—he has taken away my bullocks! Far better to live by begging. At least I won't have to face the fire of four hungry stomachs!" So, Govind Master also left. Everyone had left. And now the school would be closed. "It will have to be closed. Now I don't even feel comfortable in this place," Panchu reflected. What next?

Panchu looked around with vacant eyes to find an answer to that question.

Even though not a single boy turned up, Panchu visited the school regularly. He sat there the whole day and kept entertaining his mind by thinking about long-forgotten as well as current things. But today, with the death of Ganesh, his mind was completely wearied and his thoughts turned away from the school. He could not keep his mind engaged. How could he distract his mind from the present? Where could he go?

Quite unconsciously, Panchu's hands started fiddling with termite-infested drawer. He withdrew his hands with a start. He had a sudden feeling of having committed a grave blunder by keeping his hands on that drawer with all those termites.

"This drawer ridden with termites!" he mused. "It means that swarms of termites have installed themselves here. Now they won't leave this place. And why on earth should they leave? They thrive on wood, paper etc. Man too has come to possess those things, but not as food! Oh, such injustice! Just imagine, for thousands of years since man acquired control over wood and started using it for himself, these termites must have starved. Oh, they have been starving for thousands of years—poor things!"

Tears welled up in Panchu's eyes. All through the famine he had suppressed his tears. But today, if there were tears in his eyes at the thought of the terrible plight of those white ants that had been famished for thousands of years, it did not mean his patience was running out. No, his patience was enduring. It was unflinching.

And, in order to strengthen that feeling, he started musing in superlatives in English about his shedding tears over the famished termites: "Just imagine, their children, sons, daughters, nephews, nieces—yes, nieces too. Yes, yes, nieces too should be there, ought to be..."

Panchu experienced a slight stirring of conscience within himself. He felt that he was swayed by his own thoughts. But he was not happy about that inner stirring. He had no other means to distract his mind except by entertaining illusions. He reflected: "We've starved the white ants and now the white ants are starving us... remember this always, my boy! There's limit to everything... For the present, you may tyrannize the white ants, but even their patience can come to an end. But, in what way can they harm you after all?"

Panchu brought his hands close to his face and looked intently at them. Since he had kept his hand in the termite-ridden drawer for so long, it was likely a couple of them had crept on his hands! "What if they've got on to my hands?" he asked himself. "They will sting. When they can eat up wood and paper, what's the problem about human flesh—soft human flesh and hot human blood? Suppose the white ants develop a taste for these? What will happen? *Arre*, so far only six persons have died of starvation, but if white ants start invading human beings, there will be six hundred deaths, six thousands, a lakh, a million, a billion, a trillion... There will be disaster, disaster!"

Panchu thus went on detracting himself. "The world is coming to an end because of white ants! Can such a thing happen?"

Then he suddenly remembered: "*Arre*, Valmiki! Imagine a human being so oblivious to his surroundings that he did not realize white ants were creeping all over his body! Nonsense! As a matter of fact, it means that this time the white ants will have victory over human beings! It will be a victory for Valmiki. Absolutely justified. In the first deluge, Manu was the only one to survive, and his progeny, the human race, proved to be worthless. This time, after the disaster, a new world will come into being, a world inhabited by Valmiki's children... This is disaster indeed brought about by white ants!"

Panchu had ceased to have any control over his mind. He felt a sudden need for some medicine to get over this weakness. What could he take? He had some aspros. One day during winter, when he had had a headache, he had sent for a strip of aspros. He had taken one dose and left the rest in the drawer of his table. They should be still there.

But suppose there were white ants in his drawer too? *Chhi!* He diverted his mind again. You can't afford to do this, Mr. P. Mukherji! he told himself. You've so much responsibility on your head—the responsibility of the whole family.

"But what am I thinking? I'm fully conscious. I've committed no wrong so far. I'm absolutely fine. Then why the medicine...the aspro tablets...?"

By this time Panchu had walked up to his table and was about to sit on the chair. The thought of Aspro tablets brought a power to his face. Objectively, he took stock of himself: "Do I have a pain anywhere—in my hands, my legs, my stomach? Do I have a headache?"

As he spoke to himself thus, he experienced pain from head to foot, in every nerve, in every pore. He felt his eyes, and his body grow hot. He brought his hand near his nose and felt his breath. His breath was hot. "I've got fever, malaria!" he said to himself.

The thought of malaria reminded him of his hunger. And again he was overcome by fear. He felt dizzy. His hands trembled and legs became numb as though there was no strength left in them.

With a terrific mental effort he stood erect. "I'm absolutely fine. I'm not ill at all," he told himself. "I've no fever. These are all futile thoughts. It's stupid of me to go on thinking about such useless things. I don't know why I'm letting my mind drift. No, no, I shall not allow such foolish thoughts to cross my mind."

Panchu immediately applied his mind to some activity so as to detract his thoughts. He looked around himself. The table and the chair were on a raised platform. Panchu narrowed his eyes to restrict the span of vision. Then, with a semi-circular movement of the head, he looked to the left and then to the right, along the edge of the platform. He saw the concrete floor at the foot of the platform. It seemed as though the builders had drawn the squares on the floor simply to give the impression that square cement slabs had been fixed on the floor.

Then he saw was the corner of a table, and his eyes passed over three or four desks. Panchu persuaded himself that the boys were present. Only after imagining the presence of his pupils could he be sure about the presence of the desks. He saw the gradually approaching light and his gaze fixed on a spot on the floor. The sunlight, somewhat dimmed, entered the room through the door. It was as if it fell on the damp floor. Panchu felt quite contented and happy.

During that brief moment of surveying the classroom Panchu's heart was filled with a happy excitement, and with that same feeling of enthusiasm, he let himself think that there were boys seated on all the benches and he had assigned some work to all of them— that he had asked them to write an essay on a cow and he was himself bending over the register on the table, calculating the tuition fees.

He put his fountain pen on the table. He unlocked the drawer and pulled it out. He found a half-full box of chalk-pieces, a duster, a bottle of black ink and a bundle of papers.

How children love to steal chalk. Everytime the drawer remained open, half a dozen pieces would disappear!

Panchu started tickling his mind: "I would like to leave this drawer open and go out for a while...but where are the boys?"

Panchu could deceive himself no longer. The truth slipped out of his mouth: "Where are the boys?"

Panchu beheld his deserted classroom in the manner of a martyr walking up to the gallows.

The room was still and silent. Four rows of unoccupied benches and desks, ink stains on the desks and layers of dust. Panchu had placed the lock on the desk in front. His attention concentrated briefly on the brass lock. One never kept a lock like that, he reflected. He saw the maps of Bengal, India and Europe, the globe kept on the stool. The poem on the blackboard was also covered with dust. Panchu felt suffocated. An intense pain, whizzing like an arrow, shot up in his heart and he thought his heart would break with the feeling of desolation, a sense of failure and inactivity. Where were the boys? Had they been in class today, he would have said: "Here, take these—take away all the chalk pieces, but come back to school. He would have parted with all his possessions to see those benches occupied.

He was infuriated by his inability to act. He flung the chalk box on the desk in front of him and as they scattered on the benches, and rolled on the floor, the sound filled his ears: thak-thak thak-thak.

Panchu looked triumphantly at these chalk pieces—as though he had humbled their pride. "Oh, their misfortune!" he philosophised. "The chalk pieces are lying today thus abandoned!" There was no one to show love for them—those naughty eyes gleaming with joy, those shrieks of delight, the jostling and wrestling with wild excitement, the boxing and fisting to grab as many chalk pieces as possible. Panchu felt as though his heart was choking. The wasted body and the mind corroded by anxiety could not bear the weight of that emotion. He experienced within him a kind of irritation that struck like a streak of lightning.

This feeling of irritation worked like smelling-salts and overpowered his state of stupor. The body refused to accept the command of the mind and started behaving in an erratic manner. His eyes smarted and his face flushed. His hands moved restlessly. He pulled out the duster and flung it aside. His hand moved towards the ink-pot, and suddenly stopped short.

He remembered that while writing a letter to Jordan Saheb day before yesterday, his pen had run dry. So, Panchu started filling ink in the fountain-pen. Suddenly a thought flashed in his mind: "This fountain-pen is luckier than I. At least it has food!"

Panchu felt something crawling in his empty stomach, like a child sobbing in sleep. His breath grew heavy. He felt depressed. But again he pulled himself up: "What's this, Mr. Panchu Gopal? Look at others—the whole town, whole of Bengal is starving!"

Whole of Bengal! Panchu's eyes roved over the map of Bengal on the wall. It had happened only a few days ago. Hardly five months had passed. How every farmer in the town was happy to sell rice at twelve rupees a maund. Not even in the good old days had fate been so kind that they could sell rice at that price! It used to be sold at three or three and a half rupees a maund. People grew blind with greed. They even sold the grains meant for their homes. Going without food for a couple of days and living with half-filled stomachs all their lives—the farmers in India had learnt to do it from birth. They had become almost indifferent to the fact that their hunger had to be satisfied. But money—oh, that was something one always dreamt to have! It was only the big people who were born with the luck of being blessed by the

Goddess of Wealth. This time, the Goddess of Wealth had been merciful to the farmer—that too on the eve of Durga Puja!

The pale faces of the farmers flushed red at the sight of bundles of hundreds and thousands of rupees. Married women's capricious demands were met and fortune smiled on goldsmiths! New clothes and new ornaments and cosmetic items—and even gramophones started playing in a few houses in the town! People began thinking in terms of building *pucca* houses. The old and the aged became impatient to visit holy places. The farmers, when they did not have money, had always imagined what they would do when they did have money. Now they could fulfil all their desires. In this euphoria of the moment, they felt greater than the big shots of the town. They felt Dayal Babu or Monai could humiliate them no more. They went crazy with the warmth of money they had come to possess.

Dayal Babu and Monai started receiving back the money they had lent. Intoxicated by the power of money, the farmers forgot on the occasion of Durga Puja that they would have to repay the money they borrowed. They started spending money for their innumerable pursuits of pleasure.

Soon came the time when farmers started receiving court summons on behalf of Dayal Babu and Monai. Like a nine days' wonder, gold and silver ornaments were gone from the bodies of the farmers' wives. The gramophones stopped playing. *Pucca* houses would now be built only in heaven! Goods worth ten rupees were sold for two rupees. Whatever grains, clothes and household things remained unsold were looted by bandits.

> People watched with mouths agape.
> Rice sold at eighteen rupees a maund!
> Rice sold at twenty-four rupees a maund!
> At thirty-five, forty rupees a maund!
> What was happening? What would happen?

Many hanged themselves. Some dead body or the other was lowered in the lake of the town every other day. People left their villages and went to the city in the hope of getting in the city money they could send home. Only a few young men remained in the villages.

Mothers consoled their hungry children: "We shall buy rice when your *Baba* sends money from the city. How will Monai give rice without money?"

Aged parents would ask the postman: "Have you brought the money order from my son? He is bound to have sent the money. You fellows from the post office have conspired to swallow our money."

Their hunger did not wait even as they kept expecting their money.

People sold their houses, they sold their fields, granaries, clothes, rags and quilts—they sold everything in order to fill their stomachs. Monai bought everything and sold rice to them in return.

After facing lathi blows from Dayal Babu's men, they could not get much fish from the ponds. Plants and leaves, grass, flesh of dogs, cats and rats, whatever was available, was consigned into the fire of the hungry stomachs. With all that, their hunger was unsatisfied. They felt hungry everyday.

At the thought of hunger, Panchu's consciousness returned. Even though he had been looking at the map of Bengal all that time, his eyes had not been seeing the map. Awakened from his thoughts, his eyes once again saw Bengal. Even from a distance, the innumerable crooked lines and the names of hundreds of towns and cities stood clear in his mind although they were too hazy for his eyes. Every village and every house must be facing the same problem of getting rice. And a Monai in every village must be demanding exorbitant rates. People must be pleading in flattering terms as they had been doing at Monai's shop. They must be pleading and prostrating before him with more than heavenly happiness. They must be hovering round him, weeping before him. And the Monai of every village must be listening to people's blessings and curses with the same nonchalance, sitting back calm and unmoved. He must be making his own calculations, unconcerned about the plight of the public. Thousands of people must be dying. Others would have deserted their villages and gone away. The boys too would have left, and schools must be deserted like his school. And the teachers...!

Panchu was reminded of his own family. For four full days, the famine had struck his home. No one in the family had eaten even a grain of rice. His ten year old sister Kanak too had forgone her share of food being given a couple of morsels and rice broth to drink. But this was not enough to fill their stomachs. They clamoured for rice all through the day. His eight month old niece Chunni was half dead, crying with hunger. She was on mother's milk, but how could the mother feed the child at her breast when she herself had nothing to eat? Even the little one was made to suck a little rice broth. Panchu's mother, father, elder brother Shibu and his wife, his own wife, his two sisters and he himself had been starving and subsisting just on water for the past four days.

Well, he would definitely get rice from Dayal Babu in the evening. But how long could things go on like that? How long would he be able to keep up his prestige? Ultimately, who would keep up his prestige and before whom? Hearths had gone cold in every house. Who was respectable and in what manner? With the exception of Monai and Dayal Babu and hardly ten others, in whose house was fire lit regularly in the kitchen? At this rate, the whole village would die with hunger and thirst. Parvati aunt died, Haren died, Tinkandi died, Ganesh died. People were dying in the town all the time. Likewise, in his family too, one by one...

In spite of himself, tears welled up in Panchu's eyes. He felt outraged by his tears—why did he have such thoughts at all? Had he nothing else to do in the world?

Panchu wiped his tears with the end of his dhoti and looked at the open drawer. Right at the back was a bundle of papers tied with a jute string. Some letters and notes, degree certificates. Once, after his elder brother had torn off one of his certificates in anger, Panchu had started keeping his personal papers in school.

Panchu looked through the papers... A certificate given by Professor Bannerji, a letter from Jordan Saheb, another letter from Jordan Saheb, a letter from Rai Bhuvan Mohan Sarkar, a letter written by Ganesh... After learning to read and write properly in Bengali, he had once gone to spend his holidays with his uncle at Dacca. He had written from there: "My respectful greetings..."

Deep within Panchu had a feeling that if he paid even the slightest attention to that letter from Ganesh, he would again start thinking about death. Till death clearly dominated his mind, he should divert his attention somewhere else...

Oh, yes! Had he not been calculating the tuition fees of the last month?

Shaking off the dust on the papers with his left hand, he pushed them to one side. The papers lay in disorder on the table. He opened the lock of the other drawer and took out both the registers. Something slipped out and fell on the platform. Panchu's eyes gleamed with delight as he sighted the aspro tablets.

Dumping the registers on the table, he bent down with alacrity and picked up the packet. There were two tablets left.

"Should I take these tablets? That is, am I feeling sick?... No, this is no sickness, just a headache. Really? Of course, with all these silly and crazy thoughts crowding my mind, won't I have a headache? Of course, my head is paining."

Panchu looked hungrily at the two white tablets in the packet. Then he tore the foil and kept both the tablets on his palm. And before any other thought would cross his mind, he promptly popped them in his mouth, as though stealthily even from himself.

"Shall I swallow? No, I must chew. At least I must feel the taste!" Crunch—crunch, he crushed between his teeth. But the tablets started dissolving. Realizing that his teeth were weak, Panchu brushed the small particles of the tablets against his palate and started dissolving them further. His mouth was filled with bitter taste as he went on dissolving the tablets in his mouth. Collecting the saliva in his mouth, he continued the process till both his cheeks bulged—so much so, his jaws started paining. Ultimately he had to swallow his saliva.

Even though bitter, Panchu's taste-starved tongue had found at least some taste after four days. He felt some kind of satisfaction.

He wanted water to drink. He went out of the classroom.

The bitter taste had gone and his tongue was gradually becoming dull again. That irked Panchu. His hunger was aggravated. The numbness in his head increased. There was a pond right behind the school. Panchu marched in that direction. Cupping both palms together, he drank water. Water hurt in the empty stomach. Yet he drank again. He drank a third time, a fourth, fifth, sixth time. The seventh time, he let the water fall back into the pond from his cupped hands.

Panchu's stomach became bloated. He dared not drink any more water. But he was not yet satisfied. He washed his face, splashed water on his head, gargled his mouth and finally got up wiping his face and hands with the end of his dhoti. Deliberately he made himself feel fresh and persuaded himself that his stomach was full and he was feeling fine.

And now his thoughts were diverted to his family. They too would have drunk water and must be feeling fine. Now there was hardly much time left. As the sun went down, he would go to Dayal Babu's house and...

Panchu estimated that it was about half past two. It would be better to spend about an hour near the pond. He could leave at half past three. But everyday he went to Dayal Babu's house at half past four or even five. If he went particularly early today, Dayal Babu would think he had done so because he was getting rice from him. Ugh! Let him think what he pleased. He would tell Dayal Babu he had arrived for tuition early since there was no work. And, if he had to go early, why not start this very minute? But no, it would not be proper. If he went so early, it would become very evident that he had gone early for the sake of rice. But that wasn't too far wrong either! Of course, it was a question of reputation. And a man, once he lost his reputation, became worthless.

"But," Panchu asked himself, "have I not already ruined my reputation by asking for rice? Well, no, it's not a question of reputation at all. I've only asked for rice in lieu of salary!" However, one could buy rice even from Monai's shop, couldn't he?

But eight days ago when he requested Dayal Babu to give him rice instead of salary and Dayal Babu had agreed, he had hoped that Dayal Babu would not measure rice exactly in terms of the amount of his salary. Dayal Babu was no Monai after all! Dayal Babu was such a big zamindar and people of the town held him in high esteem. Panchu was his children's tutor, he read the newspaper to Dayal Babu, wrote his letters in English addressed to big officers. For all that extra work, he had not charged anything so far. People took their own different views. In any case, he did not expect Dayal Babu to give a maund or two of rice for eight rupees of the salary. He would give at the most ten seers instead of five. Or, maybe more, zamindar that he was! Could one ever imagine shortage in a royal family? He could certainly give a maund or two if he wished. Well, even if not that much, at least fifteen seers? Even with that much rice he could comfortably pass a month. The whole family would manage with a daily consumption of half a seer. It would not fill the stomach, but something was better than nothing at all! What was the alternative? Oh, what hard times had come! The famine would not end as long as the war continued. It was the war that had brought about the famine!

Panchu had read in the newspapers about foodgrains being sent to Bengal from other parts of the country. Union Boards were being set up in every village to sell rice at low rates.

Dayal Babu had laughed when he heard about it. Monai had also laughed. And because of his longstanding relations with them, Panchu also realized that in their laughter was the hidden warning that the golden land of Bengal was going to become a cremation ground. Even then, if he and his family continued to have a daily quota of half a seer of rice, he was willing to allow his human consideration die along with Bengal.

Panchu thought: "The zamindar can't be expected to provide fifteen seers of rice for a salary of eight rupees. Of course, he can give fifteen seers if he agrees to increase the salary. Well, in that case, I shall request him to increase the salary. Will he agree? *Arre*, I shall do some other odd jobs for him. Even a clerk's job if my family can be somehow saved from being devoured by the fire of hunger. If he wants, I will sweep his entire estate. There's always hope as long as there is life. One can think of reputation when the stomach is full... God, let it be so! Oh, Lord, listen to this appeal of mine. Make Dayal Babu agree to this somehow!"

With that prayer, Panchu's heart choked with emotion. He had reached the door of the classroom by that time. He noticed the torn poster. Panchu immediately turned round and looked in the direction of Monai's shop—police constable? No, no, he wasn't coming.

Panchu entered the classroom and heaved a sigh. He sat on the chair, deliberately withdrawing his eyes from everything in the room.

He would not think about the deserted benches any more. Nor about the white ants. To hell with the school! What purpose would it serve any way? If only he could get some additional work at Dayal Babu's house!

Panchu picked up both the registers to return to the drawer. Under the registers lay scattered personal papers. He suddenly noticed his master's handwriting. Two and a half years ago, she had prevented him from going in for I.C.S. The upper portion of that letter lay hidden under other papers. Panchu started reading the visible portion of the letter:

"... Last night he (Shibu) lost in gambling all the jewellery I had made for Tulsi's marriage. His wife had noticed him taking the key from under my pillow. I was on the terrace talking to Ramtanu's wife. He had already done the job by the time his wife came to inform me. Your father heard the cluttering sound of the opening of the door and the lock of the box, and he cried out: "Who's there?" You know very well how he keeps his ears alert even seated in his room! But when your father cried out, that fellow did not utter a word in reply. I came down in panic and shouted after him: 'Shibu! Shibu!' But had Shibu ever listened to anyone? There was a time when he showed consideration to me as his mother. But, my dear, he has now become his own master! What should I do? I've got to suffer whatever I'm fated to suffer.

"Your father had gone blind. In Shibu's form, Narayan is testing my strength. I do not know what all is in store for me in future. Had Shibu not turned out to be such a worthless fellow, I would have prostrated before God and pleaded for death. Which other woman would have to face such a humiliating situation? Should a mother with two young men as her sons have so much to worry? But, my son, I didn't do enough penance, did I? My condition is like that of a sinking man who, in spite of being blessed by God with vast fortunes, cannot enjoy the benefits of his wealth.

"Now I'm not thinking about Shibu or you, my son. You two, God bless you, are now on your own legs... Shibu had sold his wife's ornaments even earlier. Twice he was given a beating too on that account. Till yesterday, his wife had kept everything hidden from me. She did tell me earlier about his taking to gambling. When we protested, he said it was all a matter of luck—if he put something in stake, he would bring tenfold, if not often, then just once, in a single game. He talked about lots of other things too. He also started terrorizing his wife. I knew he used to quarrel with his wife. But I had no idea he had gone so far. If Shibu continues to be like this, God save the family! As for me, my son, I shall keep worrying about his wife and about Tulsi's marriage as long as I live. Kanak too is now going to be ten years old. Then I have to worry about Dinu and Paresh as well. How would those little children know that their father is a gambler and the children of gamblers have only to depend on others!

"I discussed yesterday's incident with your father. He said: 'I could not see the world till I had my sight. But I can clearly see now how the world would end whose frightening state I had already seen!'

"Then he started saying: 'It's only because of your over-fondling that Shibu has gone out of your hand. If you treat a child as a child even after he has passed that stage, the blame for his irresponsibilities would come only on you.' My son, had I known that mother's love, instead of being a blessing, could turn out to be a curse at times, I would have tried to keep my feelings under check. Shibu was born after we had consigned five children into mother earth. Hence, I was afraid of keeping him away from me.

You've studied so much and perhaps you will understand a mother's heart. But how much more will you study, Panchu? You may be feeling that your mother is not happy to see you making progress. But son, if I go on thinking only about you, what will happen to Tulsi and Kanak? What will happen to Dinu and Paresh? Tulsi is now sixteen. How long can I conceal her advanced age? I had striven hard to make those ornaments over a period of seven years. And now, God had snatched away everything! How can we come out of this entangled situation?

"You have written in your letter that you won't be coming home during the holidays. You say you want to go to England to study. That's alright. But tell me one thing. You will go to England, but where will your mother go? To whom will she unburden her heart?

"I've told you what is in my mind. As for the rest, you are a sensible person. Otherwise, God is of course there to see, my son! Be happy wherever you may be. That is the only blessing my heart can give you."

As he finished reading the letter, Panchu heaved a sigh. He leaned against the back of the chair. One by one, memories of the past days flickered in his mind. However unwillingly, he had to surrender himself after that letter from his mother. And he had gone home.

Shibu always got irritated with Panchu. And Panchu knew that it was because of Shibu's lack of education. All that Shibu desired as the one whose younger brother was bright in studies was to be a step ahead of him. That obsession had driven him to gambling. His father was not wrong in thinking that mother's indulgent love had made Shibu stubborn, selfish and worthless. Even now she had a soft corner for him.

When Panchu had gone home after receiving his mother's letter, Shibu had missed no opportunity to show off his superiority over his younger brother.

After coming home, Panchu still wondered what he should do to earn a livelihood. And one day Hiru Bagdi suddenly approached him with eight-year-old Ganesh. He said: "Do me a favour, learned young man! When I see you, one thing always comes to my mind: Seven generations of my ancestors passed their lives at the feet of high caste people like you. But these boys won't be willing to do that. Right from now, they've started raising Gandhi Baba's flag. By the time they grow up, they will go completely out of hand. Instead of that, if you would be kind enough to give them some education, they can find some jobs in the city. And I too will feel happy in my old age."

Panchu realised only that day that the backward communities like Doms and Bagdis of his little town had become so sensible. However, even after that realization, his conventional upbringing prevented his taking up the responsibility of teaching English to low-caste children. He was on the point of declining, but suddenly, old Ramanlal Chakravarty appeared from nowhere. He stopped to hear the conversation between Hiru and Panchu and then burst out with an angry glare in his eyes: "Oh, the low-caste people are becoming so bold! Even Doms and Bagdis have started competing with high castes!"

Hearing such abusive remarks from the mouth of another person, particularly a high-caste, Panchu's social consciousness which had been kindled by the political and social movements in the city was reawakened. His heart rebelled against the high-caste people. He looked at Ganesh. He was struck by the simple expression on the boy's face as he gazed at Panchu with hope. As a reaction to Ramanlal's outrageous comment, he felt that he would be insulting the Goddess of Learning if he refused to teach Ganesh. And right in the presence of Ramlal, he assured Hiru that Ganesh could study as long as he was in town.

How the people in the town had been offended by that! In his own house, his mother did not approve of what Panchu was doing. Shibu said all the repugnant things he could think of. The whole town started abusing him. As protest in the town became stronger, Panchu's resolve became firmer. "Everyone has a right to education," he said.

Panchu had acquired a new interest in life. A mere angry reaction had strengthened his resolve. In that same excitement he collected low-caste boys from the town and started teaching them under a tree.

He had been of some help to the family, and now he had taken up that bother on his head! But it had become a *fait accompli*. He resolved to start a school. In course of time, he would make that very school his source of income.

When the whole town was against the school and against Panchu, it was only Kanai Mistry who had stood by his side. "Go to the city and get funds for the school," he had said. "And make your school so great that even the *laat saheb* himself feels compelled to come here for a visit."

Kanai's good wishes bore fruits. Panchu went to the city and with his irrepressible zeal and the cooperation of Principal Jordan he obtained financial help from several wealthy and respectable citizens. How happy and excited the children were when he came back to town with books, slates, pencils and so on. And one day, when the American missionary Jordan Saheb came with his English and Indian friends to see the school, how the people of the town were impressed!

Principal Jordan promised to build a *pucca* building for the school. With the help of the government contractor Rai Bhuvan Mohan Sarkar and through him with the help of several zamindars in nearby areas, the school building came up in no time. The collector came, many big shots came, functions were organized, sweets were distributed to the children. Dayal Babu patted Panchu's back and engaged him as a tutor for his sons. After Ramanlal Chakravarty's death, his son Govind also joined as a teacher in Panchu's school, completely ignoring the people of the town and helped in the good work.

The whole town was astir when Govind joined Panchu's school as a teacher. Right from the beginning, Ramanlal had been the staunchest opponent of Panchu's school. When his own son started teaching low-caste children, many accusing fingers were raised. But Govind thought out an irrefutable argument in support of his action: "Collector Saheb has specially asked Panchu Babu to open this school. He wants to teach the state language to everyone. Tomorrow, these very children of Doms and Bagdis will learn English and become the rulers. They will force the Brahmins and Kayasthas to carry human excrement. Just wait and see. Just a small request and a big man came to pay a visit to the school. Do you think Panchu Babu is an ordinary man? He is a very close friend of Collector Saheb. Anyone talking against the school would be sent to jail."

In spite of a certain amount of exaggeration in Govind's words, the people of the town had to acknowledge that Panchu was not an ordinary man. An opponent of his school may not be jailed, but he could be certainly fined. People were impressed by Panchu and even started respecting him. But, in order to save the face of the Brahmins and the Kayasthas, they made a condition by way of a compromise that they would send their children to his school if the low-caste children were made to sit separate from the high-caste children. The proposal had come through Panchu's mother and because of her insistence, Panchu had to allow such an arrangement.

Even today Panchu remembered how excited he had been—like a child—over his tremendous success. Patting Ganesh on the back he had said: "Ganesh, if you hadn't come to me, there wouldn't have been this school in our town."

And the simple face of the child had glowed with pride and happiness. That simple face floated before Panchu's eyes.

"Today there is no Ganesh and there is no school!" Panchu felt like breaking into bitter tears. Ganesh and the school were like the body and its life. Without one, the absence of the other was also natural. Panchu was very agitated at the thought of his inability to bring back Ganesh and revive the school. A feeling of protest rose within him.

Just as small children kick their feet and sulk in order to get what they want, Panchu, at that moment, longed intensely to have Ganesh with him. His eyes searched for Ganesh all over the room. He felt as though Ganesh was entering through the door. Ganesh was at all the desks. He was collecting pieces of chalk. Near the globe—yes, it was Ganesh standing near the globe. He had set the globe spinning. Was the globe really spinning? He even saw Ganesh emerge from the map. He felt Ganesh was coming towards him simultaneously from all sides.

"Sir...!"

Panchu was startled. He looked back. No one. But it was definitely Ganese who had addressed him. Exactly his voice.

Suddenly Panchu thought he heard a boisterous laugh. Panchu's heart started beating fast. At the same time, he felt himself going numb. His head swung sideways.

With all his might, he thumped on the table with his hands that were hanging behind the chair. Then, resting the whole weight of his body on his palms, he tried with all his strength to raise his body. And stood up at last. Bewildered, he darted out of the room. Looking towards the room from the verandah, he felt his heart still pounding. He was breathing fast. Had he really seen Ganesh?

Panchu was awakened to reality. He pulled himself up with a reproach: "Again you've allowed your mind to stray! No...no... But then, those sounds...and that face...!"

Panchu's breathing slowed down. His heartbeats became normal. "I was only imagining, nothing else. There was nothing at all...nothing..."

He wanted to go back to the room. But...

Suddenly Panchu turned round and saw the sunshine. It must be nearly half past three. Actually, it may be a quarter to four. He should be going now.

But what about these registers, papers? "Oh, let them remain here. Who ever comes here?"

The lock was kept on a desk a couple of steps away from where he stood.

"I shall take it...yes, I shall go and pick it up. There's nothing to worry," he assured himself.

Panchu moved in with measured steps, and to his surprise, his courage prodded him to rush in and pick up the lock. Then, with both hands, he pulled both the doors of the room and closed them.

Panchu faintly smiled as he closed the latch of the door. "I got scared for no reason at all. Oh, no, I wasn't in the least! It's good that I've to go to Dayal Babu's house. I got up in time. Otherwise, I would be still sitting there lost in my own thought."

As he locked the door, he thought: "Did Dayal Babu really promise me rice? Or have I imagined even that?"

But no, the zamindar had actually made that promise. With all the strength of his soul Panchu convinced himself that Dayal Babu had really promised to give him rice.

And then, Panchu broke into a sudden laughter.

2

"*Badi Bahu!* come, come quickly! Don't waste time! Light the *chulha* right now, child, and keep the water to boil. As soon as Panchu comes, put rice in the boiling water. It will be cooked in no time!" Parvati Ma said all in one breath, holding an empty tumbler in her hand from which she had first drunk. And then, with remarkable energy, she started polishing the tumbler.

Bakulphul, Shibu's wife, was seated in the verandah, patting Chunni who lay on a mat nearby. She had been trying to put the little girl to sleep. She had just slept after giving lot of trouble to her mother who continued patting her.

Kanak too was sleeping closeby. Bakulphul smiled at her mother-in-law's words and raising her head, observed in a soft voice: "But isn't it still morning for my brother-in-law?"

As she said this, she looked at Mangala who sat leaning against the wall. Using her knees like a work-table she was embroidering 'Good Luck' on a pillow-case with green and red thread.

At Bakulphul's remark, Mangala looked up. The pupils of Mangala's dreamy eyes, a special characteristic of her face, glowed and mingled with the eyes of Bakulphul and a mischievous smile played about their lips.

Bakulphul then let out a soft sigh that Mangala could hear. It caused a stirring which had a cooling, soothing effect on her empty stomach.

Mangala resumed her work and then with fake anger in her dreamy eyes, said: "*Arre*, there's still some time before the zamindar's clock shows afternoon and evening. And then, who can be sure when it will be afternoon and evening in the zamindar's clock? I say, Bakulphul, hunger has made you like a child!"

"Say what you will. But today, I'm also waiting for him like you, my dear! God, how much you've to wait everyday!"

Bakulphul again heaved a prolonged sigh as she looked at Mangala. But this time, her stomach started wriggling with that cool feeling.

Even while joking, Bakulphul felt depressed. The wriggling sen-

sation in her stomach made her restless and she stood up in order
to forget it. Seeing that she had stood up, Mangala also gathered
her things and got up with an idea of helping her in the household chores.

A streak of sunlight, passing through a broken arch in front of
the verandah, had reached up to the wall. As Mangala got up, the
light fell on part of her neck, lips, nose and head. The red stone
in the golden nose-stud glowed in the light. For the past four days
since hunger visited the house, Parvati Ma had given the few
remaining ornaments to the daughter and daughter-in-law to wear.
The utensils clanging in the kitchen were more in number than
required. Women engaged themselves in more work than was
needed. As usual, they tried, unsuccessfully, to behave as though
their minds were completely free from worry.

The previous evening, Panchu had burst out laughing when he
saw this. He said: "Ma, if any newspaper reporter visits your house
today, he will find no trace of famine here. I don't understand from
whom you're hiding the real situation. It is the same story in every
house."

Parvati Ma said with an embarrassed smile: "Whatever it is,
we've to keep up our prestige, isn't it? That's how God has made
us different from low-caste people. Otherwise, won't we too be
begging in the streets and wandering from village to village or
looting and plundering?"

Panchu laughed again at his mother's remark and said: "How
long shall we keep ourselves from doing that? After all, prestige
cannot fill our stomachs.Then what's the point of saving it?"

Parvati Ma could not think of an appropriate reply. In a defeated
tone she said: "Your thinking is so different from the whole world!
Tell me, can we ever free ourselves from the restrictions of prestige? Respectable people keep up their prestige till they die, my
son!"

"But Ma, like a thousand patches of an old dhoti, the prestige
of respectable people cannot hide real facts, no matter how much
they try."

"That's true. But what can we do? A naked person exposes his
legs, but even he somehow hides his shame, son!"

In the meantime, Ramtanu's wife arrived and Parvati Ma started
talking to her. Everybody in the house got busy with something
or the other. Then suddenly, Dinu started clamouring for food and
Paresh soon joined him. Scolding and threats, coaxing and

cajoling—nothing worked. Seeing that his mother was getting defeated in her effort to save the prestige of the family, Shibu also appeared on the scene and started beating up the children.

Panchu somehow separated both his nephews from their father and took them to his room upstairs. Later he wrote in his diary: "If there be a gallant person in this country who can keep his distance from the unreality of prestige, it can only be a young child who is never ashamed of the human weakness of hunger."

A small cane table was covered with a table-cloth that Mangala had embroidered. In the centre of the table was a small pen-stand with the ink in both wells having run dry. On the left were two pieces of bricks covered with coloured paper and decorated with a string of wax beads made by Mangala. A few books had been arranged between the two bricks. On the right was a brass incensory in the shape of Om. And right above the table hung a calendar on the wall advertising Indian tea. On both sides of the wall were two windows opening on a view of the town. A nicely made bed was kept close to the wall on which hung a picture of Radha-Krishna in the centre with pictures of Subhash Bose and Jawaharlal Nehru on either side. On one side of the room were three boxes piled one over the other. In the niche above were kept a mirror, a comb, bottles of *alta* and hair oil and a wooden *sindoor* container from Banaras, all neatly arranged.

Mangala had kept her sewing and embroidery kit near the incensory on the table.

Panchu's diary lay open on the table right in front with a pencil kept between the pages. Mangala read Panchu's writing once again. She picked up the pencil and put it in the pen-stand. Then she shut the diary and placed it near the books. After that she had a look at herself in the mirror, passed the comb lightly through her hair and started going down. But she returned from the doorway in order to close the windows. As she looked out she saw Shibu telling half a dozen men around him at the top of his voice: "Monai himself told me that the Government forcibly buys all the foodgrains from him to feed the army..."

Mangala shut the windows and came down. "My husband should be on his way home with rice."

She had hardly walked down the stairs when she saw Tulsi, Dinu and Paresh entering through the outer door. As they saw Mangala, the young children cried out in chorus: "Aunty, we ate *Chandech (Sandesh)*—two each!"

Everyone in the house turned to look at the children.

Parvati Ma and Bakulphul who were in the kitchen came out. Kanak was also awake by that time. She lay with her head resting on her palm and chewing the straw she had broken from the mat. Now she too sat up. Parvati Ma asked: "Where did you get the *sandesh*, Dinu?"

Before the children would say anything, Tulsi cried: "Brother of Aunt no. 8 has come from Calcutta."

Parvati Ma interrupted sharply: "Again you said Aunt No. 8? You too have picked up Panchu's habit. What will Ramtanu's wife think if she hears it? Don't you ever say it again, do you hear?"

Tulsi became silent and the children stood petrified.

After a moment's pause, Parvati Ma again observed affectionately: "He must have brought a message from Gopal's father. When did he come?"

"Just today. He will take Gopal with him," said Tulsi, lowering her head.

Paresh went up to the grandmother and said: "I ate *chandech*, grandma! It was sweet!"

Dinu also could not keep himself away. He came to Parvati Ma and said: "Grandma, uncle gave only one *sandesh* to me and Paresh, but gave a lot to Tulsi Aunty."

Tulsi had brought one *sandesh* with her which she was hiding. Quietly she gave it to Kanak and sat on the mat by her side. She fired Dinu: "You liar! He gave me only two. I protested so much, Ma!"

But Dinu did not keep quiet. He retored: "No, uncle put two in your mouth with his own hands. We had counted—one, two— yes, and then Aunt came into the room...yes!"

"You also got two pieces each!"

"That was given later by Aunt no. 8..."

"You said that again! Just you wait!" Parvati Ma scolded him angrily.

Dinu immediately ran and clung to Mangala's legs. She was sweeping the ground around the *tulsi* plant. When Dinu suddenly clung to her, she stumbled a little but quickly regained her balance and cried: *"Arre, arre!* what's the matter?"

"Aunty!" Dinu told her very softly. "I'm telling the truth, Aunty! Uncle gave only one *sandesh* to us but gave a lot to Tulsi Aunty. And he also fondled her. Uncle didn't even fondle us!"

Dinu said all that in a slow, sulking tone. In between, he glanced at Parvati Ma as though to suggest to her: "Grandma, if you don't listen to us, we won't even complain to you. We'll tell everything secretly to our Mangala Aunty!"

Tulsi controlled her anger with great difficulty and gave Dinu an astounded look. After listening to what Dinu had said, Mangala looked sternly at Tulsi. Tulsi looked aside as their eyes met and lowering her head, started pulling straw from the mat. She was feeling irritated with herself that she had taken Dinu and Paresh with her when she went to the house of Aunt no. 8. But she had had no idea that uncle had arrived. And she had never imagined that he would behave with her the way he did!

Tulsi experienced a tremor in every pore of her body when she thought of it. To hide her flushed face, she lowered her head between her knees. A tress of her hair fell over her face. In the form of that uncle, a man entered her world of imagination for the first time. Through him she had experienced all those things she had found happening between man and woman in her own home and in the neighbourhood, in the life of married girls of her age, things happening in the novels of Bankim Chandra and Sarat Chandra and for which she had been yearning for the last couple of years.

Suddenly Dinu and Paresh had created a row and Aunt no. 8 had entered the room. The moment she saw her, Tulsi had trembled with fright. Aunt no. 8 had directed a significant look at her brother and Tulsi and distracting Dinu and Paresh, had taken them out of the room.

After that, uncle's juicy talk and his amorous gestures. Out of sheer shame she had perspired profusely and escaping from his embrace, had fled the room. Uncle, in his restlessness, had impulsively held her hand at the door and said: "Come in the evening—definitely! Uma Didi won't tell anyone... she won't let anyone know about it..."

"Come in the evening! Come in the evening!" She dared not lift her head... How would she know that it was beginning to get dark... that it was evening...!

And then Kanak shook off her hand and asked: "How many pieces of *sandesh* did uncle give you, Didi?"

"Did I not say two—one I've already stuffed in your mouth!"

Tulsi stood up uneasily; but she could not decide where else she could sit in the house by herself. She could not be by herself anywhere. She read hostility on every face. Her whole body had stiffened. She had no courage to stand. She wanted to lie down quietly somewhere, to be lost in herself.

"Are you listening? Get me a glass of water!" Baba called out to Parvati Ma from his room.

The moment Tulsi heard that voice, her thoughts changed their course. "Come in the evening!" Tulsi knew that when Baba asked for water, he meant that only Parvati Ma should go to him. Tulsi experienced a surge within her. Her eyes rose to look at her mother.

Parvati Ma was irritated. Irritation made her nerves tense. Her sagging cheeks were burdened with shame—at her age it was hard for her to bear that burden. If only she could have gone deaf! But he had lost his eyes and did not know when it was day or night!

"Oh, Tulsi! Didn't you hear? Tell your mother to bring me a glass of water!" Baba called out again.

Tulsi who was standing in the verandah, promptly said to her mother with some excitement: "Ma, Baba is asking for water!"

It was like a blow to Parvati Ma's soul. She writhed in impotent anger. Grown-up girls, daughters-in-law and a grandmother of three grandchildren—she felt her status badly shaken. She took out her anger on Tulsi: "Lazy girl that you are—why don't you go and give him a glass of water? After going blind, he has become a great bother for me. Night and day—he just goes on clamouring for one thing or the other. One moment he would want water, then paan, then tobacco... Why can't he recite God's name like an old man should? Ugh!"

Keshav Babu lay on his cot in a half-reclining pose. Every word of Parvati Ma pricked his heart and his blind eyes. Agitation showed on his pale face. At first, Keshav Babu sat up. He felt something like a surge of energy because of his impatience and irritation. But the very next moment, he slumped back and rested against the cushion. He folded up his legs and heaved a gentle sigh.

It was now five years since Keshav Babu had gone blind. How long could one go on reciting God's name? Lying in the room for all twenty-four hours...eating a couple of rotis like a dog in hell—that was all! There was no one who bothered about him... *Arre*, when even the wife had stopped listening, what could he expect from anyone else? Now she was the mother of two grown-up sons who were earning and were married. Why should she now bother about him? But who made her the mother of her sons? She wouldn't listen to him because he had gone blind—was that it?

It was more than a minute that Tulsi had been standing there with a glass of water. But she was simply staring at her father.

Even in the dim light she could see that his face had become heavy and gone red with excitement.

Keshav Babu heaved a sigh and spreading out his legs, leaned a little more on the cushion. Tulsi said in a sharp voice: "Baba, I've brought water for you!"

The moment Keshav Babu heard Tulsi's voice, he got furious and asked her to take back that glass of water. "Now I'm going to be neglected to this extent, is it? I don't want her obligation! I don't need any water! Take it back! When God has deprived me of my sight, even food, then what shall I do with that water?" He shouted angrily and judging from the direction of the voice, fixed his blind eyes on Tulsi.

"I loved her more than my life—and this is the reward she is giving me! I could have married fifty times if I had wanted. Women, one better than the other and beautiful like heavenly nymphs would have bowed at my feet. And this woman is treating with disregard the man before whom so many wealthy and learned men used to stand respectfully with folded hands! A woman, after all! She can be your companion as long as the body is young. And when that time is over, she starts riding a high horse even when you just ask her to come! But actually, the fault is mine. I have spoilt her by pampering her. I allowed Shibu to be with her in order not to hurt her feelings. Only because of her I couldn't educate him. Otherwise he too would have been a man of learning like Panchu. I say, the sons of learned men cannot but be learned. But this foolish woman—how could she appreciate my good points? And she considers herself a devoted wife and an intelligent woman! Such intelligence be damned! She can find a hundred excuses if she's really keen to come. But no, she won't come! Having a moment of happiness in my dull life...but she would grudge me even that!..."

Keshav Babu's blood started boiling again. He thought about his life of dependence and tried to control his agitated mind. His mind was fatigued because of the blows and counter blows of the hunger of the stomach and hunger of the flesh. His head whirled. The body was fagged out. He breathed heavily.

Keshav Babu felt defeated. She would have certainly come, he thought, had the sons and the children not been around. He felt hostile to his sons, daughters-in-law and the grandchildren—they were like poison he thought. Only because of them he could not have his moments of joy whenever he craved for them. He was enraged with his wife too: "Can't she get the hint? But she has a heart of stone! If she wants, she can come to me throwing dust into the eyes of the whole world. But she must want to do it in the first place! After becoming a mother-in-law and a grandmother, she has forgotten that first and foremost she is a wife! Scriptures have ordained devotion to husband as a wife's highest religion. But whose scriptures? Whose wife? They are all illusions. An illusory creature—that's woman! She casts a spell of illusion. She has tempted and lured the greatest of sages leading to breach of their penance. But why should I go far? This woman has misled even me! Otherwise my life in this world and the other world would have been far better. But a woman opens the gate to hell. Oh, God, how did I go and entangled myself in the fickle attachments of a householder! This woman really led me astray!"

Keshav Babu's blind eyes roved round the room and imagined the bundles of innumerable books and manuscripts piled up on the shelves. He had been an authority on scriptures and logic himself, and in addition, he was the son of a great scholar. The greatest men acknowledge the great power of his scholarship even today. He had been a professor of Sanskrit at the Dacca College. But now his blindness had deprived him of everything. And the woman...the gate to hell...

The door latch lightly clanged. All philosophy, knowledge, learning suddenly vanished like volatile camphor. "She has become... perhaps her heart has softened!" Keshav Babu's sightless eyes gleamed with hope. But...it was only a sparrow which had fluttered its wings and flown away after sitting on the latch.

Out of helplessness, a sigh escaped Keshav Babu's mouth. "Oh, how would she come? Now nothing would happen. I should renounce the world. What is the point of living in the house like this? What happiness can such a wife bring for me? Even otherwise, God's wrath has visited the earth. On the top of that, if one's own wife becomes hostile and denies me happiness... Well...the woman is the gate...of hell! God! Oh God!"

The excitement of physical desire turned into anger and deep in his heart, gradually changed into detachment, and he was overcome with the idea of renouncing the world. But that was nothing unusual. He got into such moods quite often. When the male in Keshav Babu could not satisfy his physical urges, his mind turned to the idea of renouncement. Once when he was overcome by such feeling, he was so infuriated that he had banged his head against

the wall till he started bleeding. When the mood of renouncement dominated his mind, he would start reciting stanzas from
Charpata Manjari of Sankaracharya. That day too his defeated mind
resorted to Sankaracharya:

> Who is your wife and who your son.
> This world indeed is very strange.
> Think of who you are and whence you came.
> Oh, you stupid mind worship Govinda,
> Worship Govinda!

Bakulphul was seated near the *chulha* and Mangala who had
brought firewood to light the *chulha* was standing in front of her.
Parvati Ma was seated on a plank a little away from them. Hearing the recitation of that stanza, Bakulphul meaningfully raised
her eyes and looked at Mangala. As their eyes met, a naughty smile
played about the lips of the two women.

Mangala was standing with her back to Parvati Ma. Bakulphul
looked aside to hide her smile. But that smile did not escape Parvati Ma's notice. The pride of her status and the irritation because
of her age compelled her to turn into shyness. The daughters-in-
law knew that even their mother-in-law was a woman.

Keshav Babu went on with his recitation. Parvati Ma feared that
if the recitation continued even a moment longer, he may start
banging his head. That fear gradually drove Parvati Ma to surrender. As she prepared to bring herself in the line of her
daughters-in-law who were in their late teens, her forty-eighth year
peeped with the colour of youth through the veil drawn on her
face. "What else can I do when he doesn't listen to me?" she seemed
to say.

But how could she, the aged wife, raise her foot in front of the
young daughters-in-law and unmarried daughters and go to the
husband to bring him back from the mood of renunciation to that
of a married man?

The recitation continued...

At last Parvati Ma broke her silence: "Tulsi, child, go to Ramtanu's wife and ask her when *ekadashi* should be observed."

For Tulsi it was like a blind person getting back his sight. She
at once got ready to go. Kanak took the hint. She said: "Ma, I'm
also going with her."

"What will you do there?" Tulsi gave Kanak a startled look.

Mangala looked sternly at Tulsi and said: "Why don't you take
her? Kanak, take Dinu and Paresh along with you. All of you can

spend some time with uncle there."

Tulsi was infuriated: "In that case, where is the need for me to go? Let Kanak go and find out."

The recitation in Keshav Babu's room...

Parvati Ma said sharply: "Why don't you take her with you, Tulsi? She hasn't gone anywhere the whole day. And how can I remember about things like *ekadashi* in any case? She would forget it in her play and I won't be able to observe my fast. Go and come back before it gets dark. And listen, don't let anyone ask for *sandesh*, do you hear?"

Kanak, Dinu and Paresh had already gone ahead. Tulsi lowered her head in anger and hurried out without paying heed to her mother's words.

The recitation became more insistent.

"Oh, unfortunate that I am, even death doesn't come to take me away," Parvati Ma muttered with a sigh and got up from the plank. For a while, she stood in hesitation, and then, lowering her head, walked towards her husband's room.

Bakulphul and Mangala now raised their heads to smile freely. Dragging the mother-in-law's plank, Mangala sat on it and said: "Why are you smiling, my dear? You'll know it when you become a mother-in-law. Your husband is the son of his own father, after all! Do you think he'll spare you to say rosary in your old age?"

The courage of cracking a joke and smiling vanished all of a sudden: "I would end my life should any such thing happen." And as she said that, Bakulphul's face reddened. She knew very well that while rebelling against her helpless situation, she could only talk about ending her own life. She knew that she was the property of her husband till her last breath. Year before last, he had not spared her even when she was running very high temperature, and it was with great difficulty that she was saved from death.

Bakulphul shivered with that thought. On an empty stomach, such excitement made her feel giddy. Somehow, she kept her cool and muttered with a sigh: "Is a woman's life a life at all? I really feel pity for Ma."

"But I think the fault lies with her. If she is firm, what can Baba do? He will bang his head once, twice... In the end, he will cool down and stop doing that," observed Mangala.

"You think he's so simple-minded. You think all men are like your husband! A man like him...," Bakulphul stopped midway.

Chunni was awake in the meantime and had started crying. Bakulphul glanced in the direction of the verandah. Her face and eyes clearly showed her physical and mental fatigue. She straightened her back with a jerk and said to Mangala meekly: "At least pick up the child, dear! I've no strength left in my body!"

Between Chunni's crying and mother's duty, the tender feeling of affinity was caught in a tug of war. There was no milk in her breasts and the little one would keep crying and ultimately become silent forever. How could she produce milk in her breasts? And would not a mother's heart burst with anguish at the thought of her own child, her very flesh and blood, crying itself out and starving itself to death?

Chunni's tears filled the eyes of Bakulphul. Tears streamed from her eyes. Her helpless mind, because of its inability to carry on her physical function, cried convulsively like a small child held in someone's arm.

Chunni's crying reached Bakulphul and was lost in her ears. Mangala had taken Chunni to the kitchen and Bakulphul had probably noticed that through her tears. Those eyes, out of habit, were just functioning as a matter of course, but her heart, separated from her mind, was sinking in tears. No relief anywhere, there was no relief anywhere. She felt suffocated. It seemed she possessed no mind, no body, only breath which was suffocated with the weight of tears. With those tears, she was losing consciousness of her surroundings. Darkness, dusty smoke...smoke...

"Oh, my dear Bakul!"

Bakulphul felt that somewhere in far eternity her breath was getting connected again with her body. She felt the movement of breath, its rising. "My dear..., oh, my dear!" Movement in the body. And from a far distance she heard the familiar voice: "Oh, my dear Bakul!"

Bakulphul's sinking heart had now the support of words. In that darkness, away from consciousness, those familiar words were beginning to re-establish the breaking link between breath and consciousness.

"My dear...oh...oh my dear Bakul!"

Those words rescued her from the suffocating darkness. She now felt a certain contentment, stirring of life. Renting the screen of her torrential tears, she was now eager to convey her conscious message to that familiar voice.

That voice now grew more uneasy and more agitated. Once

again, life was fast gathering its strength. Voice had found its own strength. Her voice, with its full strength, wished to break out... and it did: "Yes, yes... oh, yes!"

Mangala was taken aback. She came back with Chunni and found Bakulphul crying. "*Arre*, what''s the matter? Why are you crying?" But however much Mangala asked, she did not answer. She just went on crying, shedding profuse tears, and her recurring sobs choked her. Bakulphul had no control over her body and was about to fall. Chunni lay in Mangala's lap and she too was crying. Mangala was in panic for a moment. Then she controlled herself and quickly leaving Chunni on the floor, rushed forward and caught Bakulphul in her arms to save her from falling. Shaking her vigorously by her shoulders she cried: "Phul, oh, Phul... Phul!"

Bakulphul responded: "Ye...s...s!"

"What's the matter with you? Why don't you say something? Please say something!"

Bakulphul was fairly in control of herself by that time. She was trying to suppress her sobs and now she could successfully fight them back. She coughed and cleared her throat.

"I say, Phul, what's wrong with you?" Mangala asked again. Wiping Bakul's tears with the end of her own saree she said: "You're mad, I tell you! Must you simply ruin yourself like this? Crazy! To what length you can carry things! Here, take charge of the girl. Poor thing, her voice had gone hoarse with so much crying!"

Mangala picked up Chunni and put her on Bakulphul's lap. She had recovered quite a bit by that time. Wiping her eyes and nose with the end of her saree, she lay Chunni comfortably on her lap and moving her knees, patted her to make her stop crying.

Mangala fixed her dreamy eyes on her dear Bakulphul's face. From her very first day in the house, there have been sisterly relations between them. Not even once did they behave like the younger and elder sisters-in-law. After marriage, Mangala had once gone to her mother's place. With the permission of her mother-in-law, she took Bakulphul along with her. Bakulphul had no parents. Her maternal uncle had somehow fixed her marriage and thus discharged his responsibility. Since then, he had not bothered about her at all.

In childhood, that uncle's daughter had always treated her with disdain. His wife saddled her with all the household chores as though Bakulphul was a maid in the house. Hence, she had not been able to make any friends outside the house. But her fatè completely changed after coming to her in-laws' house. What she found there was not a mother-in-law but a mother. Panchu, Tulsi, Kanak, Baba—everyone was so nice! At first she was very fond of Shibu too. Even now she loved him, but...

Bakulphul and Mangala looked at each other and at the very first sight, their relationship deepened into that of love. Moist eyes glowed with attachment. Lips quivered. An affectionate smile was drawn on two pairs of lips...

"You devil! You scared me so much by crying so much! You wretch!" Then turning towards the door of the kitchen Mangala said: "Starving as it is, and then your crying face—my head whirled as I looked at you!" Then she added: "Will you drink water? Drink a little—I'll bring it."

Without waiting for Bakulphul's reply, Mangala went out of the kitchen. For a while, Bakulphul kept staring at the door. Then she lifted Chunni and pressed her to her bosom and started fondling her.

But Chunni did not become quiet. Now she was not even able to cry. She was breathing heavily. At last Bakulphul put her to the breast and the child was quiet. Harassed by hunger, that little girl pulled at her mother's breasts and strove hard to fill her stomach. It was very painful for the mother, but she could suffer pain at that moment. They were facing the consequences of the sins of their elders. But what sin had that little one committed that she had to face famine the moment she was born into the world?

"Here, drink this water," Mangala said as she entered the kitchen with a glass of water.

Bakulphul's train of thought was disturbed. With a dry smile, she extended her hand. "We can manage to live on water, but what will happen to this little one?"

"What will happen?" Both of them knew the answer to that question. They also knew that the whole town, the whole of Bengal was aware, yet everyone hesitated to mention death by name. Their hearts trembled with fear.

Mangala was silent and grew serious. Under the pretext of a fast, the whole family had been keeping hunger at bay for the past four days. With grains stocked in the house, one could fast even for eight days instead of four. But here? Well—it did not matter. Panchu would be arriving any moment carrying rice with him.

"He'll be home soon and he'll bring rice. Why do you worry?"

Mangala consoled her. "God will do everything good. Give Chunni to me. She'll kill you the way she's pulling at your breast!"

Mangala came up to Bakulphul and picking up Chunni from her lap smiled at the child: "I say, that's enough! Don't drink away all the milk. Leave something for your brothers and sisters to be born!"

Mangala pulled Chunni on her lap. Chunni was not at all prepared to give up support of her mother's dried up breasts. She clung to her mother's breast with all her strength, like a leech and pulled at the breast. Bakulphul's hungry and weakened body could not take it and she cried in an enraged voice: "Oh, shee... why don't you die, you devil?"

She wanted to curse the child. Like all Indian mothers, Bakulphul too habitually cursed her children a hundred times during the day: "Go and die! Go to hell!" She always showered such "blessings" on her children. If anyone commented about it, she retorted: "If children ever died because of their mother's curses, this world wouldn't have been in existence at all!" But today, while she cursed Chunni, her heart suddenly cried out. As such, death was always ready to come uninvited every moment. Just a little groan, and then the hard breathing, and then the breathing would stop. What then was the need for such curses?

Bakulphul felt uneasy and suffocated. She wanted to take back the curse or render it ineffective. She wanted to say: "May these children remain safe. May all human beings remain safe. Troubles are a routine matter. May God be pleased to let me die in place of all of them..."

When death was distant and only occasionally visited some families, one was not so scared. But today, death was dancing on people's heads. Taking advantage of war and the famine, death was becoming indiscriminate and its hunger was becoming insatiable. Hence, Bakulphul did not wish death for anyone, from her children to herself. She wanted to run away from death to save her life.

Just at that moment, Shibu's voice was heard at the main door: "Have no worry, Sir! I shall go to S.D.G.'s house as your leader. I shall go and tell the Government officials: 'You rascals are going to kill our people with hunger.'"

Two or three other persons had crossed the threshold and entered the outer room. Shibu came in first, followed by Somen who was Panchu's very good friend. He often visited the house with Panchu. Bakulphul, Mangala and all others knew him well.

Shibu led all his friends to his room upstairs...

Chunni was still crying. Shibu asked in an authoritarian tone: "Why is Chunni crying? Give her milk...or..."

Looking at his companions, Shibu said: "Will you have tea, Somen? Very well. Make four or five cups of tea. And also some snacks. Make *halwa*...and shall we have some salty dish too?... Yes, I was telling you that I shall speak to the Government officials..."

Shibu and his friends had gone up the staircase and were in Shibu's room. Mangala and Bakulphul exchanged amused glances. Bakulphul said: "Make tea, dear! and make *halwa* also! If your pantry is empty, then go to Monai and ask him to open the bags of semolina and sugar! Today your brother-in-law used all his authority to bring *swaraj*..."

"Swaraj?" Shibu was thundering in his room. "You'll ask for *Swaraj* and I know what they'll say. They will say, 'You Indians, rascals! You want *swaraj*, is it? Alright, you bastards, we shall bring death for you!'"

Shibu was merrily talking away upstairs in the style of a leader. He was saying: "I say, friends, I know it's the government policy. Forty crore Indians, wretches that they are, will die of hunger and thirst, the famine will end, and now you ask for *swaraj*, they will say. I shall tell the British Government that India is ours—it's our thing!"

There was something grand in Shibu's leadership. There may be ten persons or ten thousand—he gave no chance to anyone else to speak. Whether or not people were in need of a leader, Shibu Mukherji was always available. Shibu Gopal Mukherji, a born leader of all parties from the Congress to the Communist Party, the Hindu Mahasabha to the Muslim League, in fact, leader of all human beings, had just paid a sudden visit to the office of the Ghoshpada Famine Relief Committee. Somen was the Assistant Secretary in that organisation. A few young men who had gathered in that office had decided to take a deputation to meet the D.S.G. Immediately, Shibu had become their leader.

Once Shibu had become leader, nobody could make him budge. He had become aware of his leadership qualities first during the Quit India Movement of 1942. Those were the days when Panchu's school was doing very well. Panchu's name was famous in several towns and villages around. Being Panchu's elder brother, Shibu considered it a matter of right to do big things and earn a big name. The Quit India Movement gave him a boost. Shibu thought out a very good plan in the interest of the country...

Who showered lathi blows and bullets on the revolutionaries?—The police. Hence, the Movement would become successful if the police could be prevented from playing an active role. With that idea in mind, Shibu Mukherji picked up a spade and started digging on the road opposite the police station. When he was arrested, he started shouting the slogan "Inquilab Zinda-bad!" Then he tried to scare away the police by presenting himself before the police in a menacing stance: "You're not doing the right thing by punishing me... I know from birth that I'm the incarnation of Chanakya in this Kaliyuga. I'm the son of a Brahmin. In a single sweep, I shall completely wipe you out, you bastards!"

Subsequently, in the face of cane blows from the police, he held the police officers' feet at the very second blow. He begged to be pardoned. The news spread. People teased him. But that did not deter him from asserting his leadership.

Somen was really exasperated with him. He respected Shibu because of Panchu. But there was a limit to his paying such respect. All the members of the Famine Relief Committee left one by one after Shibu entered the office. Poor Somen was badly caught. Two young men from a nearby village had come to consult him. Along with Somen, they too had to suffer Shibu's presence. Somen closed the office to get rid of him. But Shibu forced Somen and his friends to come to his house. All along the way, his commentaries on the British policy, the ways and means of attaining *Swaraj* and the list of abuses meant to be hurled at the D.S.G. kept him and his colleagues from thinking about serving the famine-afflicted people. All protests and dilly-dallying by Somen to escape from Shibu were of no avail. He stopped saying anything more, but Shibu's non-stop speech in what Panchu called his 'Made in India' English did not stop. He was obsessed with himself. He forced everyone to listen to him.

At last Somen thought of a way out—"Dada, we're going with the deputation tomorrow, right?"

Shibu was shocked: "What do you mean by our going? *Arre*, I go..."

Somen was forced to cut him short. "But we don't wish our leader to go in an ordinary manner!"

"That's right, that's right..."

Somen did not allow Shibu to proceed. He said emphatically:

"Then I'm going. I should make arrangements for a procession. You'll be taken out in a procession of people who will be collected from about a dozen nearby villages. Then alone will it have the desired impact."

"That's what I also want..." Shibu again said in the manner of a leader. Somen sprang to his feet and said: "That's fine then. You write down an application in English. Show it to Panchu. I shall now take your leave."

Somen's hurried behaviour unwittingly pricked Shibu's sense of greatness. "What can Panchu see? What he see my English? *Arre*, I teach him ten years!"

Somen vowed to himself never to repeat this mistake, and quickly said to remedy the situation: "You don't follow my point, Dada! What I mean is that in any case, you'll have to show the application to the people. So, show it to Panchu and take his signature."

Shibu replied in a serious tone: "Panchu should not sign first. The D.S.G. will think, headmaster no price—a worthless fellow. But a leader means a leader. He would impress by his striking appearance and influence. The first signature should be by public leaders. You sit down. I'll write the application. You sign it as one leader and..."

"In that case, let your signature be the first. Actually, there should be only your signature as the leader of Bengal. And now we're off to make arrangements for the procession. Come on!" Somen said to his companions and did not wait even for a second.

3

Panchu had gone to Dayal Babu's house in the hope of somehow manoeuvring to get some help from him. Instead, he lost even the tuition he was giving in his house as Dayal Babu was sending away his wife and children to Pachhant the following day. Even he was scared by the increasing incidents of loot and attacks by the starving people. Robbers were afraid of robbers. In spite of fifty cudgel fighters from Bhojpur guarding him and having two guns by his side, Dayal Babu often woke from sleep with a fright.

Panchu's passive revolt against Dayal Babu provoked in him some kind of sarcastic reaction against his own helplessness and it pricked his mind. Panchu was irritated by that reaction which lay hidden in his unconscious mind. Thinking about his irritation from all possible viewpoints, he felt that those people persisted in their evil ways because of the weakness of the general public. The passive sacrifices and tolerance alone encouraged them to tyrannize people through their selfish pursuits. That habit of several centuries had given them a false sense of power. Even the greatest wrestlers, when forced by circumstances, became nervous in front of moneyed men who suffered from dyspepsia and sat with their flabby bodies on huge cushions. Even great intellectuals considered the intelligence of those feeble-minded men of wealth as big as their safes and considered themselves well-protected by obliterating their own existence. Was it not so because those people possessed the power of wealth?

One Dayal, one Monai swallowed up the stocks of grains meant for the entire population of the town, took away the clothings meant for the whole town. They kept very carefully in their safes food and clothes of the people in the form of bundles of currency notes and heaps of ornaments of gold and silver and precious stones. They had the cudgel fighters from Bhojpur for their protection. They had their guns. The police and law were on their side. What did the common people have to protect themselves?

Panchu's lowered eyes rose and looked in the direction of Mohanpur. Dayal Babu's mansion stood beyond the limits of the town. The mud houses could be seen. It would be sin even to describe them as houses. They were a mere pile of four broken mud-walls—the bamboos of those houses, the roofs, rags and quilts were all sold and other household items were looted.

The bodies of two children lay near Ramu's hut. Perhaps they were Ramu's children. Panchu could not hold himself back. He went close to find out. Death was still playing tricks with those children. They would be dead any moment. Ramu's wife had already run away and Ramu himself had joined a band of robbers. Home, parents—those children were deprived of everything. At the moment, it was only their tired breathing that was trying to keep company with them till the last moment.

Panchu observed death from very close quarters, gazed at it very intently. In the days of famine, even he and his family would be in that state... But right now, he had some rice. His family must be waiting for him at home—Dinu, Paresh, little Chunni, Kanak...

Panchu quickly withdrew himself from that spot and started walking towards his house...

There, it was Fazl Chacha taking a tin sheet from his house to sell. And there was that aged Khetramani seated like a lost soul, her eyes looking down. She wore a strip of cloth wrapped round her waist and held an earthen pot in her hand. She used to go round in the village at one time. Panchu had named her Naradji. How did she come to the fishermen's settlement from that hillock near the Brahmin's colony? She would die one day, seated like that.

By now, Ramu's children were probably dead. Who would pick up their bodies? Would their dead bodies simply rot there? Would the dead bodies of human beings just rot? Perhaps, someday his own body too...

Panchu paused and pondered. He felt like going back to Ramu's children to see what had happened. But he must rush back home. Dinu, Paresh, Chunni, Kanak—everyone at home would be hungry.

Forcibly breaking away from all those thoughts about the unclaimed dead bodies which provoked him to think about himself in that condition, he quickly walked ahead...

That was Beni's hut. Beni was seated right there. His wife too was there, sitting with her head resting on her knees. She was married two months ago. Fresh in youth, new-born excitement of life... and now the famine. Beni had no equal when it came to playing the flute. Panchu saw that the youth of that couple had aged.

Though seated so close, the woman was not conscious about her man nor the man about his woman. What honeymoon for a young couple afflicted by the famine, Panchu thought... He remembered Mangala, her dreamy eyes, her carefree movements, her smile...

Mangala had been starving for four days. Panchu's steps quickened.

Right before his eyes at a little distance was Monai's shop. God's godliness streamed in the thin membranes of the flesh of emaciated figures that wavered and stagged as they moved. Along the path, eyes glaring and sunk in their pits, they roved around Monai's shop in search of foodgrains. Innumerable skeleton-like beings were bending low, looking for a few grains of rice in the dust. The wild growth of men's beards and women's matted hair, and all the veins and bones of their bodies had a peculiar shine. Children did not look like human children. That entire colony did not look like a colony inhabited by human beings.

Evening twilight gradually faded and those swaying creatures seen in that dim light...

Panchu thought: "Will these creatures ever be considered human beings in the world of the rich and the government officials? They'll call them ghosts—yes, ghosts, even though those people are themselves riding on our heads like ghosts of dead humanity! They've built their golden mansions on the foundations of our hunger. They're man-eaters... savages!"

Panchu's mind, flourished on the political atmosphere of the city, was now agitated in an amateurish manner. He had with him five seers of rice at the moment. He would be able to have his meal for the day. Before he got rice from Dayal Babu, he too belonged to the group of starving men and women. He too experienced the same pangs of hunger like those skeleton-like beings. But his satisfaction that his family would be able to have a meal today, set him apart from that entire starving lot. At the same time, he was aware that his feeling of satisfaction was only momentary. Hence, his mind was reluctant to part company with his starving fellow creatures. From day after tomorrow, his family too would be facing the same harsh future. But he was happy at least at the moment. At the same time, he was honest with himself. He felt irritated for his intellectual superiority over people like Dayal Babu who were responsible for making his satisfaction momentary. In the matter of eating a meal, he was today in the same condition as Dayal Babu and Monai. Why then should he not be irritated with them and why should he not side with his future companions?

Suddenly, Panchu's reverie was broken. In front of Monai's shop, half a dozen living skeletons had surrounded a single creature who was just like them and were engaged in scramble and skirmish. Their vague and frightening voices made the growing darkness of the evening ominous. Then Panchu saw that the shrieks of the surrounded man created a pang of pain in the ominous clamour and were suddenly stifled. The man slumped to the ground.

Panchu rushed to the spot. It was Munir, the carpenter. His breathing had stopped. He was dead. A heart failure, perhaps. Rice lay scattered around Munir's body. People had been pouncing like vultures to gather the rice. They had become oblivious to the fact that close to them lay the body of a man who had been one of them. With all their excitement, they were trying to collect as much rice as possible. With a lost look in their eyes, they glanced at the dead body, then at Panchu, and again resumed their job. Their hands started grabbing and snatching rice.

Panchu shouted: "You've killed that man at last!"

Hearing Panchu's words, those skeletal creatures lifted their irritated faces. Those dried up wrinkles, those sunken eyes seemed to ask: "What nonsense! We're doing our job!"

A couple of them also noticed Panchu's bundle of rice. Panchu was startled. He stood up and again glanced at Munir's body. Munir had done lot of woodwork in the building of his school. He was a good man, poor thing!

Panchu feared that those people may start scrambling for his rice too. He was not worried about his rice being snatched from him. His only concern was to avoid one more death resulting from such a scramble. That would mean one more dead body. Dead bodies—the dead body of Munir, of Ramu's unclaimed children, and one day his own...

No, no! He would arrange for Munir's burial. It was the demand on him as a human being. Moreover, Munir had worked for him in the school.

For the past four days, Nuruddin the carpenter had had his two square meals. He passed his hand over his filled stomach and blushed. He was a guest at Azim's house. Every evening he sang in his melodious voice:

"Flowers have bloomed in my life today,
I'll come, he said, at evening hour!"

That voice, ringing nonchalantly, dashed against the walls of the hungry houses, filling their hearts with lingering agony. There was no one in Nuruddin's house. His father had died long ago. He had a sister who had been married. He had his mother on whom he took out his anger for seven days of starvation. The moment he strangled her at neck, that hungry, lean old woman's soul writhed in pain and went to lodge a complaint with God Almighty, penetrating through the heavens. With his mother's death, his anger cooled down. But his hatred for his partner in hunger was such that he did not regard his act as a crime. Persuading himself that his mother had died of hunger, he took Azim's help to arrange for her burial. That day, Azim even gave him a meal at his house.

Azim was Monai's right hand man. He had been working at Monai's shop since he was a child. The famine could never visit his house. Nuruddin was his childhood friend. They were like two bodies and one heart. It was sheer human duty to support a friend in his time of trouble. Apart from that, Azim thought Nuruddin was a very useful man. For instance, in business he was capable of bringing unexpected gains. At a mere hint, Nuruddin could go and bring down with him any nymph from Indra's palace. Ever since Azim became Monai's trusted and important man, he had come to regard himself as one of the respected men of the village—next of course to Monai.

As a result of his friendship with Nuruddin, Azim also occasionally got his minor share in a big gain. That was why he always remained under his thumb. When he lived with Nuruddin long ago, Aziz had tried to molest Munir's wife. Since then she had been his target. But now he was not inclined to lick the left-overs. That was why he never complained to Nuruddin about Munir's wife.

As a joke, Nuruddin often used to humiliate him right in front of the woman. Now he was caught in his grip. He had a good chance of performing the duty of gratitude. Azim arranged the sale of Nuruddin's house and four *bighas* of land to Monai and helped him get twenty-five rupees. He lodged him at his own house and gave him two meals everyday. In lieu of that, Azim urged Nuruddin to call Munir's wife. Another condition was that he himself would have a lion's share and Nuruddin a small share. It was a hard condition for Nuruddin, but he was getting rice from Azim. Apart from that, the twenty-five rupees also were in Azim's house.

Then Nuruddin started his frequent visits to Munir's house. For the past seven days, nobody in Munir's house had eaten even a grain of rice. Without any food, those two little girls, Chand and Rukia, lay like corpses. Munir had been battling with hunger as well as malaria. Even then, Munir's wife still derived strength from namaz five times in a day.

Nuruddin came to express his sympathy. But Munir's wife reacted as Nuruddin had expected.

Now Nuruddin changed his tactics. He pretended to share her belief and trust in God. They started having discussions about revelations of God...

The mosque of Mirganj stood on the borderline of Mohanpur and Mirganj. It had been famous as "the mosque of ghosts" for several generations. Nuruddin said: "A ghost resides in this place and does miraculous things. Last week, I was passing by. I had been starving for six days. It was time for evening namaz. Then I thought that God was greater than the fear of ghosts. Mustering courage, I offered namaz right there. After namaz, I came out of the mosque and found rice and fried fish on a banana leaf on the steps. My mouth watered but I was afraid of ghosts. Then I heard a voice: 'Oh, you devotee of Allah, these things are meant for you. After two and a half centuries we have found only you who considered fear of God greater than us. The world is facing today increasing danger. The world has disregarded God. But God loves those who do not forget him. Here, eat this and offer your namaz in this mosque everyday. You have nothing to fear. I am the leader of the ghosts. By God's command, I put His devotees to rest. You will get your food here everyday. God's devotees cannot go hungry."

One evening, Nuruddin took Munir's wife with him to see the miracle. After namaz, they found food served for two persons.

That day, after a full seven days, Munir's wife had a meal to her fill. She did think about her daughters. She also thought about her ill and hungry husband. But Nuruddin had made it absolutely clear to her that she was not free to transfer her right even to her dearest person.

After her return from the mosque, Munir's wife could not look straight into the eyes of her daughters and ailing husband. She bemoaned her plight but her feelings could not be expressed in words. But as evening came, she remembered the food on the banana leaf which, by God's command, no one else was entitled to eat.

Fear of God taught Munir's wife to tell lies. Her conscience became numb and her selfishness grew stronger. She started going for namaz everyday.

Nuruddin had already served food on the plate. Azim was also to join them for the meal that day. Clever Nuruddin was well aware that he was in Azim's hands everyday. He used Munir's wife for his own selfish purpose. He first extracted his twenty-five rupees with a view to go to the city and search for a carpenter's job in a military camp. But he must have the necessary implements for that. Earlier, he had been selling household things as well as implements and filled his own stomach and pulled on as long as possible. Now he thought he could buy the implements from starving Munir.

Nuruddin came to Munir's house. He told Munir's wife: "From today, I'm transferring my right to you also. By God's grace, your daughters and husband would also benefit from it."

Munir's wife was very happy and she went to offer namaz.

That was the first occasion that Nuruddin did not accompany her and Azim got his chance to prove to her his manly powers. That day, Azim was to come personally with the food. After recovering his twenty-five rupees from Azim, Nuruddin had told everything to him: "By prodding her to eat food without the knowledge of her starving daughters and husband, I've completely shattered her conscience. She no longer has even the slightest sense of truthfulness or purity in her. Show her the plate and then pull it away. She will simply come behind you. Lead her down the garden path—yes, do that!"

After Munir's wife went to offer her usual namaz, Nuruddin cast his net. He persuaded Munir who was reduced to a state of utter helplessness because of hunger, to sell all his implements for a mere eight annas. With that amount in hand, Munir hurried to Monai's shop, staggering on his weak legs. It was there he met his pathetic end with rice bought from Monai's shop scattered around him. It was then that Panchu arrived on the scene.

Panchu persuaded the 'able-bodied' starving men who were sympathetic to Munir and as afraid of death as himself, to carry Munir's body to his hut. Panchu tied his bundle of rice at his own neck and flung it at the back. As he walked, the five *seers* of rice swung from side to side, and he felt suffocated. The weight of the dead body on his hands and the heaviness of heart made walking difficult for him. Chand and Rukia broke into loud lamentation at the sight of their father's dead body. They were in terrible distress. Weakness due to starvation and grief proved too much for Rukia. She became unconscious. Ten-year-old Chand was a little more mature and more capable of exercising restraint and hence she suffered more.

Mother was not at home, and father's dead body had been brought home. And the younger sister was lying unconscious. What could she do? She wailed. She felt suffocated. That one sad event brought several such events to her mind. "*Abba* had gone to get rice, but he came empty-handed, and like this!"

Her memory of her father also contained the pang of starvation which was as close to her as her father—in fact it was even closer than her father!

Close to that haunted mosque, Munir's wife was having her meal behind the bushes and Azim was stroking her body. There was savagery in Azim's eyes, there was impatience. Because it was difficult for him to control himself, he bit his lips every now and then. His eyes turned red with anger. The pressure of his hands on the body of Munir's wife grew heavier. And Munir's wife? She was having her food and wished to keep herself absorbed only in the act of eating...

In the meantime, Nuruddin heard about Munir's death and rushed to his hut. He pretended to lament—there were no tears in his eyes. And his mind got busy manipulating his next step. "Now the woman is free," he thought. "Let me take her to the city. She will be of great use. Even though she's mother of two daughters, she hasn't sagged. She has a good physique. I shall give her good food for a few days and she will bloom again."

None of the three men who carried Munir's body had strength enough to take the body up to the burial ground. At a little distance behind the hut was some fallow land. Nuruddin brought a spade from somewhere and somehow managed to dig a grave. His mind meanwhile was working in several directions: "I will cast the die if she comes back. I do hope she doesn't come excited or enraged. I shall dupe her. I shall give her two rupees as a token of sympathy in her moment of trouble. But even Azim may give her some money—though he's a cunning fox. But in the matter of women, his senses take leave of him, *sala*. And then, he has already fallen for her. He's sure to give her some money!"

Then what should he do, Nuruddin wondered. The only way was to make use of the girls and thereby prevail over her motherly feelings. What else to do? Must feed those girls, the wretches! Yes, that was the right thing to do. Master Babu seemed to have rice in his bundle. He should be trapped. But he must first make sure that the bundle did indeed contain rice.

Nuruddin kept aside the spade and started panting as though he were dead tired. Another man came in his place. Nuruddin went and sat by the side of Panchu. While talking he touched the bundle with his hand, as though by accident. Yes, it was rice. In that case, Panchu should be really trapped. But the man won't come round easily. He should play some trick. He should instigate the girls.

"As it is, educated people are always stupid. They tend to be full of sympathy and kindness. As for Master Babu, his heart is soft like wax. I must prod the girls to cling to Master Babu's legs when he leaves. I must tell them to entreat him to give them food. That's all. I'll then see that he parts with his bundle!"

But suppose Panchu's heart did not melt? But no, that was not possible. Had he become so heartless as all that, he wouldn't have come to carry Munir's body. No, his trick would not fail. God willing, the purpose would be served. When Munir's wife came back, such a gesture of consolation and solace would work wonders in her moment of grief. "Then she would be under my control!" Nuruddin said to himself.

But what about the girls? It would be foolish to take them along. But how to separate the girls from the mother? Well, he would think about it later. But right now, Master Babu's bundle of rice!...

Nuruddin heaved a prolonged sigh. Then he looked at Panchu and said: "Master Babu, Munir's poor wife has gone to the mosque to offer namaz. When she finds on her return that Munir..." He pretended to wipe his tears and covered his face with the front of his shirt, and even produced a sobbing sound. "What can I say, Master Babu," he resumed. God alone knows what all we'll have to face in the days to come! Only a little while ago, I gave two rupees to Munir. But you're all people well-set in life. I'm in no position to do anything more. But I know what people in my condition have to go through. I spent ten days without food. My poor mother died. I sold my house and land and it brought me a little money. I gave two rupees to Munir from that amount. But his luck was bad! He lost his life, poor Munir!"

Then Nuruddin narrated to Panchu how Munir's family had been starving for twelve days. And from the time he went to Monai's shop with the money, his poor girls had been waiting for him in the hope that he would bring rice for them. As he said that, Nuruddin's voice chocked again: "Poor girls! They never imagined their father would come home dead! Oh, God!" Nuruddin sobbed again.

Panchu was stunned. He stared in a daze, imagining himself in Munir's condition. Like the hand going numb after holding a piece of ice for a long time, Panchu's hand had become numb by the fear of death which had completely overshadowed his heart. Every word uttered by Nuruddin touched him on the surface and he reacted to it as though it was the story of his own family, and Nuruddin had been narrating it to somebody else.

Panchu stared at Munir's dead body. He saw in it his own dead body. The grave had been dug by that time. Munir's body had been lowered in it without a shroud. Now they were covering the body with earth. Panchu stood and stared. The weight of the earth pressed on the body. Now the body was not visible. The pit was filled with earth. Panchu heard Munir's daughters wailing. He also heard Nuruddin's loud lamentations.

The pit was filled. People pressed the earth with the mattock and their feet...

Munir had departed from the world. Now Munir would not be seen anywhere. Munir had made the benches and desks for his school. He had made the blackboards. Munir used to laugh and talk, move about and work. Till a little while ago, he was a living being to be reckoned with. He was a man who had existed. He had now become a story. Kalidasa had existed. Shakespeare had existed. Akbar, Caesar, Chandragupta had existed, Muhammad, Jesus, Buddha existed. Munir had existed. Panchu...also had existed. This famine would ultimately turn this country into a thing of the past. People would say...there was once a province known as Bengal!

Panchu had prided himself on his intellect. But at this moment he had absolutely no doubt about his utter foolishness. Looking at the pathetic grief of those two fatherless girls, Panchu had contented himself by shedding secret tears. Even after hearing Nuruddin and other three or four men praise his generosity and large heart, Panchu's thoughts were centred on his own hungry family. Nuruddin had said: "You are well settled in life, Master Babu! If you give a handful of rice in the bundle, it wouldn't hurt you in any way. Whereas, it would give some relief to these girls in their grief." By that time, Panchu's selfishness had grown so tight around him that it seemed impossible that he would part with even a grain of rice.

When people said he had huge stocks of rice in his house and that he was a big man in town, Panchu, because of his upbringing, felt secretly happy. That happiness aroused his deep sympathy for people. He could not bring himself to say that he too, together with his family, had been starving for four days, and that with great difficulty, he had been able to get five *seers* of rice. If the people who considered him a big man came to know about his real condition, he would lose face. But he would lose face even if he did not part with rice. Well, let it be so. At the most, people would say that even Master Babu had become hard-hearted like Dayal Babu and Monai. In that way at least his status would be equal to that of Dayal Babu and Monai.

Panchu's mind received a sudden jolt from Nuruddin: "You're a Brahmin, Master Babu! How will you take home the grains that has touched a dead body? That too, the body of a Muslim? You've no use of the grains any more. Whereas, the same grains would satisfy the hunger of these girls."

The argument was irrefutable. How could Panchu, coming from a respected Brahmin family, take home that rice with the knowledge of the people that it had been contaminated by contact with a dead body. It would be a blot on his religion and reputation. He gave away the bundle.

The revolt in Panchu's mind was eating him up. Why did he give away the rice? Why did he feel ashamed? Would his shame, his reputation and religion save him and his family from death?

Panchu was going home with empty hands. It was already dark. Here and there, lamps flickered in some homes. The prestige of the families in those houses was still intact. Panchu saw the light in his own house. His mind wavered and his steps hesitated. He was going home empty-handed. His family must have waited for him in expectation. Kanak must be lying as though she were lifeless. Dinu and Paresh must be crying and clamouring for food. The whole house would be restless with hunger. Panchu thought: "At first the family will greet me with expectation, but the very next moment, when they realize..."

Panchu retraced his steps. He had no heart to go home. He could not face the family suffering pangs of hunger, particularly when he himself was responsible for their plight. It was only his foolishness that would force his family to perish with hunger.

He walked on aimlessly. Anguish and anger made his steps slacken. He had been full of excitement when he was coming with the bundle of five seers of rice. That strength was now drained. Starvation for four days, despair and weakness, along with the fatigue of carrying Munir's body had made him terribly weak. And now, this fresh blow of self-remorse and despair. His head whirled and his steps staggered. With great difficulty, he saved himself from falling.

All around Panchu, at a little distance, were several living skeletons swaying and staggering just like him. He felt disgust. He felt disgust for all those affected by famine. He felt disgust for Munir who was dead. Why did that wretch have to die on the road where Panchu was going? And if he had to die on that very road, could he not have done it some other time? *Sala!* Death came only when he, Panchu, was passing by with his bundle of rice!

Panchu felt enraged with Munir's daughters. And he was equally angry with Nuruddin. He was angry with all those writers of scriptures who ordained that rice became contaminated by the touch of a dead body. He was angry for his being a Brahmin and a respectable man. Impotent rage brought tears in Panchu's eyes. But this time he was not angry that he had shed tears. Only tears could give him solace.

Panchu's tears became irrepressible. Panchu's ego was constantly getting hurt at the thought of his own lowly and helpless state. And he had such bouts of pain that his mind started surging like the stormy sea. Tears flowed from his eyes in torrents. He wept bitterly, drawing long breaths.

Panchu had no strength in his feet. He just slumped down on the ground near the fields. He muttered God's name to himself. The name of that unknown Power helped Panchu regain his composure. His tears stopped. His sobs subsided. His eyes dried up. Only a couple of sighs escaped from his heart.

But again, the same anxiety: "After all, how long can I remain out of the house like this? By now, probably all of them would have learnt that I've given away the rice to Munir's daughters. And they must have worried all the more since I've not yet got back home. But going empty-handed! Oh, I went to light the lamp outside, leaving my own house in the dark!"

Then it suddenly occurred to Panchu that it was possible to buy some rice by selling the school furniture to Monai. With that thought in his mind, he felt suddenly very energetic. He experienced new excitement, new strength within. He got up at once and went towards Monai's house.

As he walked, he asked himself if he had the right to sell the school furniture. It was not his personal property after all. But who was there to question? And who would question him in any case? He was free to sell the whole school if he so chose. It was he who had built up the school. Every brick of the school building was a symbol of his sacrifices. He had gathered things for the school bit by bit, without bothering if it was day or night. And now he was going to sell it all!

His conscience said it was a theft. His conscience enraged him. What would he eat? Should his family starve? Those ideals, precepts of religion, concepts of sin and merit—they were all the luxuries of those whose stomachs were full. When famine came, even sage Vishwamitra had stolen meat from a low-caste man and had eaten. Vishwamitra had committed theft outside, whereas he would be doing it in his own school. In fact, it was no theft at all. The white ants had already invaded those desks. If the desks remained in the school any longer, they would be completely destroyed. If he did not sell the desks, the whole school, built at the cost of so much money, would be destroyed.

The argument in favour of selling the desks filled Panchu's heart with greater excitement. At that moment, he felt extremely proud of the intellectual powers that had enabled him to deceive himself so cleverly. The whole family would be freed from the haunting fear of hunger. And under that pretext, one by one, he would be able to sell many other things from the school. Thereby, he and his family would be able to fight the famine for many days.

Monai's house was right in front, barely ten steps ahead. Panchu hesitated. How would he tell Monai about selling the furniture? What would Monai think about him? Monai regarded him with great respect. And today, he would be forever disgraced before Monai. The real condition of his house would then become common knowledge and his theft would be exposed. Using public money for personal ends...suppose Monai raised such a point?

All his excitement subsided. His head started whirling again with despair. But he did not stagger. Nor did he move. He simply stood still and stunned like a stone statue. He saw visions before his eyes. And he could see nothing—nothing at all. At that moment, life seemed to have drained out of him.

"Oh, Master Babu!" Panchu heard Monai's voice. Again a wave of excitement came over him. Panchu was startled. He found Monai standing at the door of his house.

"Tell me, Master Babu! What brought you here at this hour?"

"Nothing...I just happened to be this side."

Monai came closer. He said: "You performed the last rites of poor Munir. Somebody else in your place wouldn't have even bothered to look at him."

Panchu remained silent. He was debating with himself whether he should make his proposal to Monai or not. Finding him silent, Monai said: "I've heard that you even gave rice to the daughters of the poor man! Nuru was praising you skyhigh. You're so generous, Master Babu! Otherwise, think of these times! Oh, no one bothers about anyone else. What days God has brought for us? How can we get over the hardships?"

Monai heaved a sigh. Panchu also did the same. He had almost abandoned the idea of offering his school furniture to Monai for sale. He just did not know how to say it. But if he did not ask, the whole family would starve. Then...

Monai, a practical fellow, guessed what was in Panchu's mind. He was trying to read the expression on his face. But he was not able to see in the dark. With folded hands, he said: "Master Babu, since you've already come up to my door, do come in and grace my humble home, please!"

Panchu followed Monai who made him sit on the cot in the outer room and started talking by the light of the hurricane lamp. He himself sat on the ground after giving him a place of honour. Monai could discern that Master Babu had come with some special purpose. But when the opportunity came, he would hear it straight from Panchu. He provoked Panchu: "Master Babu, what do newspapers say? What news about the war? Do you think prices will go higher?"

Panchu felt disgust for Monai. Did that selfish fellow want to loot the public still further? Would he devour the dead bodies of the villagers or what? Panchu's disgust was conveyed through an ironical remark: "You're asking about the news? You're going to prosper!"

Monai laughed stupidly and turned his pockets inside out. He said: "Hi! Hi! Hi! What prosperity, Master Babu? I'm distressed. In the *Gita*, Arjuna asked Lord Krishna what use was it to have three worlds to rule when our own kindred people cease to be ours? That's my situation too. I swear by these sacred beads I wear. I can't tell a lie, seated under this light. I can't swallow my food these days. But Lord Krishna also wanted us to do our duty. Birth and death are the law of life. I only think that..."

Monai noticed that Panchu was still silent and lost. He said: "You're looking very sad today, Master Babu! Now, don't grieve so much about Munir. He had come into this world, and now he's gone. He came and bought rice for eight annas today. But I gave him more rice for that money. I believe in silent charity, Master Babu! But he was not fated to have that rice! Every single thing is stamped for a specific person... But Master Babu, from where did you get that rice?"

"From Dayal Babu."

"Really!" Monai became serious and looked down. He asked: "What price?"

Panchu felt irritated. That wretched man was asking about what was lost and gone! He was adding insult to injury! Panchu said in an indifferent tone: "Why do you want to know the price? You all belong to the same tribe!"

"No, Master Babu! There's a difference. I shall charge you a little less than Dayal Babu. You're like a family member. I shall give you as much as you want."

Panchu was overjoyed. He imagined that Monai had already brought and stacked several bags of rice before him.

Monai went on talking in the same vein: "Now Dayal Babu has started being cunning with us. He is afraid now that I've become partner of half his business. He has gone and provoked the government to open Union Boards. He has sold his foodgrains directly to the government. He did not give a single paisa to the middleman. And now he will get his stocks sold to the Union Boards at the rate of ten rupees a maund, so that I'm completely ruined. But he doesn't know that I can also play tricks with him. I'll get him in such a noose that he'll simply stare at me with a gaping mouth. Yes, I'll do that!"

With a conceited air, Monai changed his posture, and looking towards the inner room called out: "I say, Nyada, bring me the chelum, my boy!"

Panchu's hope revived. He felt like doing something himself in the game of tricks and manoeuvres. He said: "*Arre,* I know very well, Monai! Do you think Dayal Babu is capable of fighting you? And don't I know that you're far more capable than he can be?"

Monai felt flattered. He was so moved emotionally that he touched Panchu's feet and said: "It's all by the grace of God, Master Babu! Ever since I became a Vaishnav, I've never thought ill about any Brahmin, sadhu or the sacred cow, Master Babu! I'm telling you the truth. Then who can think ill about me?"

"That's right! You're right indeed!" Panchu said with some excitement. "Of course, you've so much pity in your heart and you're a religious man. Don't I know it?"

Nyada came with Monai's *hukkah*. When the boy found Master Babu seated there with his father, he was a little confused. Putting the *hukkah* on the floor, he fell at his teacher's feet.

That awakened the teacher's pride in Panchu. He asked Nyada in a stern voice: "Why didn't you come to school today, boy?"

Nyada looked scared. Monai explained: "I didn't send him. His mother has been unwell for two days. Hi! Hi! God is going to bless this house!"

Panchu got excited. He said flatteringly: "I see! When will it be?"

"There's still time. She's in her sixth month. But she feels heavy in the head these days—and who can serve the mother better than the son? So, I thought..."

This was Monai's third wife. Nyada was the child of the second wife. The present one, being a stepmother and the young wife of an old husband, took the fullest advantage of the son.

Monai looked at the boy and said: "Go inside and do your studies with your mother."

Nyada left with his head bent. Monai took a puff at the *hukkah* and said: "All I want is that Nyada should pass his examination... God! Now your school is almost closed down. You also worked a miracle, Master Babu! In the past seven generations in this village, not a single man has done what you've done! Really, I tell you!"

Panchu said with a sigh: "Well... But now the termites are eating away the desks!"

"Oh, God!... I would like to suggest something if you would listen to me."

Panchu was startled. Perhaps his purpose would be served. He said: "Do say. What's it?"

"Why don't you sell those wooden articles to me? What's the point of letting the white ants feast on them? *Arre*, even otherwise, you'll have to make new desks after the famine. If you sell now, you can at least show some money in the school account!"

It was like a windfall to the needy. However, that still did not solve his immediate problem of getting rice. But having come so close to the fulfilment of his purpose, Panchu would not go back disappointed. He said to Monai: "Your suggestion is fine, but..."

"What is it?" Monai asked with eagerness, as though he had

grown wings. "I only said it in the interest of your school. But I won't insist. To tell you the truth, I've no need of those things." Saying this, Monai got engrossed in puffing at his *hukkah*.

Panchu came out of his euphoria. He was anxious not to spoil the situation which was about to be resolved. He started saying confusedly: "No, I don't deny that. But my point is...well, you know very well that these are the days of loot and plunder. And right now...I mean...I'm under some financial strain. You can well understand that if the school closes down and..."

Monai produced a bubbling sound as he puffed at his *hukkah*. He shook his head and said in an emphatic tone of understanding: "I understand everything, Master Babu! I've also seen good times as well as bad times. I'm even ready to give you rice!"

Panchu realized that Monai had thoroughly understood the purpose of his visit. He felt very embarrassed. To seize his opportunity, he said with a show of authority: "Yes, I shall certainly take it for the present. But I want you to know that I shall take that money only as a debt. Whatever money you give me for the furniture, I shall withdraw from the bank and credit to the school account."

As he said this, Panchu himself felt he was going out of his way in making this clarification. Monai stared at Panchu intently and shaking his head, started gurgling at his *hukkah*. He assessed the depth of Panchu's intention. With a view to confirm his guess he said: "Very well, I shall come and see the wood in a couple of days. The deal will be done."

Panchu saw that the possibility of getting the rice had again receded. He became impatient. Panic-stricken, he pleaded: "Please finalize the deal today, Monai. There's not a grain of rice in the house. I lost five *seers* of rice by touching the dead body of a Musalman. I'm in great dilemma."

Monai kept mum. The *hukkah* produced a gurgling sound. Panchu's pleading eyes were fixed on Monai's face. He felt that by entrusting his prestige in Monai's hands, he was begging him to protect him. Panchu felt he had fallen in his own estimation. His self-respect shattered like a fallen earthen toy. But suppose Monai refused even after this? No, no, he would not let that happen. If such a thing happened, he would place his head at Monai's feet. He was prepared to suffer any humiliation so that he could enter the house today with a bundle of rice.

Monai put aside the *hukkah* and said: "I shall give you ten *seers* of rice right now. Manage with it for the time being. We can settle the amount later. Don't worry at all." Monai stood up. He stopped hesitantly at the door and said: "Master Babu, let me have the keys of the school building if you're carrying them with you. The benches will have to be removed during the night, so that your reputation doesn't suffer."

Monai's show of intimacy touched Panchu's heart. He promptly pulled out a bunch of keys and handed it over to Monai and said: "There are some papers and registers in the drawers of the table. Please see that they're kept apart carefully. Right?" Panchu's tone was extremely polite. Monai said as he took the bunch of keys from him: "Don't worry in the least. I shall just get you ten *seers* of rice."

Monai went inside. He was happy that by God's grace, he had saved fifty-sixty rupees so easily. He had sold away all the benches by taking ten *seers* of rice. Otherwise who would have bought such things? Monai said to himself: "Master Babu won't be able to look me in the eye. God is great. He is great indeed!"

On the other hand Panchu reflected: "God is so kind! I lost five *seers* of rice and now I'm getting ten *seers* instead! I'll get rice in future too. I should easily get two maunds. At least Monai has a godly heart. He came in useful during a crisis!"

4

In spite of exercising great economy and barely filling half their stomachs, six *seers* of rice were consumed within four days. By this time, Monai would have probably sold away the school furniture at a ·discount. Panchu said to himself: "Let me go to settle the account with Monai. As it is, he is a notoriously cunning fellow. He'll offer two rupees when you expect ten. But at the present critical moment, whatever he gives will be of great value... There are forty-eight benches and as many desks. He should give at least fifty rupees. If not fifty, let him give at least forty. I can get at least a maund of rice with that amount and carry on for a month without any difficulty. Of course, the furniture is worth much more than that. The value of that furniture should fetch him at least one and a half if not two maunds of rice. Besides, there has been an announcement about controlled price of rice today. In view of this announcement, Monai will have to sell rice at ten rupees a maund. Monai is expecting the Union Board rice today. In that case, I can buy four maunds of rice for forty rupees. We can get along for four or five months. After that, God will take care of us. Yes, He who has created this mouth, will also provide food to eat!"

But the very next moment Panchu felt that proverb was utter nonsense. So many people had died of starvation. In their foolishness, people had imagined God to be kind. But where was God— that Universal Supreme Spirit? Could He not see with His own eyes lakhs of innocent people dying of hunger? If he saw that, it only meant that he created their mouths but did not give them food to eat.

All those skeleton-like creatures—men, women and children, rushing and walking with all the strength of their weakened bodies, passed before Panchu's eyes. Their sunken eyes gleamed with happiness. There was excitement in their dried up bones. Some carried rags in their hands, some carried worn out utensils of aluminium, copper and brass and rushed to Monai's shop. Legs of cots, ploughshares, fishing nets and hooks, implements used by carpenters and blacksmiths—they were carrying with them whatever was left in the house.

Today there had been an announcement in the town about rice to be supplied at controlled price. Even small coins were useful now after a long time to buy rice. Now the famine could not hurt them any more. Its impact would be gone. The Government had heeded their appeals. It was said grains would be distributed free after a few days. Good times would return once again. God willing, there would be a bumper crop in the current year, and once that was harvested, the whole country would be like heaven once more.

The control order brought fresh life to those battling death. Panchu looked at them and pondered: "The people of this country are so simple-hearted! Even a small thing is sufficient to please them. A strip of cloth and a handful of rice—that's the only heaven they yearn for! They don't aspire for cars and mansions."

Panchu remembered that Dayal Babu had once sent a special man all the way to Calcutta to get a dozen bottles of Scotch whisky. But even though he was willing to buy at as much as eighty rupees per bottle, he could not get the stuff in black market. How agitated Dayal Babu had been! In a pathetic voice he had said: "Look at this, Master Babu! What hard times we're facing! Scotch isn't available even at eighty rupees a bottle!"

"Yearning for a drop of liquor," mused Panchu, "made Dayal Babu restless, whereas the poor people under Dayal Babu's heels are restless without a grain of rice. What an odd similarity! A few days later, how happy Dayal was when he heard the news about Scotch whisky being sold at the controlled rate of thirty rupees a bottle! And today, when rice is being sold at controlled rates, the people are so happy and excited! And look at Monai's enthusiasm!"

A large crowd had collected in front of Monai's shop. It was impossible to hear what people were talking about. Monai, with silver-framed spectacles resting on his nose, was busy examining with disdain every rag and quilt brought to him. Seated next to him, Azim was following Monai's instructions and noting down the amount due for the items exhibited in front.

A few steps ahead of Monai's shop was a tree on the left. The leaves of that tree had been already used to quench the fire of the stomach, and many of its branches had been broken. The bare skeleton of that tree now stood like a silent witness, a symbol of the starving Bengal. Panchu stood under the tree, looking on at the farce going on in front of Monai's shop...

"Two bowls and a dhoti...you call this a dhoti, do you? Ugh! The thing would be costly even if one got it free! Write, Azim, write six paise in Bholu's name. He'll eat controlled rice, *sala!*" Monai said with contempt and flung those items on the pile of utensils and clothes.

Azim was writing non-stop and as he wrote, he repeated: "Six paise for Bholu!"

A skeletal figure bearing the name of Bholu pleaded in a low, trembling voice: "That won't fill our stomach, Monai. Four annas... write at least four annas! We've been starving for ten days!"

Monai retorted sharply: "Oh, oh! If you're hungry, who ever gets a full meal around here? Looking at your condition, I can't even breathe properly. Six paise won't be enough, you say? These bastards! The more you give them, the more they plead and ask for more... Lord Krishna has said in the *Gita* to be content with what you have. But you fellows can't be content! Ugh!... Here's an aluminium bowl and a plate. Write four paise for Patal."

Those who had come to sell things were not entitled to bargain. The buyer gave the price he fancied. People were eager to sell their things as quickly as possible and buy rice. About seventy-eighty persons were standing there. In Monai's shop, there were heaps of old and broken utensils and piles of clothes. Iron scraps, fishing nets, legs of string cots were piling up. But rice was nowhere in sight. Monai's cash-box was not there either. Monai was just blabbering, shouting abuses, keeping things and instructing Azim to note down the price in the account book... He had informed the crowd that the money would be given after the amount had been written against each name.

Every man was in a hurry. Every man wanted his things to be bought first. Once the name and price were noted down in the account book, everyone felt that his right to have the rice was ensured. The harassment caused by hunger was not so acute at the moment. Once their names were noted down in the account book, people came away from the shop and either stretched themselves on the ground nearby or sat in small groups gossiping. Some of them had been starving for eight days, some for ten, even twelve days. They were all gripped by hunger, and, viewing impending death with its increasing frightfulness and experiencing the dull feelings of fear and anxiety, they had been fighting against void. Like an ant crushed under a foot, the enslaved man, crushed under the heavy weight of the ruling authority, had been concentrating on death, and, tearing himself away from his attachment for life, he awaited the final moment. As he got some relief through the controls, he escaped from the clutches of death. Nothing would make man happier than being able to extend his life even briefly.

Panchu stood against that tree and observed the farce. Mingling his own self with all those struggling creatures, he identified his consciousness and mind with the picture before his eyes. His eyes, his mind would rush to seek refuge under it. His Bengali mind, nurtured in the political atmosphere of the city, was seriously thinking about the conditions of those hungry and naked slaves who were still human beings and were caught right up to their necks in the shackles of helplessness. Panchu reflected: "This can't even be called an ideal of non-violence. Nor can it be called renouncement by a yogi. This is just dying the death of cats and dogs!"

Then he thought: "Even cats and dogs cannot be easily pushed away from what they are entitled to have to satisfy their hunger. Even while dying, they would fight with all their might and rise in loud protest against every tyranny coming before them in the form of death. But we are dying the death of insects—without voice, without strength!"

Panchu continued to ponder over the situation: "Would man in any country, any community in the world, like to die in this manner? Then why doesn't man think of the consequences of his doings? Why does he forget that the very people upon whom he perpetuates atrocities carried away by the blind fury of his power and authority, may some day turn round and sit in a higher position?"

Panchu also looked at the other side of the picture. Suppose, in his place, Bholu, Patal, Tinkaudi or any other man, harassed by starvation, forces his way and sits in Monai's place and starves Monai for ten-twelve days as he himself has starved and tempts him with the consolation of giving him rice—imagine how Monai would plead and beg for food and how he would suffer... That very thought filled Panchu's heart with a kind of delight. He grew impatient to see the fun of starving those very people who had been starving their helpless fellowmen all along.

Dayal Babu, Rai Bhuvan Mohan Sarkar, Mr. Jordan, Lady Chatterji, Lord... Panchu indulged in malicious pleasure of imagining every 'big man' suffering pangs of hunger. Let those who are fighting for personal power, fight against hunger for once! Let those claiming to provide the divine gift of relief, those self-appointed messiahs—let them ask the question while suffering pangs of hunger if their empty stomachs would be able to take abuses? Had anyone ever been able to do it? Then why did they want to abuse others? Why did they abuse those who were starving?

A glow of happiness spread over his face, revealing more prominently the arrogance of his mind. He felt like a child who had happily touched the moon in the water in a dish. Allowing his feeling of self-importance to grow by going on giving a longer rope to himself, Panchu listened to his own voice like a voice of his soul.

Panchu's stomach was full at that time. He had come to settle his account with Monai, but he found instead the accounts of those starving people. All around him were groups of people seated in different places, raving with satisfaction and happiness in the expectation of getting rice. Today, after a long time, Panchu was excited.

In between, Panchu looked around with roving eyes to catch a glimpse of joy on the faces of those starving people. Right behind him, on the other side of the tree, Keshto Nandy was trying with all his might to raise his cracked voice to his former high-pitched level. It had become a common saying that whenever Keshto spoke, his voice could be heard up to the distant Mir Ghat. In an attempt to convey something, he was speaking hurriedly in a very loud voice: "He pushed my sister out of the house. He said there was no food in the house. He asked her to go to her brother and come back after the famine. Now, tell me, if I'm her brother, is he nothing to her? If you talk of religion, he's her husband, her master. He held her hand to live with her till death. And now, when trouble came, he dragged her by the hand and threw her out, eh! Can there be anything more mean? At that time, believe me, I felt so disgusted! How man has fallen! I swear I really wanted to renounce everything. My heart tore away from this life. Still, I did not fail in my duty. Promptly, I too dragged out my wife and threw her out. I told her that since my sister had come to me, she should go to her own brother! That rascal must be thinking that because he threw out my sister, she would have nowhere to go. But, I say, Keshto Nandy would save his sister even at the cost of his wife! That blasted fellow must be thinking that only he's capable of throwing out his wife. But I'm steps ahead of him. I'm made of sterner stuff. I say, I'm very particular about my reputation, ye...e...s!"

Panchu felt that as Keshto Nandy uttered the last sentence, he had stretched his voice so much that he had once again established a record of its high pitch. He thought that when man became utterly shameless, he proclaimed everything at the top of his voice.

Discarding the appearance of shamelessness he consciously presented himself as a proud champion of justice and truth, and saving man from a feeling of inferiority. He had noted it happening all along among the people of his town. Every man with even the slightest strength in his body and almost all people with reputation hid their pain behind false pride and sulked within. They had nothing to eat. Menfolk in the families constantly worried about their responsibilities, and, feeling helpless, went crazy. They saw the protruding bones in their children's bodies and their flesh drying up and their legs and arms looking absolutely emaciated. With each passing day, they and their children lost hope of getting food. In that situation, which father would not curse himself for being born a male? Which heart would not shatter in the face of inability to fill one's own stomach and the stomachs of their family members? Man could not feed himself and his children, could not feed his aged parents, his brothers and sisters who depended on him. Yet he was alive.

Man had been writhing in agitation as he received the blow of his worst failure. He rebelled against everyone. He rebelled against himself and against God. There was a constant tug of war between the snapping thread of life and attachment to life. As the day dawned, man woke up with a fresh mind, hoping to find food for the day, that there would be some miracle and everyone would find a plate of food before him. If such a thing could happen, there would be a wave of excitement all around. The face of the whole town would completely change. And then, Monai, with a crestfallen face, would wonder who would come and buy grains from him.

Man detracted his mind the whole day by sustaining himself on hope. But at the end of the day came the night and darkness loomed on his hopes as well. He became grim and irritable. As he looked with hungry eyes at the stars in the realm of death, some sudden painful moaning filling the air. In the dark night, he heard over long distances shrieking and groaning sounds. Together with hysterical human beings, crying and shrieking as they ran helter-skelter, one heard the loud barking of the dogs and people's hearts trembled with the terror of death. They spent nights without sleep and in course of time, birds started chirping on the bare branches of trees, feeling stimulated by the silvery light that came like a miracle.

Man became irritable in the face of fading hope. Hunger had reached a point where there was no refuge and no hope. People wanted to forget their hunger and think about something else, but they were unable to do that. With depleting physical strength, relations between man and woman were beginning to break down. When aroused, they pulled and grabbed each other's bodies and soon started panting. That weariness, along with the weariness caused by hunger, enflamed the fire of their hearts. In spite of the desire for sensual pleasure, man had started consciously hating physical contact between man and woman. Wives were driven out from so many houses. So many women deserted their husbands. Relations between young children started breaking. The presence of even parents, brothers and sisters became irksome. At the very sight of one another, they were filled with wild fury. Every man started thinking that he would not have starved if he had been the only one alive in the world. Every man considered another man his sworn enemy. Neighbours and relatives started remembering things of three generations ago and sought every opportunity to pick up a quarrel.

Respectable people of the middle class concealed the affliction of their hearts under their torn sheets and went round the town. Their condition was even worse than the poor. They talked about Shantipur's pairs of dhotis and the lavish dishes they used to have in the days of their forefathers. Every respectable man boasted about his grandfather or great-grandfather. All their efforts of keeping their pangs and nostalgia confined within their hearts by distracting their minds from their empty stomachs were of no avail.

Panchu had noticed that in his own house and in the houses of his neighbours, people were more worried about maintaining their prestige than about satisfying their hunger. They had been thinking of so many ways of doing that, but all their efforts and plans had fallen to the ground...

Haran Bhattacharya's family had been starving for two days. Even behind the closed doors of his house he always had the lurking suspicion that the outside world have come to know that his family had been starving. He was constantly worried about it. On the third day he thought about a solution. He came out of the house. He provoked the people to talk about their plight and then announced that as for him, he was going to get the digestive powder from the *vaidya* as he was suffering from indigestion.

Relations among people were becoming unpleasant... One day, Paresh Ghoshal suddenly pushed out of the house his younger brother and widowed sister accusing them of incestuous relations...

Kanai Ghatak had lost his father some time ago. It was essential to perform the religious rites on his death anniversary in order to save the family reputation...

Kanai clicked a deal with Paran Haldar who was a well-to-do manager of Dayal Babu. He forced his wife to sleep with Paran. When Paran tried to escape without paying the agreed amount, Kanai turned mad with rage. People from the neighbourhood collected in his house when they heard the two men shouting and abusing each other. Kanai had tried to save his own reputation by pushing his wife into selling her body. And now, in the twinkling of an eye, that reputation was gone! Kanai's starving wife stood mute, her womanhood dishonoured. Paran Haldar pushed aside Kanai Ghatak and cutting through the crowd, ran for his life. Now, Kanai wandered in the town like a mad man, though he harmed no one. He boasted about his family reputation day in and day out.

Everyone knew the condition in the house of everyone else. Still no one could give up the supporting crutch of the reputation he once enjoyed.

Almost eighty per cent of women from reputed houses had taken to prostitution in the expectation of getting money or food or in order to forget their sorrows for a while.

Communities remained only in name. Nobody bothered about distinctions of caste. Distinctions between Hindus and Muslims had ceased to exist. All were hungry and sailing in the same boat. Everyone, even though apparently worried about the plight of the world, was actually worried about himself.

Panchu wondered if in his house too family relations, reputation, attachment for one's kith and kin, character, courtesy and so on would remain intact in the absence of food.

This thought gave a severe jolt to Panchu. It alarmed him. But once the question arose in his mind, it was difficult for Panchu to get away from it. He could not bear the glare of that naked truth. In the context of the things happening around, Panchu started assessing every member of his family in the light of the grim reality of the days to come.

Shibu was the first to come to his mind. Anything wrong happening in the family would be primarily Shibu's doing. Mother would be dead before any untoward development in the family. She would certainly be dead—she should be dead. Shibu was capable of forcing his wife into prostitution—though Bakulphul was surely not that type of a woman. She was, in fact, a woman of very strong character. As for Tulsi, she did not seem to have good character. Mangala said she had done something fishy with the brother of Aunt no. 8. And Mangala...oh...no—no!

Panchu grew restless when he found that while thinking along those lines, he was losing control over his imagination. The veins of his head became tense. His mind became overburdened and agitated with the excitement of a murderer gone berserk. He was wild with rage, his fists clenched, his jaws closed tight. His body shuddered with the force of his feelings. For a moment, his consciousness and power of thinking vanished. Then suddenly his attention was drawn to an incident—this saved him.

Tulsi Boshtam was pulling his wife's torn saree. And she was crying and shrieking and struggling with all her strength, trying to wrap that dirty saree around her body though it was torn to shreds.

Tulsi Boshtam shouted: "Give me your saree. I'll bring rice from Monai."

His wife retorted: "Why don't you sell your own dhoti?

But his contention was that he was a man and he could bring some food only by making several trips outside. Whereas, she was a woman and what did she have to lose? She could well remain confined to the house behind closed doors.

The spectators took the side of both. But more were in favour of the husband. They cited several such incidents and commented that in many houses women remained naked in the house.

In the end, the woman had to surrender to the male power. After that terrible blow, she reacted like a weak female cobra making hissing sounds. Her trampled ego asserted itself with greater force and gave new strength to her starved body. Tears had long since ceased to flow from her eyes. But today, when she had to strip herself openly, her heart cried out in anguish: "Go and fill your stomach by selling the honour of women. How long will you be able to eat like this?"

Tinkaudi, in his good days, was counted among notorious drunkards. Even today, he had been hiding the pain of his heart by taking refuge in the same attitude of a libertine. He added the final touch to the biting comment of Boshtam's wife: "Not merely women's honour, Lakkhi, women themselves would be sold. What remains after that is only stomach, ha, ha!"

With that villainous laugh emanating from his throat, Tinkaudi presented the reality in the garb of ominousness...

Glamour and uproar! The enraged, pathetic cry of distress of helpless wild beasts being strangled to death...

Startled out of his thoughts, Panchu looked in the direction of Monai's shop. People were beside themselves. They had rushed into the shop, crushing their own fellowmen in their excitement and moving forward. They could not find even a couple of words from their heart-rending pain and anger. Like man of primordial days, individual pain, in its natural form, cried out collectively. The echo of that cry, moving like a saw, pierced through Panchu's being from his ears to his soul, as he sat under a bier-like tree.

Man had discovered a language which lay hidden under a civilization thousands of years old. Monai was surrounded on all sides and abuses and curses were being hurled at him.

From where Panchu was sitting, nothing could be seen clearly. He wondered what the row was about. It seemed Monai was up to some new trick. Panchu got up and went near the shop. All the others nearby also rushed to the shop.

Monai was saying: "The rice is lying with the government. You can take your money!"

But what would they do with the money? Money could not be eaten. You may go on looking with pleasure at all your gold, silver, diamonds and jewels—all that humbug belonging to the people whose stomachs were full. Those things had no value to the starving masses. A diamond worth millions or billions would well become a grave danger to one's life if it were eaten. Man had equated poison with the Koh-i-noor. In his love for self, man became so clever that he started regarding himself his own enemy. Man started valuing himself in terms of glittering stones and metals. A selfish man gratifies himself by stuffing the glitter of gold and silver in bags made from dead skin. Whereas, life insists on attaining its right by filling empty stomachs of millions of beings and will rest only after attaining this.

Their rough and itching skin with gypsum-like scales showed the distinct shapes of their ribs. Many of them had swollen hands and feet. And they had oozing wounds and scars in many parts of their bodies. Those bodies, rotting with diseases like syphilis, gonorrhoea and oozing blood, brushed and jostled against one another. They were rushing into Monai's shop to express their impotent rage. Surrounded by so many striking bodies, Monai felt he could not breathe. Accusations were hurled at him from all sides, casting aspersions on him. They plagued him with their heated questions: "Why didn't you tell us earlier that you had no rice? Why did you buy our things? Why did you deceive us? Monai, you won't be happy by causing misery to thousands of people by starving them. Worms will breed in every pore of your body. Your wealth worth lakhs of rupees will be reduced to ashes in the flames of our hunger. You will die the death of cats and dogs. You'll die rotting."

Monai rose to his feet and thundered: "Right now, only you are rotting and dying. How can you blame me? I don't cut anyone's throat. I don't rob anyone's house. I'm satisfied with whatever little God gives me through my business. Why don't you ask the government to give you rice? The government has brought these controls. Get away, all of you! Clear out from my shop. Take your money and out you go!"

For a while people were overawed by Monai. They stepped back as he came forward fretting and fuming. But their wrath at being cheated was stronger than Monai's overbearing posture. People pounced upon him like hungry wolves. They beat him up. They threw everything that came in their hands. Some people tried to break open the door of his house. Azim vanished from the scene.

In their frenzy to take revenge, people even entered his house. They started breaking and flinging his household things about. Monai's wife, wailing and beating her breasts, showered curses on them. But she too got beaten up. Nyada was beaten up as well. As for Monai, people spat on him, pulled his hair and he was beaten blue and manhandled in the worst possible manner. They plundered his house. They took out their anger on anything they could lay their hands on. Some people rushed into the kitchen and quarrelled among themselves while they grabbed the food that had been cooked. The food lay strewn all over. They rummaged every room of the house. Some people discovered there was a basement in Monai's house. The collective strength of all the hungry creatures smashed all the doors of the house.

There were stacks and stacks of grain bags. Such huge stocks that even the whole town could not have eaten in a month. The crowds got mad with excitement at the sight of those bags. There were uproarious cries all around.

Monai's wife and Nyada wailed and screamed. Monai, beaten blue, stared in a silent, passionless manner at the looting and plundering going on in his house. The rice bags were being ripped open. Rice got scattered in the godown. The crowd laughed hysterically.

Suddenly, in the midst of their laughter came the sound of bullets being fired. Dayal Babu's armed men were firing at them and wielding their lathis. Many people were hit. The cries of joy turned into death-cries.

Azim had come back with Dayal Babu's toughs and armed policemen and was instructing them to shower lathi blows and bullets on the crowd.

With people writhing in pain and piercing shrieks rising from all sides, Monai's house was coloured with stains of blood. It became a cremation ground—out of seventy or eighty people, twenty or twenty-five became martyrs at the altar of hunger.

However, Monai was saved. Nyada was saved. Monai's wife cried and cursed the crowd. People ran helter-skelter. They ran in all directions to save their lives. Their courage gave way. Rice had come to their hands and had slipped away. So many lives perished. The anger of defeat got buried in the bloodshot colour of their eyes. The crowd, making a great hue and cry, ran out of the house with staggering steps, pushing the burden of their defeat on to their legs.

Panchu stood in a corner, a witness to the scene. He saw the terrible revolt of the people and its inhuman suppression and his concern for family reputation and selfish considerations had made him a coward. How could a middleclass man like him, a gentleman from a respectable family and an English-educated headmaster, side with those people? He stood passive and limp when they were fighting for justice. He remained as passive even when they were

being beaten up. Of course, he did exhibit his intellectual power. He was happy when they looted and plundered
Monai's house. And when they were being lathicharged and fired
upon, he grieved within and stood there, contemplating that
Monai, Azim and Dayal Babu should be strangled to death. But
Panchu loved his reputation more than he loved his family and
his own self. How could he, poor man, take the side of the people?
He needed rice from Monai. If he took the side of the people, he
and his family would have to starve. So, he stood there passive
and withdrawn, taking care of his self-interest and his reputation.
Unaware of his cowardice, he felt remorse and a kind of unhappi-
ness within at the thought of the atrocities of capitalists and the
plight of the working people and the peasants.

Monai was now in command of the situation. Blood-soaked
bodies lay scattered in the godown and the threshold of his house
and verandah. His whole house was in disarray. Several wounded
persons lay sprawled all over. Many were in their death throes.
It seemed as though even the walls groaned with pain.

Monai shuddered. He was terror-stricken at the sight of the dead
and the wounded. In his heart rose a prayer: "God, I'm not to be
blamed at all. You dwell in every heart, my Lord! You're a witness
to everything. You're the Supreme Spirit; and know the heart of
every living being. You're kind and merciful!"

At the same time, Azim was bragging about how he had
sought Dayal Babu's help and had brought his armed men and
the police.

Dayal Babu's armed men were twisting their moustaches,
boasting about their bravery and courage. They demanded from
Monai the reward for their bravery. Monai gave five rupees to each
one of them. Then he raised an outcry about his losses and
cursing the wounded and the dead lying about his house, started
pleading. But in the end, he was compelled to give five rupees
more to each.

Monai looked at Panchu and said in a complaining tone: "Did
you see, Master Babu! This is the reward you get these days for
doing good to somebody! Doing good has given me a bad name!
Prompted by my religious feelings, I said to myself that I may as
well buy their rags so that the poor wretches can satisfy their
hunger at least with controlled rice. I took pity on them, but these

bastards turned out to be such devils that they rewarded me thus for being good to them!"

Panchu stood speechless.

Then pressing his hands on his own back Monai observed: "These are not the days of being pious. Really, I tell you! *Sale...e!* They've given me such a beating that my bones are rattling. These mean bastards! They've gone and sold their women. They've indulged in so much sin that even God would look away from them. Yes!... Now tell me, how mean of them to raise their hands on my wife! The way they beat her! And they also beat up my Nyada. Demons, all of them!"

"What's the matter, Monai?" a commanding voice was heard at the door.

Monai, Azim, Panchu, the policemen and musclemen were startled by the voice. They all stood respectfully. Monai came forward, pleading guilty with folded hands. Dayal Babu stood in the doorway.

A *kurta* of crinkled mull, a dhoti of fine mull bordered with gold and silver threads, an unwrinkled silken shoulder cloth round the neck, a gold watch on the left wrist and on the fingers of both his hands glittered the rings studded with four gems. In his right hand he held an attractive stick with an ivory handle. He wore pump shoes and in his ears were scented cotton buds. He had stuffed a *paan* in his mouth. His eyes showed the hang-over of the liquor he had consumed the previous night. He was escorted by four ruffians. Dayal Babu had sanctified Monai's house by the dust of his feet. He surveyed the verandah, the threshold and the basement. Dead bodies lay strewn all over. Monai followed him with folded hands, muttering every other moment: "I'm completely ruined, oh my saviour!"

Dayal Babu conducted an enquiry. He heard all the details. He abused the lewds of the town and informed Monai that the matter had been reported to the Daroga. He advised Monai to have the dead bodies hidden in the basement behind the grain bags before the Daroga appeared on the scene...

A thick mattress was spread on the wooden divan for Dayal Babu, who soon made himself comfortable. Dayal Babu's umbrella-bearer tucked the umbrella under his arm and started fanning Dayal Babu. One of the servants held out a *paan*-container and another servant hurriedly came forward with a spittoon. Dayal Babu spat out the old *paan* and stuffed two fresh ones in his mouth along with a pinch of tobacco. The servant held out before him a silk handkerchief with which Dayal Babu wiped his hands. Then he bowed respectfully to Panchu and beckoned him to sit by his side. He gave two rolled *paans* to Panchu and started complaining about the heat. The servant fanned him all the more vigorously.

Dayal Babu's respectful behaviour provoked Panchu's suppressed sense of dignity. One was the son of the goddess of wealth, he thought and the other, himself, of the goddess of learning, and both deserved to occupy the same seat.

Accepting the *paan*, Panchu raised his head with pride and looked around. Monai sat on the floor at Dayal Babu's feet. His posture was pitiable and he folded his hands before Dayal Babu. Panchu briefly fixed his contemptuous gaze on Monai. But the next moment he remembered his own act of stealing the school furniture. A mean creature like Monai had known Panchu's secret about selling the desks. His fear of losing his reputation pushed aside his fear of learning.

Panchu shuddered as he sat on the plush mattress. He shifted his gaze. There in front of Dayal Babu in the sunlit threshold lay the bodies of the people who had given libations with their blood. Those bodies lay before Panchu's eyes as well. And Panchu was seated next to Dayal Babu!

Panchu felt a tremor in his body. The crinkles of Dayal Babu's *kurta* that touched the sleeves of his shirt were like heavy fetters and he was impatient to be free of them. Dayal Babu had his legs stretched over almost the whole divan, while Panchu sat crouching in a corner.

Now Panchu felt that his status in society was not the same as that of Dayal Babu. It was only because of Dayal Babu's grace that he had the good fortune of sitting on the divan and eating his *paans*.

Panchu glanced at Monai. His status was not equal even to Monai who was in a position to oblige him. But being forcibly entangled in the knots of high-caste and low-caste distinctions, Monai was also obliged to honour Panchu. But Panchu was afraid of Monai's velvet-covered leather shoes. The scholar in him was shocked. His urban mind was shocked. His diligent life received a shock. And his sense of respectability was greatly hurt. Suddenly he felt a loathing. He thought with contempt: "Whatever happens, I will never sit before anyone with folded hands."

Panchu forced himself to look at the corpses. They had no consciousness that would have forced them to pay their respects to Dayal Babu. They had no consciousness about themselves. They were the corpses of people who had died fighting to reclaim their God-given right. They had a higher status, higher than Monai, higher than Dayal Babu. Higher even than kings and emperors. They had risen higher than everything in the world. No one could dominate them any more. They were now free and emancipated.

"If only they had become aware about their rights a little earlier!" Panchu reflected. "They and the whole country would not have been reduced to this plight if realization had dawned earlier. It is against human dignity to die bearing the yoke of slavery. It does not matter if we are not in a position to take the life of somebody else. But we have the power to lay down our own life. And this power is something really very great. He who takes life cannot experience even in his dream the pain experienced by one who gives life. One who lays down his life, dies with a particular experience which gives him a sense of satisfaction. And he who kills? He is a great coward. He covers his cowardice by repeated killings and hence he's never free from anxiety. Night and day, he concentrates all his efforts on maintaining his false sense of power. Is this life? Not a moment of freedom. Not a moment of peace. Always surrounded by fear—ugh! Slaves of seats of power!"

In a flash Dayal Babu seemed to Panchu very insignificant. He felt proud of his own greatness. Supporting his elbow on Dayal Babu's cushion, he sat stiff.

Then Panchu started musing: "This nitwit who always lives in a world of insincere praise, this enemy of intellectual power is a thousand times inferior to me. No man becomes great merely by inheriting wealth. Only he who has the courage to die fighting for his right is great." And Panchu felt that he possessed that power. "My place is among those corpses lying in the scorching sun," he said to himself.

Once again, Panchu looked intently at those corpses. But now he felt that there was a slight distinction between himself and those corpses. Suppose those men lying dead had been confident about their courage to die? They would have died, but they wouldn't have suffered so much before dying. They would have died the type of death he wished for himself.

Panchu remembered all the impressive funeral processions he had personally seen or about which he had heard or read. He imagined for himself such an honourable death and was lost in that thought.

5

There was a huge gathering at the garbage mound in front of Monai's temple—kites and crows in the sky, and on the ground a whole army of dogs and human beings, all engaged in a regular tug of war over the left-overs in the leaf-plates thrown on the garbage mound.

Twenty-four persons had died in Monai's house ten days ago. Monai, who had become a Vaishnavite, wearing a string of sacred beads and a vermilion mark on his forehead, had arranged the customary feeding of Brahmins in order to pacify the hungry spirits of the dead persons.

Every single member of all the Brahmin families in the town had come for the feeding. A large number of their relatives and sadhus had also come. Seventy to eighty persons were fed on the occasion.

Not all those who came for the feeding were Brahmins, but all of them were famished. Had there been no famine, it would never have been known that the scriptures permitted Brahmins to eat in the houses of boatmen, a low-caste community. Ever since a boatmen had drunk the water with which he had washed the feet of Lord Ramachandra*, the members of that community had become sanctified. And now, the Brahmins, who had been starving for seven or eight days, had gone to have food at the temple built by Monai, originally a boatman. Innumerable hungry eyes stared at them greedily. Two toughs stood guarding the entrance of the temple. The people could not enter, but they stood at the entrance and looked on eagerly as the Brahmins were being fed. Many of them had not even seen anyone eating for a long time. However, the guards at the entrance with their big moustaches and blood-shot eyes, their thunderous threats and the knocking of their staffs, prevented them from advancing in the direction of the feeding.

A gang of boys from five to twelve years of age also joined the

* Reference to an incident in the *Ramayana*

crowd that went staggering opposite the temple entrance. Completely naked, with emaciated hands and legs and swollen bellies, they sucked their thumbs as they looked with hungry eyes at the tough-looking Bhojpuri men at the temple entrance.

Leaf-plates were being flung on the garbage mound one after the other. Up in the sky were the hovering kites. Crows assembled in large numbers on the parapets of the temple, waiting for their chance. On the ground was a tussle between human beings and dogs. The kites occasionally missed their mark and struck at the heads of men and women bending to pick up the leaf-plates. The dogs strove hard to lay their claim making full use of their paws and jaws. And the hungry man fought with might against all these in his self-interest even, against himself, for the sake of a handful of left-over food.

Panchu heard about it and reached the spot to witness the scene. He and his family had gone without food for six days. That day, Monai had done him a grave injustice when settling the accounts. He had told him bluntly: "All my money has gone down the drain, Master Babu! The benches were all rotten. No one was willing to buy them even for the price of firewood. I could not get even ten rupees for that stuff. To tell you the truth, it's you who should give me two seers of rice. But I won't talk about it as I comfort myself by thinking that I've been of some service to a Brahmin."

The unexpected turn in the situation left Panchu absolutely bewildered. For a while, he stared in amazement at Monai's face. It was a simple unlined face with no evidence of cunning in it. A vermilion mark on his forehead and on his lips the usual pitiable smile and the same humility in his manner of speech. Nothing blameworthy, no flippancy, nothing to suggest any manoeuvring.

Panchu was stunned. Overpowered by a feeling of despondency, tears threatened to well up in his eyes. But Panchu disliked showing his defeat to anyone. In any case, what was the point of giving an answer to Monai? He quickly walked away.

Dayal Babu had broached the subject of the feeding of those Brahmins. The Daroga was also present. It was revealed that Monai had given two thousand rupees to the Daroga in cash, and after undertaking to pay the fine for feeding the Brahmins by way of expiation for the hungry men dying in his house, he had been pardoned by Dayal Babu and his coterie as well as by the government of the Daroga. The details of the riot were entered in the report, with Panchu Mukherji's name as a witness. And as he left,

Monai obliged Panchu by giving him two seers of rice.

From a distance, seated on the bamboo bridge, Panchu witnessed the scramble for the left-over food. People fought like mad creatures, glaring wildly at one another. A boy was injured when a kite's beak struck his head and he collapsed on the spot. People climbed the garbage mound, trampling the boy under their feet.

Panchu thought the boy must have died. He did not feel inclined to go near and find out. But he realized that he had not heard the boy shrieking, but then there was hardly any strength left in the voices of those starving creatures. While breathing his last, the boy must have cried out with all his strength, but his cry would not have been loud enough to be heard even a furlong away.

Panchu no longer took particular notice of someone dying. It had become a routine affair and he had got accustomed to it. While suffering the pangs of hunger for six days, he had forced himself to harden his emotions. On the last occasion, he had had the support of Dayal Babu and he had entertained some hope. Then he had got some rice from Monai. But now there was no hope of getting rice from anywhere. There were just a few ordinary ornaments of gold left, but Monai wouldn't give even one-fourth of the due amount. And Dayal Babu never bargained, so he would have to respectfully accept whatever he gave. Dayal Babu was so tight-fisted that he did not easily part with even the smallest coin. And in the market-place, the police and the soldiers had devised a new tactic for blackmailing anyone who came to sell ornaments. He was immediately branded a thief. Half the amount received after selling the ornaments had to be passed on to the police for fear of being insulted in public. From the remaining amount the shopkeeper would want compensation for wear and tear. One had to give bribes to even breathe!

Panchu's family would sell whatever ornaments remained only as a last resort, to buy rice. The money they would get would be just enough to buy rice for one day. Hence, the selling of the ornaments was being postponed day after day. They would do that when it was absolutely necessary, to sustain themselves for a day. As Parvati Ma said, that was enough of a consolation to enable them to pass their days.

Suddenly, a naked woman ran past Panchu and reached the garbage mound. Having been born in an age when civilization was at its zenith, Panchu was not accustomed to witnessing such a grotesque sight in broad daylight. Panchu noticed that that woman possessed more strength than the kites and the crows, the dogs and even human beings. Everyone moved away as she came close.

Initially the people were shocked by such unseemly sights. But not any more—and not after the incident, ten days ago, when people had torn off tattered clothing from the bodies of their wives in the hope of getting rice from Monai's shop at the controlled rate. They got no rice and also lost the clothes.

Men had given up living in their homes while women were compelled to remain indoors. They stared at the four walls, honour lost and totally starved. It was common now to hear the shouts of women quarrelling among themselves day and night in their houses, even the well-bred women, using the most abusive language.

Panchu thought of the loneliness of the women who had no female company in their houses. What an existence—the same walls, the same doors, the same things around the house; a room full of many happy and sad associations! Panchu imagined a newly-wed bride who had spent her wedding night in that room. In that very room, perhaps, she had given birth to her children and had a taste of motherhood. Then, with the coming of the famine, many 'valuable' things had been sold, one by one. And now that very room was suffocating her to death. This hungry and helpless woman was confined to the home out of sheer shame.

Surely there was nothing wrong if such a woman, on hearing about the possibility of finding some left-over food, broke the constraints of feminine honour and ran out of the house in her naked condition. Why did people think this was a criminal act? Man, in his condition of slavery, wanted to unburden himself by thrusting the entire burden of slavery on woman. The subjugation of women by men irked Panchu. Anger raged within him.

The Brahmins were emerging from Monai's temple with forced expressions of contentment on their faces. Panchu saw that their condition was even worse. Having found the opportunity of satisfying their hunger of so many days, they had eaten with such avarice that the food had become poison for them. As they stepped out of the temple, many of them experienced shooting pain in their stomachs. Some felt giddy and a large number of them were throwing up.

Panchu had witnessed two scenes: the non-Brahmin human beings and the animals engaged in a scramble for food on the dumphill and the pitiable state of those Brahmins who had filled their stomachs over much. The Brahmins collapsed on the ground, they had no strength to rise. They vomitted all over. The most disgusting sight was that of a ravenous man eagerly falling on another to lick the vomit.

Panchu promptly moved away, agitated. Did the first man who enslaved another realize that the seed he was sowing would let down its roots so deep and wide?

The pangs of hunger gave way to nausea. Panchu clutched his stomach and tried to divert his mind from the scene. Every man who was a slave should be prepared to face such a day, Panchu thought.

Panchu was harassed by the fact that he was unable to forget what he was trying to forget. Even as he tried to forget, these thoughts crowded his mind. And the more he tried to divert his thoughts, the more dejected he became.

Suddenly, there was a loud cry: "Move away! Move away!" Panchu was startled out of his thoughts. Dayal Babu had arrived on the scene with his strong men.

"Oh, God! Oh, my God! All of them have taken ill, poor creatures! What did Monai give them to eat? Where is Monai?"

Dayal Babu's eyes turned towards the crowd on the dumphill. "Such atrocities on my people that they're forced to lick left-over food? A *kevat*, after all! Man of lowly birth! After making a little money, he's trying to leap up to the moon! Bring him before me!"

By that time, Monai was seen rushing from the temple with his hands folded. Dayal Babu eyed him contemptuously and said: "It seems you've saved a lot of income tax!"

Monai's heart trembled with fear. Panting, he pleaded in a piteous tone: "No, no, my saviour! You...you're our protector!"

"What has happened to these people?" Dayal Babu demanded, pointing the end of his ivory stick at the sick Brahmins.

Monai folded his hands and said: "Oh, my saviour! I very much wanted to stop them, but they went on eating. I'm innocent, my master! And even these poor creatures are not at fault. It's all the mystery of God's working!"

Dayal Babu cut Monai short and said angrily: "You've not become such a great devotee of God that you can talk to me about His mysterious ways. You've heard my name, haven't you? I'm Dayal Zamindar!"

The name struck Monai's heart like a bullet and even though he went on giving endless explanations, his face wore an expression of fear. He fell at Dayal Babu's feet and said in a subdued tone: "You're our master! It's up to you whether we live or die. What else can I say? I've fallen on bad days. God is witness. I've got a bad name though I was trying to do some good."

"Who'll pay for the medical treatment of these people?"

Monai Babu was startled by the question. Looking at Dayal Babu's face he said with some hesitation: "Med...i...cal tre...at...-ment?"

"Give a rupee to each one for medicines. Do you think they should suffer on your account? Remember, Monai, if you show the cussedness to harass my people in any way, I shall drag you down to your father's sorry state. Come on, give a rupee to each one!"

With still expression on his face, Monai straightened himself. As Dayal Babu ordered the second time, he signalled Azim to rush to his house.

Dayal Babu advanced a little towards the dumphill, and gave another blow to Monai.

"You want to force my people to do such disgusting things by throwing them left-over food to eat? Do you intend wiping out religion and righteousness. You're a mean fellow! You should have told me. I wouldn't have allowed my people to lick that left-over food. Distribute one *seer* of rice to every person in the town on my account! That job should be done by this evening, do you hear?"

After issuing that order, Dayal Babu looked at his *paan*-carrier who promptly held out a two-colour silver container. Dayal Babu took a *paan* and left. He saw Panchu seated near the bridge.

"What's the news, Master Babu?" Dayal Babu asked.

Panchu who had been starving for six days, was determined not to have anything to do with Dayal Babu or Monai. He said to himself: "All of them are selfish, mean and cunning with their bellies full. If they're so arrogant because of their money, we're proud about our poverty!"

Panchu was very happy that Dayal Babu had driven Monai into a corner. He wished somebody would pull down and trample Dayal Babu as well. He also felt like asking Dayal Babu what generous acts he had done for his people that he was going around with such arrogance. The wretched fellow did not even feel ashamed. In a town that was like a cremation ground he went around like a dandy!

And then he heard Dayal Babu's voice and their eyes met. Pan-

chu's feeling of revolt instantly vanished. Smile on his lips, meek
expression in the eyes and that same habit of springing on his feet
and bowing with respect—like the shopkeeper starting his patent
exercise at the very sight of customers. Panchu did not want to
do that. But he had no control over himself. The moment their eyes
met, Panchu behaved like a monkey dancing at the signal of the
juggler. Trying to save his self-respect so carefully protected in
his glass-house and threatening to show it to him at the same time,
he behaved with the zamindar with sham cordiality.

"I just came to have a look at all this!"

"I say, don't even mention that!" Dayal Babu observed petulantly
with the air of a man pretending to worry about the whole world.
"Did you see?" he said. "How these blackmarketeers are hell bent
upon looting, and that too in broad daylight! They're all government stooges, dear sir! The Englishmen are no ordinary creatures,
Babu! Look at their policy! They took away rice from the middleman at cheap rates and never bothered about the pubic. On
the other hand, they allow these traders to suck the blood of the
people and when the public starts clamouring for foodgrains, they
impose controls! Huge stocks are lying with people like Monai.
On whom can you impose your controls?"

As Dayal Babu spoke his eyes gleamed with arrogance and cunning. He extended his hand for a *paan*, and then for tobacco and
a silk handkerchief to wipe the hand. No signal was needed. The
servants of the aristocratic Dayal Babu bowed respectfully to
Master Babu.

Master Babu who had been starving for six days, was presented
with a rolled *paan* instead of food. But anything would do. He
wanted to chew, like a goat, all the betel leaves in the container.
Panchu stuffed two *kevra*-scented *paans* in his mouth and chewed
them vigorously.

Dayal Babu continued: "Oh, Saheb! That's exactly the policy of
the British rulers. They're provoking Indians to cut the throats of
fellow countrymen. Later on, they will turn round and say that
they were busy fighting the Nazi onslaught. And in any case, with
the Indian Ministry in Bengal and Indian officials running the
administration, how could they be blamed if Indians themselves
starved their own brethren? And they will say we don't deserve
independence! So, Sir, they achieved their objective without losing
anything! And we remained the slaves we've always been."

Dayal Babu shifted the *paan* to the other side of his mouth.

Panchu had finished his *paan* and his hunger had been aroused like fire.

Dayal Babu observed: "The real thing is that we're not united. India wouldn't have been in this state had we been united."

Panchu stared at Dayal Babu's arrogant face. Dayal Babu must have had a hefty meal at home. What would he have eaten? The aroma of pungent spices entered Panchu's nostrils. At first, Panchu liked it, but later he was enraged. Selfish to the marrow of his bones, a worthless fellow—that was Dayal Babu. Anger loosened his tongue.

"It is fashionable these days to sing the praises of unity. Everyone talks about it at the top of his voice, but no one really feels it."

Panchu felt his heart unburdened as he uttered these words and it gave him a feeling of contentment.

Dayal Babu was shocked.

Panchu felt emboldened. He continued: "This country will be free from foreign domination only when our cultured classes give up their selfish motives and false pride and act with reason. Bent under the weight of slavery, the cultured classes try to raise their standard of life with the help of their pride in family status, material prosperity, literacy and knowledge, all of which amount to nothing more than wooden chips. By saying there is no unity in India, we're only trying to equate ourselves with the British. There would be some sense if somebody belonging to an independent country asked such a question. But to whom are we addressing this question? Are we not part of India? Then, isn't it our own weakness to which we're making repeated references? Without overcoming our own weakness, we've no right to point a finger at our neighbours. We don't have that right at all!"

Having spoken, Panchu suddenly grew afraid. What if Dayal Babu got offended? Oh, hell with him! The arrow had been shot. If there was to be destruction, it may as well be total. Dayal Babu would not drag him to the gallows in any case. And there was no hope of gaining anything out of him. Then why should he, Panchu, submit to Dayal Babu's authority? Panchu was conscious that he was nonetheless doing it! That was exactly why his breath was sinking within even while he spoke with bombast. In order to keep up his arrogance, Panchu had been talking to Dayal Babu in that tone—as though he had been teaching the boys in the classroom, and that too, in the presence of a school inspector. But having uttered those words, Panchu felt scared. He coughed and turned his face to hide his confusion and spat on the ground.

Panchu, who had access to the collector and Jordan Saheb, who was learned and above everything else, son of a great logician, had overawed Dayal Babu with his imposing stance. Dayal Babu was at first startled to see himself being outdone and then felt somewhat embarrassed. He could not think of an answer and was piqued. He was at a loss for words. While taking *paan* from the servant, he took the *paan*-container as well and held it in his hand as Panchu spoke. When Panchu stopped talking, Dayal Babu, in order to give a fresh start to their conversation, first looked at him with amazement and then, opening the lid of the *paan*-container, offered another *paan* to Panchu.

The *paan* hurt Panchu's empty stomach. He did not want to have it. But Dayal Babu, with a show of familiarity, insisted in a flamboyant tone: "Take it, dear man! I don't very much appreciate that air of religiosity in you!"

Dayal Babu had softened a little and a smile flickered at the corners of his lips. Panchu relented, but arrogance flashed in his mind like lightning. On the pale face of hunger gleamed arrogance and joy. Panchu smiled and picked the *paans* from the container and remarked: "You're offering this to me, but remember that if I develop fondness for it, I'll start coming to your house and go on eating *paans*. In these days of unemployment, by God's grace, I'm free the whole day..."

Panchu wanted to use a more familiar term for Dayal Babu, but could not bring himself to do it. Even so, Panchu attained equal status with Dayal Babu by establishing a semblance of familiarity. And now he wanted to convince Monai about the power he possessed. He sought to do that by dropping his veneer of respectful formality to Dayal Babu.

Monai had been standing at a little distance, looking lost and alone. He had amassed wealth, but he had not been able to establish with Dayal Babu a relation based on equal status. First and foremost, God had made him low by birth. And then, he had no education to speak of. This lack of education was the main factor that stood between him and Dayal Babu. He did not know how to use slang words in English. There were many boys in the town who were educated. But no one gave them any importance. It was only because of Panchu that great Englishmen like the collector came to this rotten town. And big zamindars and big shots like Dayal Babu talked and exchanged jokes with Panchu. That, according to Monai, was the importance of learning.

Monai wanted to make up for his own lack of education by doing everything so that his son Nyada would grow up to be a learned man. Monai was obsessed with his studies. Ever since the school had opened, Nyada had had to stop playng with his top, even on Sundays. Studies and nothing else for the boy from the time he woke up in the morning to the time he went to bed at night. Just as Monai did his business from morning till night and concentrated only on business, he wanted his son to concentrate on his studies. He had been working from the time he was of Nyada's age. So, he considered Nyada also capable of doing the same thing. When times were good, Govind Master gave him tuitions at home for two hours every morning. After that Nyada attended the school. Once back from school, the boy would have a wash, eat something and immediately sit with his book to memorize the lessons in a loud voice. The moment his voice slackened, Monai would thunder at him. Later in the evening, Kanai Master came. He was a hard task-master. Monai had engaged him to see that Nyada remembered everything in the books by committing it to memory. He wanted Nyada to top the class always. Monai was convinced that God had been very kind to him. Once his Nyada got proper education and earned a foreign degree, he would become a big government official. Then he, as his father, would be respected by all big people and he would make millions.

Monai's greatest desire was to buy a big estate before he died. He aspired for a good reputation among the big traders of Calcutta. He wanted to build high-rise buildings in Calcutta and have in his possession one crore of rupees in hard cash. Had he been born in a city, he would have fulfilled all those desires on his own. But being born in a village, and that too in the family of a *kevat*, was a curse from which he could never be free. He needed some support to rise from this position. He would earn any amount of money, but if once he stepped out of his limits, he had to fall back into the pit of inferiority. In order to wipe off his *kevat* origin, at least to some extent, Monai got himself initiated as a Vaishnavite. But he derived no practical benefit out of this. He even built a temple in the town. After all that, he was still fit enough only to sit on the floor when he visited the homes of the high-caste. But he knew that educated men and government officials bore no community stamp. Therefore, Monai was very particular about Nyada's education.

This time, Dayal Babu had dealt him a powerful blow. Dayal Babu had himself insisted that the Brahmins be fed and now he wanted a rupee to be given to each of them! He had come to mete out justice—the rascal! Not only that, he insisted that Monai should distribute free of charge one *seer* of rice to each person in the town! As though it was his inherited property that he could do anything with it! But then it was indeed his ancestral property. Monai lived under Dayal Babu's zamindari. Dayal Babu was the ruling authority in the town. He could do anything he chose to do.

Thanks to Dayal Babu, Monai sustained a loss of about seven hundred rupees. Monai muttered angrily: "I haven't had a chance so far. But I shall ruin him the moment I find a loophole. The scoundrel is irked by the fact that half the title deeds in town are in my name. God granted that to me and I'm enjoying it. Why should this rascal burn with jealousy? These people can never see anybody going ahead in life. Bastards—they go on shouting about unity. But they cut the throats of their own poor brethren. What blessed use is *swaraj*? I say, how long will people suffer atrocities? God willing, I will buy the entire estate of Dayal Babu and live in his palatial mansion. Let him have his way for the present. It's his chance today!"

Monai sighed, and resting both his hands at his waist, stiffened his back a little. He looked in the direction of his house. Azim had not yet returned. He muttered: "Let me flaunt the money right on his face—the bastard! That will save my reputation. But right now, he has broken my back. And now, he has tasted blood. If he decides to go to the police station, he will rest only after seeing me behind bars. Rascal! He will even rob me of my shroud. But if he wanted to hand me over to the police, why did he save my godown by preventing the raid? What trick is the fellow playing? Dayal is not the type to show sympathy for nothing. I don't understand. But I am sure he will drive a knife into me in such a place where I won't get even water! Oh, God! I'm your faithful devotee—then why should this enemy of mine put his foot on my neck?... Oh, that Azim, why does he take so long? Where has he disappeared, *sala*! This rascal Dayal will ruin my reputation any moment. Look—he has started bombasting again—*sala*!"

"Perhaps you've forgotten the days of your father!" came Dayal Babu's voice. "Chheda Singh!" he continued, "Bring this chap to his senses. Tell him that I'm not his father's subject that I should be standing at his door for three hours!"

Monai's eyes closed for a second. He feared he would lose his reputation for life if he got a single blow... "Oh, that fellow, Chheda Singh, will pounce on me any moment! Oh, my God! That rascal Azim...oh, he's coming at last...walking like a great master!"

As he spotted Azim coming, Monai heaved a sigh of relief. Slinking away from Chheda Singh, he walked towards Dayal Babu with folded hands. He said: "How can I be so cheeky as to keep you waiting? God has showed me such days that I'm forced to hear abuses from the government. Now I'm convinced that your good self has taken me under your protection. When you start abusing, my master, it's only good fortune for me, your humble servant."

All the muscles of Dayal Babu's face became tense. A faint smile of conceit flickered on his lips reddened by chewing *paan*. He was leaning on his ivory stick. And the gems of his ring glittered on the right hand. Turning his face away from Monai, Dayal Babu looked up at the blazing summer sky.

Monai advanced to touch Dayal Babu's feet. Dayal Babu's heart swelled as he thought triumphantly: "Now he has come to his senses. I'll throw him down flat—the rascal! He won't have less than a thousand bags of grain in his godown. Even after cutting and overwriting, the rascal will save at least a lakh and a half. He collected grains on the sly from all over the place, and I got no inkling at all. A real scoundrel—that's what he is!"

Monai's words barely registered in his mind. He said to himself: "I won't get anything if I hand him over to the police. The police will swallow it all. Why not snatch away five hundred bags from him as part of the two thousand bags I have to provide for the army? What's wrong? If I report him to the police, he would have no face to show and he will have to do hard labour in jail. But now, I'll have to pay him only for five hundred bags. Even after that, that rascal will still be left with a thousand five hundred bags. He can easily make a lakh and a few thousands. Is that a small amount for the man of low birth? What times! Even low-born fellows like weavers, cobblers and boatmen have started becoming millionaires! But he's a big scoundrel. Agreed, he has half the land deeds in the town registered in his name. Trying to become my equal—rascal! I must force the nasty fellow to part with a thousand bags of grains!"

Dayal Babu gave Monai a sidelong glance. After singing the glory of the Gita and the holy scriptures, Monai now stood respectfully at a distance, head bowed and hands linked together in front.

Monai took from Azim five ten-rupee notes and a silver rupee coin. He placed the money at Dayal Babu's feet and said with folded hands: "Oh, my saviour! Please accept whatever little this humble servant of yours can offer and pardon him. I maintain my family with the leavings of the government. Have mercy on me, my saviour! May God always keep you in happiness."

With that, Monai pressed Dayal Babu's legs. A loud laughter was heard from the dumphill. Somebody's devilish delight—it gave a pleasant thrust to Dayal Babu's ego.

Dayal Babu had publicly brought under his feet the man responsible for the starvation in the town. He had shown Monai how powerful he was. Dayal Babu added further glory to the traditional respect and reputation of the family and thereby became a saviour of all the generations that had lived before him. He proved to the world that a low community would always remain low.

Dayal Babu thought with contempt: "Ugh! He wanted to grow wings and fly high! The rascal—he had started competing with people like us who have been zamindars for centuries. Great man that he is, he went and built a temple in the town. And after buying half the title deeds in the town, he had a great desire to have everyone come bowing to him. In order to pose a challenge to me, Dayal zamindar, he dared to show his power by starving my people. Now do you see, fellow, who is more powerful? The whole town is curious to see what harsh punishment Dayal Babu gives to this devil of a man. Just see, my people, how your Dayal Babu can protect you even now!" And he moaned: "They're ungrateful, all of them!"

What had Dayal Babu not done for the people for whose sake he had taken the trouble of coming all the way and for whose sake he had defeated his enemy in a trice? He got grains for those who had licked left-overs and medicines for the sick!... But the people for whom he did all that were utterly stupid and did not seem to be impressed at all. Nobody even raised a cry of praise for him! Not even that admirer near the dumphill who had broken into a delirious laughter a little while ago. Unlucky wretch! He did not even look in Dayal Babu's direction. He was absorbed in licking the discarded food thrown on the dumphill! They were all mean, worthless fellows! Today they didn't even pay respect, Dayal Babu reflected with irritation. Ill-begotten chaps, all of them!

The first thing that Dayal Babu noticed was Monai's temple. Then he saw the famished patients, those Brahmins, who had eaten gluttonously, who had sustained themselves for many days on the crumbs given of pity by their clients who engaged them for performing religious rites. They thought Brahmins deserved to be respected because they belonged to the highest caste. But how worthless they were in physical strength! And among those licking food on the dumphill were also the highest Brahmins! "Oh, yes! That fellow is the grandson of Dibu Bhattacharya—what's his name? Well...to hell with the name! How many names to remember, that too, of these sinning fellows? To tell the truth, it's these Brahmins who have brought this country to ruination!"

Dayal Babu felt very excited and continued thinking in the same vein: "Ever since the degradation of the Brahmins, Hinduism has vanished. When your respected Brahmins have gone downhill, how long could poor Kshatriyas go on serving their country? Even so, have the Kshatriyas spared any stone unturned for the good of their country? The great incarnations like Lord Rama, Krishna, Buddha, Mahavira as well as the valliant men from Bhima, Arjuna, Rana Pratap and Shivaji to Prithviraj Chauhan were all Kshatriyas, who could successfully aim an arrow following the direction of a sound. Germany appropriated the Vedas—otherwise the Kshatriyas would be ruling the world today. We were ruined by our mutual dissensions. Otherwise, could the British have dared to rule over India? Could the Banias ever be rulers? But they have been doing it in this *kaliyuga*. Just see, a great saintly man like Gandhi is born in a Bania family. It is correctly written in the scriptures that the terrible *kaliyuga* has arrived and is here to stay. That's why Hinduism has fallen on such bad days! Dignity and decorum of the high caste are disappearing. People from good families have been reduced to licking food on the dumphill. What a pitiable state for Hinduism! What a downfall for our country!"

Dayal Babu suddenly felt that, barring himself, the whole country; the whole world was heading towards complete ruin. Boundless compassion surged in his heart for the utterly senseless human race. Dayal Babu started worrying about the whole world. A strong aspiration for the uplift of the fallen people rose in his heart. He thought that by doing good deeds, he would earn a great name for himself and Hinduism and the country too would be uplifted. Then he wondered what great deeds he could do. Building a temple or a *dharamashala* did not bring much name in the present days. The wretches belonging to low communities too had started building temples.

He could not think of any way that would make him great. Dayal
Babu felt quite disgusted. He felt that he had wasted his whole
life. It was now time to do some concrete work. Actually, he had
been doing something. He had arranged food for the starving
people and medicines for the sick. And he had been serving his
town by standing in the scorching sun. He had set a great example before the world. If his work could be reported in the news·
papers, the whole world would come to know that Dayal Babu
was among the great zamindars of the country. Once he acquired
that reputation, he would become a political leader straightaway.
If elections were held, he would surely contest. He could stand
on the Hindu Mahasabha ticket... He could even fight the elections on the Congress ticket... But he should have gone to jail to
get the Congress ticket... Then the Hindu Mahasabha...yes, that
would be the most appropriate thing. By standing on the Hindu
Mahasabha ticket, he would be able to keep up his reputation and
also protect the sanctity of Hinduism. Yes, that would be the right
decision. He must definitely advance in life. His name should be
mentioned in history. It could be done only with the help of Master
Babu. The young man was very useful. He should be asked to write
articles in the newspapers singing his praise, and he must get them
published. Or, why should he do it himself? Let Master Babu see
that they were published. But he must have got some money out
of it. Then Master Babu would utilize his knowledge of English
to promote the image of the zamindar. Indeed, Panchu was a very
learned man. But he was an arrogant rascal. Well, nothing wrong
with that. One must be proud of one's learning. Wealth and
learning—after all, those were the two things about which one
could be legitimately proud. Dayal Babu said to himself: "I've the
power of wealth, he has the power of intelligence. He'll make me
famous in the newspapers and I shall protect him and his family
against the famine."

A new hope, a new excitement rose in Dayal Babu's mind. He
looked at Panchu.

Panchu was seated with bowed head, lost in thought.

As he chewed the *paan*, Panchu imagined for himself a status
equal to Dayal Babu. But his hungry stomach hurt him the whole
time, making a mockery of the situation.

Panchu, in spite of all his efforts to the contrary, always felt inferior in the presence of Dayal Babu or Monai. The world of practical reality had made him gradually realize that man would not

get respect for his greatness on the strength of his learning and intellect. Panchu realized that money was the greatest power. The very next moment, such ideas would seem to Panchu an indication of degradation and he would brush them aside with disdain. It made Panchu happy to think that intelligence had always been placed higher than wealth. He thought that if Valmiki had not been born to write the *Ramayana*, who would have ever known about Rama? Had Rabindranath Tagore not been a poet, who would have respected him as a relation of Prince Dwarkanath Tagore? Had he himself not been educated, would Dayal Babu have tried to curry his favour?... But with all that, how powerless and insignificant he was in front of Dayal Babu!

Like the waves of the sea, Panchu's thoughts rose high and then crashed. He felt he would have been happy had he been a wealthy fool rather a moneyless man of learning. He and his learned father had been starving like any other uncouth villager, whereas Dayal Babu lived in great luxury, stroking his swollen belly. Dayal Babu and Monai enjoyed a high position just because they happened to have money.

Panchu sank into the darkness of his mind. He felt his breath choking. A sigh escaped from his mouth and immediately subsided. Panchu's head was bent. He had been standing all the time, holding his chin with his palm, his left hand resting on his waist. His body grew restless. He was engulfed by a feeling of helplessness. His hand moved away from the chin and slid down to join the other behind his back.

Suddenly he was conscious of the collective noise of kites, crows and dogs. Panchu raised his head. Monai and Azim stood on one side and Dayal Babu with his musclemen on the other. Panchu's eyes turned in the direction of Monai's temple. The cudgel fighters were no longer guarding the temple entrance. His eyes glided over the Brahmins lying in front of the temple. Even on the dumphill the crowds had dispersed. He saw a solitary man battling with kites, crows and dogs as a powerless enemy and glaring at the dumphill.

Panchu did not relish the scene at all. At that moment, the dumphill seemed to him ominous like a cremation ground. Earlier, there were crowds of men, pouncing and falling over one another. A violent war had raged with the kites, crows and dogs. Man proved to be stronger. How lively that scene, how full of activity! And now? Man had fled the battle ground. What had happened? The food discarded on the dumphill was not exhausted. A little while ago, men were not able to eat as much as they were fighting. Then, why had they withdrawn from the scene?

Panchu suddenly remembered the firing and lathi-wielding at Monai's house. Now everything came to his mind in clear focus. Man had no doubt broken in the face of his growing hunger. But suffering it with pride for so long had also made him grow accustomed to it. With the false hope of getting food, and passing his days fighting against hunger, he was still alive. But he would have instantly lost his life if he had gone to offer resistance to bullets and lathis. Man loved life and as far as he could help, wished to keep away from death.

The hungry men fled at the sight of Dayal Babu whom they considered responsible for the starvation deaths in the town. When Dayal Babu retraced his steps, they all stood up in a collective gesture. Now only the enemies like kites and crows remained and their loud noise filled the atmosphere. Ears had got so used to that noise that unless one paid attention to it, it did not sound particularly irksome. In a way, one was hardly aware of it.

On an earlier occasion once, when the uproarious shouts and shrieks and groans of men had gradually lessened and finally stopped, Panchu had suddenly become conscious of the absence of that noise. Immediately his eyes had looked up. He had stared on in that direction even after people had gone away. But at that moment, Dayal Babu had been shouting at Monai at the top of his voice. Panchu felt a certain glee when he saw Monai being so treated. He forgot about the famished people whose steps were staggering because of their hunger, and revelled in a happy feeling of triumph over Monai through Dayal Babu's harsh reprimands. But later, that intoxicating feeling had subsided. Again he lowered his head and started wondering about his own status in front of those two capitalists, one triumphant, the other reeling under defeat. If he desired, Dayal Babu could easily humiliate Panchu right where he stood. Even Monai, if he chose, could trounce him while pretending to be soft and respectful. And Panchu, with all his strong resolve, would not be in a position to bring the slightest harm to them because he was a man without guts. Even the humblest people of the town were better than Panchu. At least they did not flatter and stoop before Dayal Babu or Monai any more!

Panchu got irritated by his sense of inferiority. But where was the escape from defeat, shame and restlessness? How could he overcome the feeling of stagnation within? On the surface, several depressing thoughts flashed in his mind like fish moving in different directions and slinking away in the clear water of a lake; but they did not come in the grip of his conscious reasoning. Panchu stood there with his mind blank and his head bent.

Dayal Babu, now determined to have his publicity done through Panchu, gazed at him. He realized that Panchu was deeply engrossed in some serious thought.

Dayal Babu drew Panchu's attention to himself and said: "Did you see, Master Babu, such are our countrymen! After swallowing lakhs of rupees, this fellow spits out fifty-one rupees as though doing a great favour to the country."

While making that observation, Dayal Babu kicked the money with his foot, and said, flying into rage: "After earning a little money, he behaves like the son of a nawab, *sala*! He has forgotten the days when there was no food in his house to eat!"

Monai stood in silence. Dayal Babu continued: "He threw so many Brahmins in the jaws of death by feeding them with rotten food and now, by flaunting fifty-one rupees, this mean chap wants to become like Ghanashyam Das Birla! Just ask what the doctor will do with a paltry fifty-one rupees? Will he save the lives of these patients with his own flesh and bones?"

Monai saw that Dayal Babu was not appeased. He said politely: "If I had money, I would not have failed to give even my own life. If I dedicate even the skin of my body in the service of the respected Brahmins, I would still be suspected. My master, you're well aware that God took away even the little money I had earned for my children. I must somehow carry on with what is left."

"Somehow carry on... Hi... Hi... Hi..." Dayal Babu jeered and made a face. Then he said sternly: "What about all those thousands of grain bags stored in your godown?

Monai was ready with his answer: "They're yours, my master! Under your rule, whatever I have is all yours!" With that Monai let out a suppressed sigh.

Dayal Babu flew into rage and said: "Do you see this mean fellow, Master Babu? In the presence of the *daroga* I saved his godown. Otherwise, he would be doing hard labour in prison. Is there any limit to the crimes he has committed? If I had been the ruler here, I would have ripped his skin and thrown it for kites and vultures to eat. In his greed for money, this wicked fellow committed such atrocities on those innocent Brahmins. My heart rents with sorrow when I look at the sad plight of my countrymen. Chheda Singh! Break his godowns!"

Monai's business sense was suddenly awakened. He thought of a tactic. Without getting perturbed and without any hesitation he again folded his hands and said calmly: "Why take all that trouble, my master! I shall send the grain bags wherever you say. After that unfortunate incident, I'm very scared. Yes, I'm telling the truth. That day, you did your best for this humble servant. You know that the eyes of the police are very sharp. Since that day, the *daroga's* man has come to me thrice. He's asking for ten thousand. If I don't give it, he wants to have my godown searched!"

Dayal Babu was taken in by what Monai said. A new enemy, more powerful than himself, was casting covetous eyes on Monai's godown. His haughty attitude softened and he asked with curiosity: "Is that so?"

Deep at heart, Monai was extremely happy; but he did not let the expression on his face change a wee bit. He replied in the same calm tone: "I don't have money, my master! And I've already become a marked man with the police. My stars are bad and luck doesn't favour me. I sent word that those bags are a big bother on my head and he could come and take them away." And Monai heaved a sigh as though he were heartbroken.

Dayal Babu's heart sank. His stern face showed slight embarrassment which Monai did not fail to notice. After a quick glance at Dayal Babu, he continued: "Master! I swear at your feet and say that I'm really fed up with my business. How long should I go on incurring losses? I shall go with my family to Calcutta..."

Monai again heaved a prolonged sigh. He glanced at Dayal Babu, Panchu and then at Azim and said: "Azim, my son, go with Chheda Singh and hand over the godown keys to him. If any man comes from the Daroga, send him to Dayal Babu. I'm now free!"

Dayal Babu was boiling within. But the Daroga had become a tough proposition even for him. He was not at all inclined to take Monai at his word, but he was sure that Monai was capable of harassing him by bribing the Daroga. At the same time, he did not even want to bow his head in the face of Monai's threatening tactics. He was really puzzled. His princely mein would certainly not permit him to accept defeat at the hands of the police, *daroga* and petty worms like Monai. He suddenly thought of a remedy. He decided that rice should be definitely distributed in the town.

Under the pretext of public good, he could humiliate even the Governor—what then to say about the *daroga*?

Dayal Babu promptly ordered: "Chheda Singh! Take the keys. Every day, the poor and starving people in the town should be given rice morning and evening. Make an announcement in the town that people should gather in the school verandah to collect their quota of rice." Then turning to Panchu Dayal Babu said: "Come along, Master Babu!"

Then, with a quick glance at Monai, he said in a dry tone: "If any man comes from the *daroga,* tell him I want to meet him. I shall settle the matter with him. "Come along, Master Babu!" he added as he left. Panchu promptly went with him.

Dayal Babu started going towards his house with Panchu trudging along. Monai stood there, rubbing his hands.

6

As Dayal Babu reached home, his manager informed him about the arrival of Mr. Das, the Union Board Secretary, who had been put up in the guest house.

Dayal Babu was extremely happy to hear this. He said to Panchu: "Even if that thing about the *daroga* is true, nobody can do me any harm. When a Union Board is set up here, I can confiscate the entire stock of foodgrains lying with Monai if I wish, and get it transferred right under the *daroga*'s eyes. The government godown will be in my house. By greasing the palms of the secretary and the sub-divisional officer, I will so defy and deride the *daroga* that he will remember me all through his life. As for Monai, I will rest content only when I completely ruin him. The wicked fellow was trying to scare me. I shall see to his police..."

After that Dayal Babu called the police-force foul names and gave vent to his wrath against the government.

Panchu wondered how even this champion of foreign rule had come to regard it as obnoxious. And he was surprised that in spite of their hatred for the British, Dayal Babu and others from his class still wanted them to continue. Why this contradiction?

Dayal Babu took Panchu to his *sheeshmahal**. The fame of *sheeshmahal* had spread far and wide. Dayal Babu had built it to humiliate another zamindar of neighbouring Gauripur. The guest house of Dayal Babu's ancestral mansion was in bad shape. He had originally intended to get the house repaired, but provoked by the spirit of rivalry, he had built it entirely anew and erected a three-storeyed structure.

The nawab of Gauripur had built his guest house in the western style. He had even taken electric connections from the city. Reacting in anger, Dayal Babu called the engineers from Calcutta. If the nawab of Gauripur had taken electric connections, Dayal Babu went a step ahead and installed a telephone. He opened the strings of his money-bags wide.

A new office was built with paved floors. His clerks, used to

* Palatial mansion with mirrors all round.

sitting on mattresses and leaning against large cushions, had to adjust themselves to tables and chairs. The manager had been given a separate room. In Dayal Babu's own office chamber, a throne-like chair had been installed on a huge carpet with a plush, luxurious sofa-set arranged on the other side. And there was a profusion of electric lights and fans. On one side of the first floor was Dayal Babu's library, the guest rooms were on the other. Right on the top was the *sheeshmahal* which few had seen but many had heard about it.

Panchu was familiar with the first floor of Dayal Babu's mansion since he had been giving tuitions to his children in the library. He had also seen the guest rooms and had been highly impressed by their interior decor and had long been keen to see the *sheeshmahal*. And today he had seen it.

As he entered the hall, he saw an artificial spring with a fountain attached on one side. On the mirrors adjacent to the spring were pictures of forests and springs. Coloured electric bulbs had been fitted at various spots in the spring. The walls were covered with coloured pictures painted on glass, interspersed with mirrors. Electric chandeliers hung from the painted ceiling. The marble floor of the hall had been decorated with expensive Persian carpets. A two-foot thick mattress covered half the hall. On the mattress was spread a white silk sheet. On the other side, a radiogram, piano, harmonium, tabla, sitar, veena and violin had been neatly arranged. Two expensive tables had been installed on both the sides for serving drinks. Silk curtains hung at the door. In all the four corners of the hall stood statues of nude women, mounted on rose wood. Exotic plants in twin-coloured pots stood on either side of the doors. Behind the mattress were huge brass spittoons. In a little passage beyond were two big show-cases along the wall. They exhibited the gifts received by Dayal Babu and his ancestors from zamindars, nawabs and English friends. Most of the items were silver or gold toys, images, sets of gold wine cups, etc., and included a figure of Buddha which had been carved in Burma and presented to Dayal Babu by a famous nawab. Dayal Babu's great-grandfather had received many titles and deeds from Mir Jaffar. Among the gifts from English officials, ninety-eight per cent were their signed portraits as well as two or three portraits of ladies. The wife of the previous collector inscribed her portrait with the words "To dear Dayal". There was also an expensive clock in an octagonal ivory frame with an engraved design.

Dayal Babu showed everything to Panchu with great pride. He said: "Master Babu, you'll see the real beauty of this hall only in the evening! After seeing that, even you'll feel convinced that you've seen the pleasure-house of an aristocrat!"

Dayal Babu drew attention to the Indian decor. "There is a policy behind it," he said. "Any Englishman, whatever his status or family connections, would be required to squat Indian style when he comes to my *sheeshmahal*. I've purposely avoided keeping chairs here. I arrange performances of Indian dance and music so that those chaps have some idea about our art and culture."

Then Dayal Babu honoured Panchu by promising to invite him for dance and music recitals in future. He then called the servant and ordered him to fill water in the tank of the spring. He had the covers removed from the chandeliers and lamps. Today the *sheeshmahal* would be lit in honour of Master Babu!

Panchu did not feel in the least excited. He did not feel happy about having had the opportunity to see Dayal Babu's *sheeshmahal*. It made him boil with rage that Dayal Babu was so opulent. He hated Dayal Babu. And he remained silent. It was mainly Dayal Babu who did the talking. At every stage he waxed eloquent over the power and glory that wealth had given him. With absolute informality, Panchu reclined against a cushion. A sweet beverage was brought which he gulped down. He went on taking *paans* from the container and stuffing them in his mouth.

Panchu was exasperated by Dayal Babu's vainglorious talk and he revolted within. But after a while he started interrupting Dayal Babu by narrating some imaginary episodes of mirth and merriment. He wanted to overpower Dayal Babu. He behaved as though he had been long accustomed to such comforts and had attended music and dance recitals in aristocratic households. He behaved as though his familiarity with the American principal Jordan had given him thousands of opportunities to see the life-style of western society and witness the freedom they enjoyed in matters of love. While longing for such opulence, Panchu, the intellectual tried to establish his superiority over Dayal Babu who was regarded as a "big man" because of his wealth. He narrated fake incidents of his debauchery and love affairs.

Of course, Dayal Babu had known some foreign prostitutes in Calcutta. But he had not been lucky enough to mix freely in English society and revel in the pleasures his English friends enjoyed. He had feasted every foreign official, but no foreign official ever bothered about him—not even the wife of the collector who wrote "My dear Dayal" on her portrait. Dayal Babu started taking interest in Panchu's stories. He made detailed inquiries about their addresses.

Panchu felt uncomfortable even as he spoke. His meaningless anger against Dayal Babu and violent contempt for him jolted his own mind.

Just then Monai arrived. Dayal Babu called him to his pleasure-house. Monai started flattering Dayal Babu the moment he entered.

Monai's servility angered Panchu. Why had that man lost all sense of self-respect? The whole town was at his feet and he enjoyed a better status than hundreds of his own and other communities. With his growing power, he had given repeated jolts even to the traditional reputation of Dayal Babu whose ancestors had been zamindars for fourteen generations and who was the ruler of ten to fifteen thousand peasants and was their lord and provider of food. Why did Monai, who was mean and petty in the eyes of the world, buckle down before Dayal Babu despite his being a millionaire? Why did he behave like Dayal Babu's slave?

At that moment, Panchu saw his own defeat in the defeat of Monai. He had been defeated by Dayal Babu because of his poverty and he did not want Dayal Babu to triumph over him. With irritation he thought: "Monai is a wealthy man. Then why does he allow himself to remain under Dayal Babu's thumb? Why doesn't he retort? A coward—that's what he is!"

At the same time, Panchu realized his own cowardice. To rid himself of a feeling of inadequacy, he reclined against the big cushion a little stiffly, and extended his hand towards the *paan*-container. It was empty. Immediately he called out to the servant. Dayal Babu asked: "What do you want, Master Babu?"

"Nothing. I felt this empty *paan*-container looked like a widow and felt pity for it." Panchu felt proud of his joke.

"Ho—ho—ho!" Dayal Babu burst out laughing. "This container is never empty, it's always full. Hundreds of *paans* are bought and swallowed during the day..." and again he burst into a laugh.

Panchu joined him: "That's why I feel pity all the more. How terrible it would be for a lamp, used to hundreds of moths, if it's suddenly left without any moths. Bring some *paans*, I say!" Panchu went on ordering the servant. He felt happy that he had deprived Dayal Babu of the opportunity of ordering the servant...

Monai, seated with his head bent low and hands folded, awaited judgment on his petition. He was not the least conscious of the conversation.

Chheda Singh and his gang had taken possession of Monai's godown. He had had the grain bags thrown out of the godown. At the sight of the bags, the people came leaping forward with excitement. The bags were being thrown out like the images of deities being thrown out of a temple. They could not believe their eyes. Nevertheless they hesitated. The blood of martyrs was on the bags.

Twirling his moustache, Chheda Singh ordered that the bags be thrown out even as he cursed Monai and his descendants. He was only a servant earning a meagre salary of twelve rupees, but he was the zamindar's strongman, and so could kick a millionaire like Monai on the face. For the same reason, he enjoyed all the rights over the life and property and reputation of the people under the zamindar's authority. Chheda Singh gifted four bags to each of the twenty-five cudgel-fighters who had accompanied him and reserved ten bags for himself. Out of these, he sold five bags to Monai and kicked him with the heel of his shoe. Then he had the bags transferred to the school building after which he made a pro-clamation in the town. The starving people of the town felt revived at the prospect of getting rice!

Monai had cooled off. More than the looting of his grain, what hurt his pride was the kicking he had received. Now that Chheda Singh had raised his hand once, he could hit him any time he chose, and Monai certainly would not be able to take that. Hence, to save himself from humiliation, he had come to seek Dayal Babu's pro-tection. He surrendered himself to Dayal Babu without any con-ditions.

"It's up to you," he pleaded. "I can be saved if you desire and I can be ruined if that's your wish. I'm your humble servant, even ready to place my head at your graceful feet. But forgive me just once, my master. You're my only saviour, and whatever punish-ment you give, I shall accept in all humbleness. But kindly don't destroy my means of survival. Please let me have my means of livelihood."

Happy at Monai's defeat, Dayal Babu expressed his joy by crack-ing jokes with Panchu. Boasting about his own importance, he informed Monai about the arrival of the Secretary of the Union Board. He had even sent a servant to the Secretary with a request to come up after his bath...

Soon Mr. Das presented himself. Dark complexioned, lean and tall, dressed in a silk suit, wearing gold-rimmed spectacles with octagonal lenses and carrying in his hand a tin of 555 cigarettes and one cigarette between his lips, Mr. Das graced Dayal Babu, Panchu and Monai by making his appearance.

Dayal Babu was promptly on his feet. Monai bent further forward. Panchu sat up straight.

At the very first sight, Mr. Das felt extreme rupulsion for Panchu. Taking care of the crease of his trousers, Mr. Das sat supporting himself against a big cushion. A couple of formal questions were asked about the trouble he may have faced during the journey. Then Dayal Babu introduced Mr. Das to Panchu and lavished praise on him. Panchu responded with a show of politeness. He did not like Mr. Das' airs either.

With the intention of getting Mr. Das to his side, Dayal Babu started giving an account of Monai's misdeeds in broken English. Referring to Monai as "damn fool" and in other derogatory terms, Dayal Babu talking in Bengali-English told Mr. Das laughingly: "To express my happiness over your visit, I offer you this greatest gift from our town." This comment provoked a laughter. Panchu did not want to laugh, but he could not help smiling.

Monai was absolutely uncomfortable. He was scared and wondered: "God knows what they are waiting to pounce upon! Every other minute they are laughing and gesticulating towards me. Any reward for it would be insufficient. One of these wretched fellows is the god of death and the other is the messenger of death. They think my house is a field and will graze away everything..."

Monai heaved a sigh. "God knows what crazy idea possessed my mind that day! If I had sold rice to those hungry people, they would have sung my praises. There would have been no firing and the zamindar would not have seen my godown. In trying to earn a profit of a thousand and five hundred rupees, I've to lose my earnings of a lifetime. Oh, God! What sin have I committed?"

Monai searched his heart. He feared that he was being punished for some sin he may have committed. At the thought of sin, it dawned on him that he must immediately expiate his sin. He decided to strike a deal with God by presenting him a sight bill.

"Actually, for what can I expiate unless I know what my sin is? To the best of my knowledge since I got initiated into Vaishnavism, I've committed no sin. I feed the ants. I maintain a cow in the temple, I worship the idols and the cow with the same veneration. It's only for this purpose that I've engaged a priest and pay him a salary. On festival days, I do as much charity as I can afford. I'm serving the Brahmins as well. Then, what sin have I committed? My Lord! I say my rosary and recite your name at four o'clock in the morning. Yes, I did wake up late day before yesterday. I woke up at four-thirty. But what of that? In fact, on the day of the firing, I was awake the whole night saying my rosary. Yes, I did it while I was in mourning. I was told not to touch the rosary during the mourning. But I was so scared of the spirits of those dead men that I could not put it aside. That was my only sin. I think God has punished me for that sin. But why do you destroy an insignificant worm like me, oh, God! Forgive me, Lord! And I've arranged the funeral of the people who died in my house. I've even fed the Brahmins. And whatever expiation still remained to be done, God made me do through the zamindar. Just see the mysterious ways of the Lord!... When the zamindar ordered Chheda Singh to distribute rice in the whole town, it was like a bullet shot in my chest. But now I realize that hundreds of people had gone hungry from my door that day. My self-interest made me blind to the situation. One has to depend on fate in the matter of business and trade. The Lord also tells us to do our duty. People in the town are no doubt hungry. But the mendicants and the beggars haven't remained hungry, have they? Yes, I would have really sinned if they had gone back hungry from my door. And now, what's wrong? It's just business. I would give grains if the deal clicked, otherwise, may God help!

"But now the very people I supported are being unfair to me. Didn't God see that I, Monai, was innocent? And suppose I did blunder without knowing. So what? I'm a man of the world after all. But that God should have punished me so! I was beaten with shoes and I was abused! I was looted. What all I had to suffer! It's too harsh a punishment, my Lord! Do forgive me, oh, protector of the poor! Just see, it's only my rice that's being given to the hungry. But the world thinks that Dayal Babu is doing charity by distributing rice to the people!

"But you, oh Lord, are the saviour of the people. You're in every heart. You know everything. I'm really a worm bothering about worldly life. But I'm devoted to you and seek your protection day and night. Save me from the clutches of these sinning creatures. Oh, my great Lord! Take me under your protection, sinner that I am! But this Dayal is no less dangerous than the *Kaliya Naag*.

This rascal has committed so many crimes that one can't keep count of them. The earth trembles with his atrocities, and now we're having this famine. When the ruler of the town has sinned so much, the town cannot but have famine. That's what our scriptures have said.

"The whole of Bengal is full of sinning zamindars. All those blasted fellows have joined hands with the government. They're the people who have sent Gandhi Mahatma to jail. They crushed the agitation of the people by calling the police to fire on them. Then that Dayal's men fired shots in my house too. I never raised my hand on anyone. On the contrary, I myself got beaten up. God is witness. All these big shots are bothered only about their own selfish gains. They cannot see the poor rising high in life. I say, they'll all be completely ruined. Just let Subhash Babu come with his army. He'll send these fellows and their government across the black waters. All poor people will be put in the position of the rich. Let's have *swaraj*. Then you'll see that we poor people will have better times."

Now Monai found it hard to sit with folded hands in that humiliating situation. An hour and a half had gone by, but nobody had even raised his eye to take any notice of him. Monai was on tenter-hooks. His business, his tactics and manoeuvres, everything depended on Dayal Babu's decision. But Dayal Babu was lost in conversation with Panchu and Mr. Das. *Sherbet* and fruits were consumed and they went on puffing their cigarettes and making merry. And time simply passed.

The *sheeshmahal* glittered with dazzling light as it grew dark outside.

The atmosphere in the hall was colourful. The bulbs behind the glass paintings shone bright. The lights in the chandeliers were switched on and the mirrors reflected a million spots of light. The spring with its flowing colours attracted attention. Down below was the coloured fountain. Its water splashed high, also reflecting those multi-coloured lights. Behind the spring, the scenery of the mountain and forest created an illusion of scenic beauty. Between the trees, one could see the figure of an undraped woman swinging from the branches of a tree, with the moon and stars in the background. There was also a painting called "Noorjehan's Wedding Night" which showed Noorjehan as an embodiment of feminine honour, standing hesitantly in the doorway of Jehangir's pleasure-house, trying to conceal with a thin veil her charming face, and Jehangir coming forward to welcome her.

Another painting, "Vishwamitra-Menaka" depicted the sage Vishwamitra and the swooning nymph Menaka who had come to the sage's cottage to disturb him in his penance on a stormy night. The painting showed the sage covering Menaka with a warm garment, her hypnotic feminine charm partly revealed through her displaced clothes.

"Heaven is Here" was another painting in which a prince was seen seated, surrounded by dancing semi-naked and naked women and a maid pouring wine. Two maids were fanning the prince and two women were held in the prince's arms.

Apart from these, there were many other paintings depicting Omar Khayyam with a woman pouring wine in his cup, Krishna disrobing the *gopis**, the bathing room of a Mughal harem, a spring scene, an enticing woman and so on—all depictions crudely aroused physical desire in the viewer.

Panchu, Mr. Das and Monai looked around startled as the *sheeshmahal* suddenly glittered with light. Dayal Babu also followed their gaze. His face gleamed with joy and pride.

Panchu was hypnotized. He thought: "Where can we find such opulence in life? How can such a dream become a reality in the life of a common man like me? Such ostentation and luxury are the leprosy of wealth. It's an unseemly exhibition of the perversity of the human mind."

Dayal Babu came forward to give judgment on Monai. He pierced every pore of Monai's being with his sharp words that were like arrows. Then he called the servant and instructed him to lay "things" on the terrace.

Panchu was beginning to think unfavourably about Dayal Babu.

Mr. Das was hypnotized by the glittering beauty of the *sheeshmahal*. And he looked at the paintings with his mouth agape and eyes bulging out.

Monai, clinging to Dayal Babu's legs, was pleading. Acknowledging his mistake, he was now begging to be punished. He was well aware that Dayal Babu would not come round unless he gave him a sumptuous bribe. Hence, he started the topic himself. He told Dayal Babu that according to the scriptures, he could not be saved unless he expiated for his crime and that he was ready to take any punishment whatever.

* Milkmaids.

Starting from five hundred bags, the "punishment" was finally fixed at a thousand bags. In between, Monai held Dayal Babu's feet umpteen times, making loud protestations in the name of God. It was decided to gift two hundred bags to the Secretary of the Union Board. Monai agreed to everything willingly. It was better to salvage something instead of being deprived of everything. With his sycophancy and flattery, he won over Dayal Babu as well as the Secretary of the Union Board.

Panchu was left alone. No reference was made to him at all. No one was paying any attention to him. Panchu felt that even that ugly, semi-educated and arrogant Secretary of the Union Board was bigger than him and the fact irked him.

Monai tried to show off and went on paying tributes to Dayal Babu in superlative terms: "No other zamindar in the whole of Bengal can boast of such prosperity. Even the great English Collector takes his hat off and becomes humble before my master... Big officials and rich people of the city are astonished by the immense wealth of this great ruler of Mohanpur and Indra's nymphs come to dance in this *sheeshmahal...*" Monai went on and on...

Dayal Babu listened with seriousness and great feeling of satisfaction. Mr. Das stared at Monai's face in wonder. In a capricious tone he asked Monai about the possible gains from the town.

Monai hesitated at first. Then he said with a pretended smile: "Sir, will there ever be shortage of pearls in a king's treasury. With your instruction, I can send right away whatever you want."

Dayal Babu made a sign.

Seizing the opportunity, Monai now adopted his trick: "All business is in doldrums. If by chance, a Union Board is set up in the town, I will be doomed to sell myself at a damn cheap rate." After that Monai urged the Secretary to stop the distribution of his rice in places for free feeding. He said he was willing to buy up the entire stock of rice lying with the Union Board. If the government sold it at the rate of ten rupees, he was ready to buy at twelve rupees.

Dayal Babu and Mr. Das exchanged glances. Dayal Babu had no objection. Mr. Das was ready to sell rice at the rate of fifteen rupees. Monai protested that he himself had been completely looted, otherwise, he would have gladly accepted the rate. But Mr. Das was not ready to come down. Monai did not press his demand. Wishing them safety and praising them skyhigh, he left with a promise to send "two" with Azim during the night.

After Monai left, the course of conversation changed. There was a mood of mirth and luxuriousness. On the left of the hall was the terrace projecting outward. The floor was paved with marble and had been sprinkled with water. Flower-pots were arranged along the edge of the terrace. Small easy chairs were laid out and the whole paraphernalia for serving drinks kept ready.

It was a bright moonlit night in June. Panchu experienced a strange kind of gloom as he looked at the fields in the distance. He felt depressed.

Panchu had never tasted alcohol in his life. But he had described himself as a seasoned drunkard to Dayal Babu. Now, however much he dilly-dallied, there was no escape. After a few bitter sips, the euphoria of inebriation got under Panchu's skin. Out of sheer weariness, he stopped thinking about himself. He became oblivious to himself and drifted into the rising waves of intoxication...

They resumed talking about their romances with foreign women. Dayal urged Panchu to narrate some more experiences of his romances. Panchu wanted to get up and run, but he could not bring himself to do it. He was going against his grain.

Snacks were served. Panchu's eyes brightened at the sight of the eats. His hand moved forward, but suddenly the thought of his starving family closed in on him. His hand stopped. The conflict in his mind grew. Suddenly, he got up from his chair. When Mr. Das and Dayal Babu looked questioningly up at him he replied: "Nothing, I just felt like walking a bit!"

"*Arrey*, sit down! Is this the time to walk?" and holding Panchu's hand, Dayal Babu forced him to sit.

Panchu sat as though he were a cog in the machine.

For a while, his mind was caught in conflict. But he was harassed by hunger. Pushing the thought of his hungry family behind the screen of friendship with Dayal Babu, Panchu extended his hand towards the table. He started eating. With every morsel that he swallowed, he pushed down the voice of his conscience. He did justice with himself by committing the crime of forgetting his crime. He had read and heard that alcohol was unique stuff for committing a wrong. Panchu tried to do even that.

"Das is talking very loudly. And he brags too much," remarked Panchu, because he was eager to prevent Mr. Das from influencing Dayal Babu too much. He went on talking excitedly about the atrocities of the British government, right from the 1942 movement to the time of the famine. He embroiled particularly the government servants, calling them selfish, rogues, corrupt fellows, devils, traitors—everything that his intoxicated mind could think of.

Dayal Babu also did not lag behind in abusing the British government and its officials. Mr. Das too rode the high wave of patriotism. Then he was overcome by self-pity. "What can we do? When we see the loot being carried on everywhere, we also feel tempted to get our share. In order to get their share in the bribes, higher officials pressurise us. For their sake also we have to resort to loot and plunder. Goods arrive from Delhi these days. Those traders come to us with their money-bags. Then tell us, what can we do? We're no saints, after all, Master Babu! The conditions will remain as they are till we have socialism in the country."

"Let there be socialism then!" thundered Dayal Babu as he put his empty glass on the table, "Socialism wanted? Then bring socialism!"

Promptly the servant appeared, thinking his master wanted something.

Dayal Babu continued in the same excited tone: "Master Babu, I want you to write articles praising me and get them published alongwith my photographs in all newspapers. Did you hear what I said? Don't I deserve it, eh? I do deserve it, don't I? Now look, who is a bigger zamindar than me? None! I arranged the distribution of rice and medicines among people...and now, I'll distribute socialism—I'll surely distribute that!"

Mr. Das and Panchu stared at the inebriated Dayal Babu. Their conversation reverted from socialism to alcohol, women, youthful revelries, and soon their tongues started rolling. The acridity of alcohol created excitement in the atmosphere.

Dayal Babu said: "Ma...ster...! Four...wo...men, do you hear? Two bo...ttles of whisky, but ne...ver down! What do you think, eh?"

Then Dayal Babu placed the glass on the table and shouted for Vrindavan, his servant. That was Dayal Babu's fifth peg. Mr. Das had downed six. And Panchu had not yet finished even the first. Panchu had taken three fourth of his first drink. Dayal Babu said to Mr. Das: "Drink, I say! Drink! Let me see how much you can drink today!"

Takind the last puff of the cigarette and blowing out the smoke very slowly, Mr. Das said: "Don't worry, sonnie! I can drink up to two bottles and remain normal!"

Dayal Babu burst out laughing. He said: "Oh, I see! You want to have a jolly time at somebody's cost! Go on! Dri...nk as much as you can! My heart is no smaller than your British Government. Vrindavan! Go on filling the glass of that rascal! I shall make him drink his master's...no, his master's country's wine...pure whisky ...and then I shall abuse his government...rascal!"

Dayal Babu broke into a delirious laugh and then burst out: "Go on, drink, you fellow! Vrindavan, thrust the bottle in the mouth of this saheb! Drink, you rascal!"

Then Dayal Babu stood up. Snatching the bottle from Vrindavan's hand, he advanced towards Mr. Das: "You bastard! I shall go on pouring this stuff in your mouth. No, you say? Look, this bastard says he can drink two bottles! You challenge me, eh? A wretched servant earning a paltry five hundred rupees, the dog of our enemy! The rascal thinks Dayal can't give him bottles of whisky to drink! You ill-begotten fellow! I'll make you drink ten bottles. *Sala!* Go and tell your government how generous this zamindar can be!"

Dayal Babu held Mr. Das by the shoulder and forced him to remain seated on the chair and, with a menacing gesture, tried to thrust the bottle into his mouth.

Mr. Das tried to push back Dayal Babu with both his hands: "What are you doing, Dayal Babu?... Look, it's not right to play such practical jokes. You're really very drunk. You're insulting me..."

Mr. Das flung his legs and hands about. His voice choked with rage. The stench of officialdom which thrives in the soil of slavery had suddenly gone stale wriggled under Dayal Babu's pressure.

Panchu was terrified. He thought: "If he starts behaving that way with me...I'll punch him, and I'll do it with such force he'll always remember...I'll certainly hit him hard... And that Das, *sala,* he's such a weakling! He's just bleating like a goat. Why can't he give him a push? Coward that he is—he deserves to die. But this is not right. After him, Dayal Babu may pounce on me. How can you be sure about a drunken man? He must be checked."

To strengthen his mind, Panchu forced himself to drag away Dayal Babu from Mr. Das: "What are you doing, Dayal Babu?"

Dayal Babu turned round and looked intently at Panchu: "I'm making him drink. You also drink. And force the stuff down the throat of this government stooge, *sala!* Drink, I say, you bastard!"

Panchu was scared out of his wits. He pulled Dayal Babu away from Mr. Das and said: "But what are you doing? Does one treat a guest like this?"

Now that he had support, Mr. Das said in an anguished voice: "See, just see, Mr. Mukherji! How he's terrorizing me! It's only because of such tyrants that our country has been enslaved. And, on top of everything, he calls me a slave!"

Mr. Das broke into bitter tears and said in a melancholy voice: "I shall commit suicide. I find this life of slavery unbearable."

Panchu was trapped between the two drunken men, both getting more and more inebriated. Panchu wondered how he could get away from them. Suppose something untoward happened?

Panchu grew restless.

Vrindavan stood silent like a statue, head bent. He had no right to witness the unseemly behaviour of his master or his friends. On such occasions, he was expected not to listen to any remarks, good or bad, made by his master or his friends. He was a symbol of blankness, a mere servant, nothing else.

Panchu was irritated to see Vrindavan standing there so dispassionately: "Why don't you look after your saheb? Take care of him!"

Dayal Babu was back in his chair by that time. Mr. Das' tears and Panchu's reprimands had calmed him down. Seeing that Panchu was scared, he said: "Don't worry, Master Babu. Mr. Das is a little drunk."

"You're drunk, Dayal Babu, not I!" shouted Mr. Das angrily. "You forgot all etiquette. And you've humiliated me..."

Mr. Das' voice choked and tears rushed into his eyes.

Dayal Babu regained his balance. He tried to pacify Mr. Das. "We've come in this world for a brief while and why should we get into such brawls. Eat, drink and make merry. That's the only way to enjoy life. Who knows tomorrow where you'll be, where I'll be? Come, let's drink!"

The atmosphere was pleasant once more. Mr. Das and Dayal Babu poked fun at each other for getting drunk. Vrindavan was ordered to fill the empty glasses, which he did with the motions of a wound up doll.

For the first time in his life Panchu was seeing drunken men from such close quarters. He was terrified by the experience.

As Vrindavan filled the glasses, Panchu picked up his glass and, looking intently at it, remarked: "If only man's blood had the golden sparkle of liquor! Then blood would also cost at least as much as liquor!"

Dayal Babu and Mr. Das were impressed by the remark and gave

Panchu an amused glance. Taking advantage of his reputation as a man of learning, Panchu was trying to extricate himself from the sticky situation through pompous words: "For the price of the liquid in this glass, ten persons can satisfy their hunger. Only the death of the famished gives us this pleasure by becoming intoxicated. Come, let's drink once more to the death of thousands!"

And with a jerky movement, Panchu brought his glass to his lips. As the liquor touched his lips, he put back the glass.

Both Dayal Babu and Mr. Das were highly impressed by the magic of Panchu's words. Only Vrindavan, untouched by Panchu's observation, carried on with his job. He poured soda in the glasses and then stood, head hanging and hands folded. The moment Panchu uttered those words, Dayal Babu and Mr. Das picked up their glasses and drank to the death of thousands.

"Drinking to the death of thousands!" The words rang like poetry to Dayal Babu and Mr. Das. The reference to the starving thousands had initially made them feel guilty. But the moment Panchu suggested drinking to the death of the starving people, they were reassured. The harsh reality became a draught of pleasure and went down their throats. Sympathy turned into inebriation and took possession of their minds. Mr. Das said he had seen with his own eyes thousands of naked and hungry people wherever he went...his heart had been overcome with anguish at the thought of his country's state of dependence...when he saw the godowns full of grain bags, he had wanted to empty them and distribute the grain to the poor. "Oh, our poor Bharatvarsha, our Bengal!" Mr. Das moaned sorrowfully. "We have fallen into such a sorry state! Rivers of milk and ghee used to flow in this sacred land of ours. Now the people of this very land are dependent for every single grain of food!"

Mr. Das, now thoroughly moved, had one more sip of whisky.

Dayal Babu heaved a sigh and said: "Master Babu, believe me, every now and then, I feel like distributing everything I possess among the poor. Oh, God! how much these poor creatures have to suffer!"

Everyone was silent for a while. Panchu was surprised at this glimpse of humanism in the observations made by Dayal Babu and Mr. Das. He thought: "Even these people have human feelings in their hearts. But then, what makes them so harsh·in spite of that? Why don't they realize their own sins? Why do they become selfish?"

Panchu was shocked by the thought: "I too have committed a sin. My family is starving and I'm seated here indulging in merry-making, eating and drinking!"

Panchu could not escape from himself. He had fallen so low in his own eyes that he dared not look up at the crimes of others. He felt a hatred for liquor, hatred for the crime and was impatient to get away from the thought of the crime. When he could think of no way of defending himself he resorted to God: "What should I do? It's God who has made me so weak and so, if I've committed a crime, it's not my crime."

Even that thought gave no relief to Panchu. He felt more restless and agitated. His relations with reason snapped with a violent jerk. He quickly extended his hand, picked up his glass and, closing his eyes, tossed down the whisky. It was too quick and he choked. His eyes smarted and the veins of his head grew tense.

Exhausted, Panchu rested his head on the back of the chair.

The clock started striking time. Panchu looked up with a start. He could not see the clock. He listened attentively. The clock struck one...two...three...four...seven, eight...nine...

Nine o'clock! It was very late! He should leave. He did not know how to leave.

Meanwhile, Mr. Das was rendering the *raga Kedara* in his own style and Dayal Babu was all appreciation.

"Fools!" muttered Panchu to himself and looked up at the sky.

Now the moonlight was quite hazy. In the dusty sky, the stars appeared very faint. The half moon is not beautiful. The moon is lovely in the crescent shape or when it is round. But the half moon looks very ugly, very ominous. This moonlight is so dull, so lifeless! And there's ominousness all round. I feel suffocated.

In this mood of dejection Panchu said: "I should now take your leave, Dayal Babu!"

Mr. Das and Dayal Babu were engaged in a discussion. Mr. Das was under the impression that he had been singing the Kedara, whereas Dayal Babu was praising it as *raga Bageshri.* Mr. Das objected, and that led to an argument between them. In an honest attempt to give an illustration of *Kedara,* Dayal Babu started singing, and, in the process, rendered *raga Bhimpalas.* Mr. Das declared that it was the *raga Malakaus* and that angered Dayal Babu.

While those two men were disputing, Panchu got up saying: "I should take your leave now..."

Both Dayal Babu and Mr. Das gave a start. Before Dayal Babu

could say anything, a servant come in and announced that Monai had sent two women.

Mr. Das' face gleamed with pleasure. Dayal Babu ordered the women to be brought up.

Azim had been standing just behind the door with the women. He came forward promptly and bowed respectfully. The women, shrinking with shame, faces veiled, bowed with folded hands. Both of them wore brightly washed sarees. For a long time one had not seen man or woman in the town wearing washed clothes. Those sarees struck Panchu as exhibition pieces.

The servant and Azim went away.

Dayal Babu said angrily to the women: "Remove your veils. They look like elephant trunks!"

The trembling hands of the women moved to remove their veils. Panchu looked at them with curiosity—one woman was the widow of Munir and the other... She was Kalirai's wife!

Kalirai was Panchu's close childhood friend who had left the town three months ago. Panchu knew Kalirai's wife very well. He held her in great respect. "She has come here—Kalirai's wife!"

Dayal Babu got up and pulled the sarees down the heads of both women.

Panchu lowered his head.

Dayal Babu was happy to see the women. "Monai has sent nice stuff!" He lifted the chin of Munir's widow and pinched her on the neck. He asked: "Whose wife are you?"

Hearing that question, Panchu raised his eyes. Suddenly Mrs. Kalirai's eyes met Panchu's. Her face went pale and she collapsed.

Panchu hurriedly left the room. His thoughts moved from Kalirai's wife to...his own house...Tulsi...Mangala....

Panchu was not aware where he walked. Tears flowed, his face turned red and as he walked, he felt a storm raging. He came out of the *sheeshmahal* and went down the stairs. Looking at Panchu's state, Vrindavan thought that he was heavily drunk. He came rushing to save him from falling. He held Panchu with both his hands. Panchu stumbled on him almost lifeless. His eyes closed. Vrindavan held him: "Babu! Master Babu!"

Panchu opened his eyes. He saw Vrindavan who said: "Shall I take you home, Master Babu?"

Panchu felt ashamed. He quickly recovered and said: "No, Vrindavan, I'm alright."

Panchu's eyes lowered even before Vrindavan. The pain in

his heart, born of shame, became a mountain. He tried hard to control his intense feeling of inferiority. He turned into stone as it were.

Vrindavan touched Panchu's feet and then, straightening himself, said with folded hands: "Master Babu, what has a swan to do in the company of storks? So far I had not thought...but today when I saw you here, I felt convinced that *Kaliyuga* had come. If even the mountains start swaying, how will the earth be saved?... What does God wish to do?"

Panchu raised his head. "You're greater than me, Vrindavan. Please forgive me."

Vrindavan gazed at Panchu.

Panchu went on saying: "The whole world, everyone is greater than me. Everything in the world is greater than me. I've no right to consider anyone small. No one is mean. No one is bad. All evil things are contained in me. I'm the most evil of all. I alone am bad!"

Finding no other way out, Panchu's anger flowed out through his tears that ran down both cheeks. And so Panchu walked towards the town.

Vrindavan, that lifeless statue that moved mechanically according to the orders of his master, that most degenerate slave, had risen high in Panchu's estimation. He appeared to him great like a *guru*.

Before the famine, Panchu's ambitions had been modest. His life had followed the accustomed and straight course without any conflict in his mind. During the famine, however, he had become painfully aware of his economic dependence and experienced the hardships that unfailingly accompany such a state. He had tried to fight his financial inferiority with the help of respectability, reputation, high education and self-respect. Unsuccessful, he grew restless. And once he lost self-confidence, his mind could not help him. He was continuously in conflict with himself. He worried too much about his status in society, with the result that he lost control over his mind. It had reduced him to being Dayal Babu's flunkey and dragged him to such lowliness in his own eyes. Panchu saw himself as the most worthless creature in the world and tears streamed.

As he wept, Panchu thought: "But who doesn't desire to be big?" The question itself became the answer. "No one has the right to assert his own authority and prevent somebody else attaining a high status. All human beings are equal..."

Then he asked himself: "But what about the distribution of the big and small in the world?" The very next moment came the answer: "It's the result of that very evil that has brought about my downfall."

In his own downfall, Panchu saw the cause of the downfall of the world. "The world is destroying itself for the sake of vanity. But what is vanity? Why does man have this trait? Why doesn't he see the awareness of his own being in the universal and collective form? Why do I see myself as being distinct from the world? Why do I remove myself from the world? Every social action and reaction affects me jointly and transforms me into consciousness. I decide about every good or bad action only according to the scales of society. Not I alone, every man does the same. In everything that man does, he's only worried about the direction or the lack of it in the world. Then why does he separate himself from the world? Why does he do it?"

The chain of questions ended, but Panchu found no answer. He raised his head, as though trying to find his way. But what he saw in front gave him a shock. In the distance the sky was growing red. Red from leaping flames! Fire! Where was it?

Panchu started walking fast. "Are hunger and epidemic not enough that even nature finds it necessary to be cruel? It's a terrible fire!"

Monai's shop came into view. He heard shouts of laughter. He saw the house surrounded by leaping flames. The fire was close to the school. Oh, no! The school building itself was on fire! Panchu's heart started thumping. The shop was deserted. Now Panchu started running.

People moved in a circle, jumping and shouting. The school building was on fire. The air was hot. Laughter, singing, loud noises, all mingled in a terrifying cacophony.

After sunset, Chheda Singh had loaded the grain bags on the push-cart and brought them to the school. The bags reserved for himself and his companions had been kept in a separate room. The bags of rice to be distributed had been kept aside. With the help of armed men, Chheda Singh had started distributing rice in the town. Even in that, they cheated as much as they could. Still, everybody got at least some rice and danced with joy.

The Spirit of Corn was pleased with man today. For the sake of that god, man had lost all money, ornaments, clothes and sold every little thing in the house, lost prestige and shame and religion...got separated from parents, brothers and sisters, wife, children and even his life. But the Spirit of Corn had remained unappeased. Today, that very god was being looted while Chheda Singh continued to shower abuses. Man who was begging for life had ultimately found support for his life. After a long time, joy expressed itself in the form of laughter and tears, shrieks and cries, singing and dancing, embraces and exchange of blows...all emerging from the depths of his heart. It was a festival of grain in Mohanpur. People danced till they felt dizzy, grains scattered all over. People simply pounced on the scattered grain. They stuffed rice into their mouths by handfuls and broke into laughter.

Azim was boiling with rage. Chheda Singh had so insulted Monai, his master, that he was impatient to take revenge on him. He could not tolerate the triumph of Chheda Singh.

People were happy to see the leaping flames. It turned out to be a matter of great fun for them. It flashed in somebody's mind that they could cook rice in that fire. "We'll cook! We'll cook!" the cry arose from all sides. Many people rushed to bring broken pots, troughs and water from the pond. They strained beyond their physical strength, all weakness and fatigue forgotten.

The flames rose high. Chheda Singh and his companions stood stupefied in the face of the flames. The situation was beyond their arrogance and commanding power. They dared not utter a word of protest.

People started keeping their broken pots and troughs filled with water around the fire and dropped rice in them. They thought the rice would get cooked. Some people started eating rice raw—this hurt in their stomachs.

In the red glow of the flames, the bones of the revellers shone brightly. No flesh, only bones. A creature called man, after eating his own flesh and blood, was launching a crusade against immorality and injustice.

Shrivelled up legs, bulging bellies, drooping wrinkles that one would associate with an eighty-year-old, cheeks sunk deep inside angular jaws and teeth shining like the edge of a sword...these were all there—the children, the young men, the adults and the old—all frames of bones, their bodies rotting with disease, people hailing from all social classes and strata. They had gathered to celebrate a festival of hunger against the background of raging flames, their hearts overflowing with joy. They were oblivious to their physical condition. Having obtained food, they had forgotten that they had been hungry for several days. There was a celebration

of human life for which they had paid a big price. Life was free—
free from fear and anxiety, hunger and thirst, respect and dis-
respect, reason, knowledge, consciousness.

People from respectable homes watched in groups from a distance. Of course, they had not publicly acknowledged that they
too had been affected by the famine. But now reports about their
real condition were beginning to be published in the Calcutta
newspapers and everywhere else in India. They too seized the first
opportunity to steal rice.

Azim had won his victory by taking revenge on Dayal Babu.
But when he glowed over his great triumph before Monai, he was
sharply reprimanded. According to Monai's plan, all that rice
should have been made available to the people and then Chheda
Singh would have been left gaping. However, Monai was not one
to cry over spilt milk. He, along with Azim, stood in a corner
watching that scene.

Azim commented: "What a sight! It's frightening! Like seeing
a ghost!"

Monai, looking in front of him, said grimly without any trace
of emotion on his face: "This is no ghost, Azim! This is the present
we are seeing right before us—the present more frightening than
ghosts. This hunger would not leave even a grain of rice untouched
in my godown. The hunger awakened today will not be satisfied
for many years. Even bullets and lathis won't keep it in check."

Azim, realizing the seriousness of the scene in front of him,
asked: "What will happen then, uncle?"

Monai placed his hand on Azim's shoulder and said in a subdued voice: "Son, go and tell your father to fix immediately eight
or ten boats. Everything should be ready within two hours, do you
follow? And listen, by the time you come back, I would have
reached home. Take two hundred rupees and rush to Chheda
Singh. Last time the boats were settled at fifty rupees. But the
situation is different this time. Any way, try to settle it at the mini-
mum charge. Everything else is in God's hands. Bring twenty
men with you. Leave fifty bags behind and load all the rest in the
boats during the night."

Azim asked: "Where will you take all that rice, uncle?"

"I shall go to Devipur. And I may go to Calcutta if I can make
the arrangements. I hear rice is being sold there at the rate of a
hundred rupees a bag."

Azim grew anxious. He said: "I've heard there is strict police-patrolling along the river."

Monai was unperturbed. He replied: "Now, now, my boy! I've faced difficult situations several times. I shall see to the police-patrolling too. As such, I'm playing this time like a defeated gambler."

"But uncle! How can that sort of logic work here? Suppose you're caught with the bags? God forbid, but what will happen in that case?"

Monai smiled. Placing his hand on Azim's shoulder with affection he said: "Don't worry about me, son. Nobody can catch me so easily. And yes, let the grain bags be found out. It means nothing. God willing, everything will work out well. As such, I've started on this venture after making all the arrangements on our side."

Monai turned towards his house, taking Azim with him. He said: "The Union Board Secretary is in town. I've instigated him in the way I should have. I met him at Dayal Babu's place. Those two women you sent there would also be a further help. He insisted on the rate of fifteen rupees, but I suggested twelve. I think he will agree to it by tomorrow. I'll leave thirty thousand rupees with Nyada's mother. Coax him to come round to accept the rate of fourteen and three quarters. But if he doesn't agree, dump the money and take the goods. The loss will be covered when I take out another lot of two thousand bags in the second trip. That zamindar, bastard that he is, has caused me so much damage! *Sala*, he too will..."

Azim shook Monai by his arm: "Uncle! Oh, uncle!..."

Panchu, meanwhile, stood by the pond, lost in thought. Unblinkingly, he stared at the flames rising from the school building. His dream was on fire. Flames were rising from his heart. In the face of stiff opposition by Ram Dulal Khudo and other elders in the town, he had started educating the children of lower communities. The noise and joyous shrieks of the children, their attending classes, Kanai and Govind Master, and Ganesh...

The day Ganesh died was also the day Panchu had last been to the school. Munir had also died the same day. That was the day he had struck the deal about the sale of the school furniture to Monai. That was the day Panchu had lost his self-confidence for the first time, and after selling the school furniture bought with public donations, his proud head had bent forever. Together with the school building, Panchu's old memories, Panchu's dignity,

Panchu' sins were also on fire. "It's my sin that is burning. My pride is burning."

Forgetting the constrictions of shame, a group of women arrived on the scene. Menfolk, delirious with joy, looked startled at the invasion of the naked, shameless women wanting to grab grains. The men were enraged. They pounced upon them, showering all the filthy words they knew.

Looking at them, Panchu reflected: "We've got to accept equal rights for all. So long as even a single woman remains enslaved, children born from her womb would only be slaves. Slavery ties life to the insensitivity of death. This famine is the result of our slavery. This famine is the result of slavery... Men sold away their women's clothes to quench the fire of their stomachs. They also sold their women's bodies. After that what honour remains to be lost that man is so horrified about their being naked?"

Two men pushed a woman back. The enraged woman bit the hand of one of the men. The flesh spat blood. The man fell to the ground with a shriek.

Panchu closed his eyes. Then it occurred to him that he should protect those women. But he dared not go anywhere near.

Panchu turned to go home. He thought: "How low man has stooped! What then is the difference between the age of barbarism and the present age? Does it mean that man's progress till today, his civilization, knowledge, science—all these have been futile?"

Panchu's reason refused to accept such a view. He carried further his thought: "The reason for this downfall is personal ego which wishes to be pleased by causing the downfall of others. It wishes to retain its position by enslaving others with the help of brute force. So long as such an attitude persists, so long as a single slave exists in the world, it will always be disturbed like this. Man will have to destroy the very root of his inherent barbaric traits in order to free himself. In the process of unifying society in his attempt to make himself cultured, man has only given prominence to his own individual self. Intellectually as well as philosophically, he has worked for the progress of society only by subjecting it to himself. It is not comradeship and does not march in step with society. An individual can go ahead not by becoming a leader in society but by matching his steps with society. Only then can man and mankind be seen as one. Actually, it is wrong to name them and see them apart. Individual and society, man and mankind are the twin names of the same reality."

Panchu's steps followed the pace of his thoughts.

7

Hundreds of vultures had been hovering in the sky for several days. They had lost all fear. With the exception of human beings who were moving around, they regarded every living or dead persons as 'food'. Cows, oxen, men, women, children—all. The town was full of skeletons half-eaten, rotting corpses.

After that fire, the town reached the ultimate point of its destruction. Along with starvation, cholera and malaria were also on the increase.

Monai left the night of the blaze after loading his grain bags. Following the instruction of the master, Azim brought a thousand grain bags from the Secretary of the Union Board and became the owner himself. He started his own ferry service.

Carpenter Nuruddin had gone away to Calcutta taking Munir's wife along. Munir's helpless daughters, Chand and Rukia, were in a terrible plight. Dinu, who lived in the neighbourhood, took them under his care. Occasionally, he still felt pity for them. There was nobody else in Dinu's house. His wife had gone away with the children to her mother's place. Later, news came that she had started selling her body to English soldiers. Dinu was shocked. Dinu showered his affection on Chand and Rukia to distract his mind. He had no food to give. He just sat by the side of the hungry girls and shed tears. He neither went out himself nor did he let the girls go anywhere. Finally he stopped talking altogether. He sat like a lost soul, staring at the house with everything looted and gone.

One day, as he sat staring at the *chulha*, it flashed in his mind that since the day the fire had stopped burning in the *chulha*, his house had been reduced to a sad state. Suppose the *chulha* was lighted again. He was sure the moment there was fire in the *chulha*, his wife would come back, his children would return and there would be no famine. There would be peace and happiness once more. This thought regenerated Dinu. He quickly got up and pulled out a bamboo shoot from the broken roof of his house. He broke the bamboo into small chips. He hurt his hand in the process, and bled profusely. But he was not even aware of it. Chand

and Rukia gave him an amazed look. Dinu placed the bamboo chips in the *chulha* and then rushed out.

Dinu was stepping out of the house after a long time. Azim's house was closeby. There always used to be some fire in a pot kept near the door for the hukkah. Like a thief, Dinu picked up the fire-pot and ran. He placed that fire in the *chulha*. "Blow!" he said to Chand and Rukia. The girls started blowing as best they could, but they soon got exhausted. Dinu held their necks and blew the fire himself and forced the girls to do the same.

A flame rose. Dinu jumped up shrieking with joy. The girls looked at him with astonishment. Something should be cooked, thought Dinu. But what could he cook? He looked around the house. There was nothing. But something had to be cooked. Otherwise, there would not be brightness in the house again. Dinu grew impatient. The flame had lowered a little. Dinu's restlessness increased. He looked around. Suddenly he said to himself: "When will these girls come to use? Let me cook them. Then the house will be bright again. Cook them!" With gleaming eyes he looked at Chand, and suddenly grabbed her neck with great force and lowered her face into the *chulha*. He wanted to make the house bright again. Without that the famine would never end. He wanted freedom from the famine. He wanted happiness and peace...

Hearing Rukia's cries of "Help! Help!" Azim rushed. Quickly leaping forward, he dragged Dinu from Chand. By that time, life was gone from Chand. Her charred face had turned grotesque, lumps of fat and flesh glistening. Dinu looked at it intently. He could not understand what had happened...

The number of lunatics in the town was growing.

The town was acquiring a deserted look day by day. Only children and aged men and women were seen. And even their numbers were steadily going down. Young daughters-in-law and daughters were being sold. Azim and Nuruddin were engaged in that business. Competition with Monai continued.

On his return Monai discovered that his very faithful and right-hand man, his disciple and assistant Azim had become a moneyed man after causing him a loss of thirty thousand rupees. Monai gave a good beating to his wife on that account, but he was unable to do anything to Azim. After burying underground whatever money he had earned by selling his foodgrains, he sighed over his adverse planetary effects and started thinking about the future. Monai, the trader, could not shed tears over his loss. He had to think in terms of making up the loss and earning his profits.

Monai heard that Azim and Nuruddin were engaged in the business of buying young women and selling them outside the town. Monai's mouth started watering.

Nuruddin had returned from Calcutta with many fascinating experiences. He had seen thousands of famine-afflicted people, begging, rotting and dying on the streets. He had even identified some people from his own town. He had seen young women being sold for two or four rupees. He had seen rickshaw-pullers inviting army soldiers and taking them to brothels. Tying big bells on their thumbs, the rickshaw-pullers would attract the attention of the soldiers by jingling them. That was the invitation to the brothel. Seeing the dazzle of that great city full of palatial buildings of the rich, motor cars, trams and buses, Nuruddin also aspired to make money. He first befriended the people connected with the brothels. He built up contacts with rickshaw-pullers and started observing the market place. He learnt that many wealthy men had set up brothels after buying women at throwaway prices. They had made ruffians their partners in that business. They also earned a little money in that business by forcing the drunken white men and military men to empty their pockets.

Nuruddin felt tempted. He sold Munir's wife to a prostitute of Sonagachi, and started working as a pimp. He started making lot of money. He saw "Sanima"* and had a jolly time. Occasionally, he felt sad about the condition of the famine-affected. Many young women in the brothels had become unemployed after falling ill. Nuruddin made a deal with a madam that he would become her partner if he got new girls.

Nuruddin came to the town. He had five hundred rupees in the moneybag tied round his waist. In the meantime, Azim had become a wealthy man by cheating Monai. Nuruddin met Azim and narrated to him all that he had seen in Calcutta. He told him about his own intention of visiting the town.

Azim's mouth started watering at the prospects of profit in that business. He cajoled Nuruddin: "Fix four rupees for each woman, my friend. We can have a fifty-fifty share. I will give rice instead of money. At the very sight of rice, the customer will fall into the net."

Nuruddin saw Azim's point and agreed to the proposal.

---

* Cinema.

Nuruddin spread the news in town that a wealthy businessman had opened a charitable home in Calcutta where poor women
were being given protection and provided food and clothing. Religious discourses were also arranged. Nuruddin said that the families sending their women to Calcutta also received rice from that
businessman.

The news caught fire. Many such homes came up like mush-
rooms in four or five towns around Mohanpur. Women started
being sold in exchange for a handful or two of rice. Old women
were not admitted though.

The mystery about those charitable homes soon became public
knowledge. But it did not matter. At least there would be food
to eat! Let the daughters and daughters-in-law become prostitutes.
Let their honour be violated. Nothing was more important in the
world than the satisfying of hunger. So, sell the women, sell!

Nuruddin and Azim started having a thriving business!

Nuruddin went to Calcutta, taking with him the first batch of
twelve women.

Monai could not bear to see Azim making progress. He made
enquiries and made his own calculations. Azim and Nuruddin
were able to get four women by giving just a seer of rice for each.
Even if he sold rice at eighty rupees a maund, he could still make
at least double the profit through the sale of women.

Monai was plagued by that temptation. But his mind reprimanded: "It would be a great sin to force the women of the town,
daughters and daughters-in-law of good families to sell their flesh."
But the next moment he thought: "But these women, poor things,
are dying of hunger in any case. In those free homes they would
at least get food and clothes. They would be happy and I too would
earn a little money. If, by God's grace, I can earn good money in
this new business, then in future, I may even open a home for destitutes. That's the great thing about religion. Even if a worldly creature succumbs to temptations and commits a sin, he can earn merit
through expiation and cross the great ocean of life. Oh, God, you're
great! Infinite is your *leela**! On the one hand, you preached to
Arjun not to fall prey to temptation and on the other hand you
made him fight a war for the sake of a kingdom! Who but you,
oh God, could have done a thing like that? You showed the real
distinction between duty and action, like separating milk and

* Mysterious ways.

water. For the ascetics you showed the path of religion and to show the greatness of action, yourself became Arjun's charioteer. You're great, oh God! You're kind!"

Monai put the *hukkah* aside and folded his hands. Tears streamed from his eyes. Voice choking, he started to pray: "Oh saviour of the poor! You be my charioteer too! Show that same greatness this time as well. What if I'm an insignificant being? I'm at least devoted to you! Appear before me, oh Lord! The world is wallowing in endless sins. Azim, *sala*! He played foul with me. It was my great mistake that I trusted Azim. Our elders asked us to block our ears even if we heard *namaaz* being offered in a mosque. They said the religion of the Musalmans was the opposite of our religion. You could never trust their religion. Our elders were right. We offer our prayer facing the east and they do their *namaaz* facing the west. In our religion, a devotee is a simple-hearted person like me who knows nothing about cheating and easily places his trust in everyone. If he had told me, I would have given him money from his deposit of five thousand rupees and helped him start a commission agency. I loved him like a son, but in the end he cheated me. God willing, I shall see that he's left high and dry. The fellow doesn't know that a *guru* always keeps one secret to himself."

Monai's little eyes flashed with pride and he resumed puffing at the *hukkah*.

Monai did not consider it a matter of shame to be beaten by Dayal Babu, the police, any government officer or a high-caste Hindu. But Azim was a Muslim and the son of a poor fisherman. He was Monai's servant and to a certain extent his disciple. Now, after being defeated at his hands, Monai could find no peace anywhere. Apart from that, seeing Azim prosper through the trade in women, Monai grew all the more jealous. And he resorted to religion in order to defeat Azim.

Monai went to Dayal Babu for help. He said: "Our Hindu religion is in great danger, zamindar saheb! Under your rule, Musalmans are tempting our daughters and daughters-in-law and whisking them away."

Dayal Babu was the descendant of a Kshatriya zamindar. He flew into rage after hearing what Monai said. Monai further instigated him: "In this *kaliyuga*, people of our town have completely lost their heads. They don't stop to think whether or not religion permits what they're doing. Azim and Nuruddin have started buying our women in the name of a charitable home..."

Monai had actually gone to Dayal Babu with a proposal. The town of Saraswatipur was under Dayal Babu's jurisdiction. A camp for British soldiers was being set up there. Monai suggested building a home for destitutes in that area. With the army camp closeby, nobody dared to think about any such thing. But if such a place of refuge were set up, women of the time would be protected and the Hindu religion too would be saved in the bargain. Monai offered to donate five hundred rupees for that religious act. If Dayal Babu came forward with his support, Monai said he would make all the necessary arrangements.

Monai took out five hundred rupees from the fold of his *dhoti* and humbly placed it at Dayal Babu's feet. The latter promised all support to save the Hindu religion.

Monai started visiting several villages and towns around Mohanpur in this connection. He started his work with much fanfare. At the same time, Monai was afraid that Azim would not sit quiet when he heard the 'destitute home' was built. The Muslim League enjoyed good influence in Bengal. It would not be surprising if the government also played some game. What would happen in that case? Monai started spying on the movements of Azim and Nuruddin.

Monai was managing four fronts at that time. He was trying to keep Dayal Babu in his grip. He was supervising the destitute home. He was keeping a watchful eye on Azim. He had posted his men everywhere for that purpose. Above all, he was keeping a watch over everybody.

Having suffered a blow in their business, Azim and Nuruddin started thinking in terms of the danger that Islam was facing. On the strength of Dayal Babu's armed men, Monai was consolidating his own business and crying for the victory of his religion. The tactics of Azim and Nuruddin did not work. They had been saying that the wretched *kafirs* were terrorizing the poor people. They said: "Power had made those fellows conceited. We cannot call ourselves true defenders of Islam if we don't take revenge on the Hindus."

Azim remembered the nawab saheb of Gauripur and the age-old rivalry between him and Dayal Babu. The territories of the two zamindars lay adjacent. Ever since Dayal Babu humiliated the nawab saheb by building his *sheeshmahal*, the nawab saheb had been bearing a bitter grudge against him.

Azim and Nuruddin went to the nawab saheb. They said: "We'll have nowhere to go if the Musalmans are subjected to so much trouble right before your eyes. That son of a *kafir* is forcing our daughters and daughters-in-law to sell their bodies. He has been ruining the Muslims in his territory."

The nawab saheb, who considered himself a great defender of Islam, was in a terrible rage. Promptly he issued the order: "Go to Calcutta and bring fifty *goondas**. Engage them to fight against Dayal Babu's armed men. Provoke them to rob his house. And I shall reward you with two thousand rupees if you can set fire to his *sheeshmahal*. That Hindu dog has been haughty with me for a long time. But remember, nobody should suspect my hand in it."

Azim and Nuruddin had not imagined even in their dreams that their purpose would be achieved so easily. They had received five hundred rupees in cash to be spent on the *goondas*. They were so happy!

It was a moonlit night. Azim and Nuruddin came out of the nawab saheb's house and walked in the direction of their town.

At a little distance from the nawab's house, Monai was hiding behind a tree. Azim and Nuruddin were coming right where he was sitting. Monai stood up and cleared his throat as he started slipping his feet into his shoes.

Azim and Nuruddin were stunned. They were taken aback.

Monai looked in their direction and said: "Who's there? Oh, Azim! Tell me, son, are you well? Now, now! Who is there with you? Nuruddin, is it? Oh, brother, you're seen after a long time!"

Monai moved closer. Azim was trembling with hatred and anger. Monai said with a smile: "Son, you'll gain nothing by killing me. I don't take you to be my enemy. No, not at all! I swear by Nyada. I swear by God!"

Monai went close to him. Azim was wild with anger. Putting his hand on Azim's shoulder Monai said: "It was I who poisoned Dayal's ears. I disgraced you before him and caused you so much harm. But God knows I didn't do it out of ill will."

Azim was enraged by Monai's words. "Then you did it to show your love, is it?"

Monai immediately raised his eyes to the sky and said: "God is witness—I played that trick out of love."

Azim jerked off Monai's hand from his shoulder and said harshly: "You don't love even your own son. How then can you

* Toughs.

love me? Did you hear, Nuru? This uncle acted out of love for us! Hi...hi...!"

Monai reprimanded him sharply: "I trained you like a parrot all these years, but you've got no sense still. You can't see beyond the point of your nose!"

Then Monai turned to Nuruddin: "Nuruddin, if I tell you why I played the trick, you'll be convinced that this uncle of yours can do the most impossible things. What does this boy know about the tricks of the trade? He's an ass. Will you come home?"

Monai started walking. Nuruddin and Azim also walked with him in silence. At that moment, they were completely over-powered by Monai.

As he walked, Monai said softly: "My wife gave me all your news when I came back. Believe me, my heart beat very fast. I told her laughingly that you've become very smart! My boy, the secret of business is only that if the need arises it won't spare even one's own father. Shall I tell you something, son? You slipped a little because of your youth. Otherwise, you could have grabbed a much bigger fortune." Monai laughed and continued: "Do you know what I would have done in your place?"

Azim and Nuruddin stared at him.

Monai said: "Son, you've learnt business tactics, but you've still not learnt to act cleverly. You're mad, I tell you! I wouldn't have let even Nyada's mother know that you've taken out the grain bags. I would have kept her in the dark. I would have first sold a few bags and then, after putting a few thousand rupees in her hands, I would have told her that in a certain village, men of the Union Board are taking out another two thousand bags at the same price. After that, I would have heaved such a sigh that your aunt would have taken off her ornaments and offered them to me. You've suffered a great loss because this uncle of yours wasn't by your side!"

Monai's trick worked. Azim and Nuruddin were hypnotized by the magic of Monai's talk. At heart, Azim acknowledged his own guilt. Monai continued: "Woman...I say, you take it from me... Just talk of profit and she will melt. She will even return the money you may have given earlier, and offer her ornaments as well. In your place, I would have killed two birds with one stone. Go slow in the matter of business and think with a calm mind. What sort of a businessman is he who can't kill two birds with one stone?"

Azim had always listened to Monai's advice with attention and veneration. Once more he did so and his guilty mind was disturbed by self-repentence. He walked with his head bent. Both Nuruddin and Azim walked on in silence, as though they were hypnotized.

Monai saw that they were totally under his spell. Suppressing a smile he continued: "Now shall I point out your second mistake?"

Azim felt embarrassed. He dared not look up. Nuruddin stared at Monai. With a faint smile, Monai said to Nuruddin: "This is called being childish. See, he's not able to look up. My son, if you play one trick, think of two tricks your enemy may play. How could you forget that Monai uncle is a businessman and would surely meet your trick with a trick of his own? You gave no thought to that and blindly went ahead with Nuru to grab the impossible! You are crazy and Nuru is crazy too. Bidding goodbye to all sense, you started doing business—great fellow!"

Azim and Nuruddin hung their heads. Nuruddin too, like Azim, became Monai's disciple.

Then Monai said with a laugh: "I laughed aloud at what you were doing. Of course, I was a little angry at first. But when I saw you playing crude tricks, believe me, I felt pity for you. Then it occurred to me that you boys were acting in haste. Really, I should teach you a few things. Otherwise you will receive hard kicks and that will ruin my name. That's why I had to manipulate all this."

Monai glanced again at his victims. He continued talking in the same vein and dealt a final blow: "You may be secretly thinking that I'm playing tricks with you. Son, if I really wanted to play tricks, I wouldn't have stopped and talked to you this way. You're both young and regard me as your enemy. Who would have known if you had just wrung my neck and flung my body away? Do you think I followed you without any forethought?"

Azim and Nuruddin were taken aback. Now another fear took hold of them. Monai put his hand on Azim's shoulder and said very affectionately: "Son, I would have played another trick if I had any evil design on you. Actually, I've a very sincere purpose in following you and talking these things with you. You know very well that I always kill two birds with one stone. I taught you a lesson by joining hands with Dayal and also played a trick in my interest and yours."

Azim and Nuruddin had lost their power of speech as it were. They had covered half the distance, and it was only he who had been doing all the talking.

Suddenly, Monai started talking in a very serious tone: "Have you instigated the nawab saheb to provoke Hindu-Muslim clashes?"

Azim and Nuruddin were absolutely stunned. Azim stammered and started saying: "N...n...o, uncle..."

Monai cut him short and said: "You fools! You did well, I say! Why are you scared? I tell you, I wanted exactly that to happen. Let the Hindus and the Muslims clash. That's in your interest as well as mine."

Nuruddin said with show of decency: "No, uncle. Do you think we can do any such thing?"

Monai immediately cried out in a sarcastic tone: "Oh, no! You fellows can simply laze—asses that you are, both of you! I tell you, I want you to arouse Hindu-Muslim feelings between the nawab saheb and Dayal Babu. Things would work out to our advantage only when those two clash. We won't get anything so long as those big zamindars hold their sway on us. Tell me, Nuruddin, am I wrong?"

Azim was unable to digest these suggestions from Monai. He had great faith in Monai's common sense. Now that very faith was giving rise to distrust for Monai. He was startled and scared. Monai was aware of his purpose in meeting the nawab saheb—in a way, he knew it. He already had an inkling. The whole thing would bounce back on him if he went and alerted Dayal Babu. Dayal Babu possessed more wealth than the nawab. In the face of the slightest competition, Dayal Babu was provoked to spend lakhs of rupees to build that *sheeshmahal*. Even now, he could easily humiliate the nawab. But if that was Monai's secret intention, why should he have come out in the night like that and tried to be so amiable? And then, he himself talked about creating Hindu-Muslim conflict between Dayal Babu and the nawab! What were his intentions after all?

Azim and Nuruddin could not fathom the depths of Monai's mind. Both were scared. Azim particularly was in a panic. Nuruddin said very cautiously: "That's absolutely right, uncle! But we don't understand why we should start Hindu-Muslim conflicts."

Monai replied at once in a serious tone: "There's a deep game in this. First of all, you must understand why Hindu-Muslim clashes take place. Isn't it because both sides consider their religion greater than the other? And when they can't decide on that point, both indulge in a trial of strength. Isn't that so? Say, yes!"

Nuruddin nodded his head and said: "Yes, of course, that's right!"

"That's right. Then it means that the quarrel is not over religion but over pride. Do you understand? I say, religion is the path of God—call Him Allah or call Him Bhagawan. It makes no difference. The difference is about who is big and who is small—and that's all due to conceit. Now, take your own case. Why did you go to the nawab saheb? Wasn't it because he follows the same religion as yours? You know that Dayal Babu and the nawab saheb are at loggerheads. Dayal Babu insulted you. And now you want to insult him by seeking the nawab saheb's help. Tell me, were you not driven by pride?"

"But uncle," Nuruddin said, "We didn't go to him for that purpose. We..."

Monai cut him short: "Son, you can't hide conception from a midwife..."

Azim and Nuruddin also felt the same. After a moment's pause Monai picked up the thread: "Truth to tell, neither you nor the nawab have the same religion. Nor do I and Dayal either. Actually I and you have the same religion. For you and me, Dayal and the nawab—rascals both—are men of another religion. And tell me, where's any religion to be found in this *kaliyuga*? Selfishness is all that's left. It's in our interest that these big people should engage in mutual strife and we join together to reap our benefits. There is an old animosity between Dayal and the nawab. But there's no obvious reason why at the moment they should indulge in strife. But you've gone and lighted the flame of religion in the nawab saheb's heart. Well, now our job is done! Otherwise, if we jump into this fire out of conceit, we too will be trampled. We can afford to be conceited when our stomachs are full. Whereas I and you are still aspiring to get rich. How can we afford to be conceited. It is foolish. What do you say, Azim? Say something. Why are you silent?"

Azim had no way out now. He said: "Am I apart from you, uncle?"

Monai was delighted. Putting his hand on Azim's back he said: "I know it, of course. Now tell me, what have you fixed with the nawab?"

Azim still dared not raise his head. Head bowed, he replied: "Dayal's house will be attacked."

"When?"

"Nuru will go to Calcutta to bring some men."

Monai considered the situation very seriously. He said: "I see..

Did he part with some money?"

"Five hundred!" Azim did not want to spell it out, but he was completely under Monai's spell.

Monai said: "Oh, no! They should attack not Dayal's house but a place in Saraswatipur where I've kept some women."

Azim stared at Monai's face with amazement. He had got over his hesitation.

Monai said: "If you attack Dayal's house, these two big fellows would no doubt be hostile to each other, but we won't be able to kill two birds with one stone. Now listen, we three could be partners in this business of women. The destitute homes serve no purpose. The army soldiers—bastards—get drunk and go berserk. Four of my women have already died. The contractor gets his fat commission. I've to pay extra for food and clothes for the women in those homes. What I want is that Nuru should settle all those women in Calcutta. Then only will it be a profitable business. That's why, the day Nuru comes from Calcutta with the *goondas*, I shall grease the contractor's palm and somehow arrange for a car. The moment those women have been bundled off, the *goondas* will raise uproarious cries in the empty house. Do you see the point?"

Azim said: "That's fine. But where does the Hindu-Muslim question come in here?"

"It'll come later," Monai said. "Listen, we'll have to play many tricks at the same time. When you bring those *goondas* with the nawab's money, they must be tutored to pose as Dayal's men. Do you get me, Nuru?"

"Why so, uncle?" asked Nuruddin.

"The trick is this—the soldiers will be wild when they don't find the women. When they see the *goondas* in the empty buildings, they will think they have abducted the women. Later, I shall convince the general of the English army that the contractor of the camp had joined hands with Dayal and had taken the women away. To prove it, I shall say that the women had been taken away in the contractor's car. Thus, in the first place, the contractor will be fired from the camp and when the *goondas* get arrested, they too will admit that they're Dayal Babu's men. The Englishman will give evidence against Dayal and he will lose his credibility with the government. His side will become weaker. On the one side, I shall manoeuvre things this way, and on the other, I shall convince Dayal that it was the nawab who arranged the abduction of the women. I shall tell him that the nawab was taking revenge on him by forcing the women to become Muslims. I shall tell him that the women have been hidden in the haunted mosque. I shall thus provoke Dayal's anger and have his men sent there. Do you understand? And Azim, you should instigate the nawab by telling him that Dayal is going to destroy the mosque during the night. You should hide his cudgel fighters in the mosque beforehand. Do you get me, Azim? Armed men from both sides will play havoc in the mosque. The matter will automatically go to the police and the court. The general of the army will write his order against Dayal. And Dayal will be hoodwinked from both sides. Do you get me? Dayal should be put under greater pressure because we're living in this town. He should be put in such a tight fix that he can't think of anything else. Then alone can we carry on our business without any fear. And I shall convince Dayal that the nawab is getting help from the League. I shall prod him to go to Calcutta and start the agitation for the Hindu Mahasabha. I tell you, if Dayal remains in town, he will suspect you because you're Muslims and he will torture you. I don't want any harm to come to you. You're like my sons."

Azim and Nuruddin were overawed by what Monai had said. Azim held Monai's legs. "Uncle, I've been unworthy of you. I'm a great sinner."

Monai immediately raised Azim and embraced him. He said: "God knows I haven't felt bad about it. But you youngsters, in your stupidity, can do some absurd things. If parents also act stupidly and start feeling hurt, how can this world go on? What do you say, Nuru? Am I wrong, son?"

Nuruddin lowered his head and said: "You're right, uncle. And I'll certainly say that it's very difficult to find a pious man like you in this world. It was very wrong of us to have misled you."

Monai immediately held his ears and looking up at the sky said: "No son, don't say such a thing. Whatever happens, is done by God. What power do I have? God willing, these Dayals and nawabs, all these big zamindars, kings and emperors will one day mingle with dust. And it is just as well they do. All these bigwigs are demons, yes, demons. The earth is crying for mercy in the face of their atrocities, son. Just see, wars are being fought. Bombs and guns and so much killing. Our villages and towns have come to this state. There's so much sin—it's the limit. God will surely be born on this earth to save this world—to protect the good and destroy the evil. It'll surely happen. Some such thing must have been written in your Holy Quran too. Because religion is only the word of God. All holy books say the same thing. Now, we poor shall rule the world; because only the poor are truly devoted to God. As for me, son, I only follow the preachings of God. You're all dear to me. Those people are my enemies. I shall destroy them and I shall save you. Now, if all these manoeuvrings succeed by God's grace, then the contractor, Dayal, the nawab—all will tumble down. Then I'll take the contract myself, follow me? Contract work, my own trade and this business in women...and this last thing is very sacred too, Nuru. There is no religion greater than providing food. Reputation, character and all other things come after it. And if prostitutes are sinful women, why would God make them prostitutes? God has devised all those jobs for filling the stomach. Do just anything, but always have the name of God on the tip of your tongue... Then you won't incur any sin, do you understand? Only when I got initiation from my *guru*, did I come to understand such things. So, my son, I'm only doing my duty by spreading out my business and I shall go on doing it for some more time. You people are very capable. The moment you take over responsibility of the business, I shall leave Nyada and his mother in Azim's charge and renounce the world. Understand?"

Azim said in a flattering tone: "No, uncle. You haven't reached that age yet, have you?"

"No, son. But I shall renounce the world. After doing my duty through action, I'll take to religion. Whatever you say, this path of religion is very hard. You have to get entangled in many attachments. Oh Lord, I've only you to protect me!"

Monai emitted a loud belch. The feeling of devotion acquired concrete form. Moving his hand over his stomach he said: "I'm getting these wretched sour belches. Nyada's mother cooked sweet rice and *loochi* today. She forced me to eat a lot. Oh, Lord!"

They were close to the outskirts of Mohanpur. All three of them were feeling light after solving many problems. Now they were thinking about some other topic of conversation. They noticed the moonlit night. They realized they had reached the town. They also noticed that the crop was ready in the fields.

Azim said: "The crop is good, uncle. But there's no one to harvest it this year."

A few steps ahead, they saw half a dozen skeletons lying on the road. Animals had hogged all flesh. Looking at those skeletons, Monai observed: "Those who could have harvested are lying here, son!"

All three men fell silent. Rows of shining teeth, pits of eyes, cages of ribs, bones of arms and legs—they stood horrified at the sight of the invisible human forms before them. In the cover of those skeletons, truth had closed in on the escaping thieves, as it were. They were struck with terror. It was nothing new. Their eyes had got accustomed to seeing such skeletons. They were to be found all over the place. So long as people had strength to cremate or bury bodies, they did it for the salvation of the souls of the dead. But now people were unable to bear even the weight of their own lives. How then could they carry the dead bodies?

Skeletons lay scattered all over town. Pieces of bones and ball-like skulls provided fun for the dogs. The number of broken and deserted mud houses, standing crops and skeletons—all symbols of the prosperity of Mohanpur. The soil, heated by the flames of life of hundreds of sages, was finding the dim moonlight cool and calm. But those skeletons appeared shrouded in mystery.

The men stared intently at the skeletons. Monai was the first to break the silence: "Those who raised the crops are lying here! Now who will come to harvest the crop? There was a time when they too were like I and you. I've sold my wares to them, talked and joked with them, kept close relations with them. I've even quarrelled with them, celebrated Holi, Diwali and Eid with them. Today they can't even be recognized. Oh, Lord, what sins must they have committed to die such a death? And what sins have we committed that we're forced to witness such things?"

Tears welled up in Monai's eyes.

Azim was like a lost child.

Nuruddin was reminded of his starving mother whom he had strangled to death in the feverish excitement of hunger. He was reminded of carpenter Munir. He remembered Munir's wife whom he had compelled to sell her body after beating her brutally. He remembered Munir's innocent daughters. He had heard from Azim about Chand. He had also heard about Rukia's death. He felt that he was a criminal of the worst kind—indeed, he was crime person-ified. He felt ashamed of himself. He remembered his own dear ones.

Monai then philosophized: "True life was lived only by these dead creatures, my son. They were always useful to the world while they lived. They re useful even now when they re dead. They're teaching us—why be attached to this body, you fool? Man dies alone. Nobody will even recognize the body. So, do the tasks

assigned to you, oh man, do your duty!"
Azim and Nuruddin stood in silence. After a moment's pause,
Monai said: "I had once been to a hospital in Calcutta. There I saw
such skeletons. Medical students have to study these skeletons."
Nuruddin, who was quite familiar with Calcutta, promptly said:
"Oh, yes! All medical studies are based on the study of skeletons.
I've seen with my own eyes. And I've also seen a lot of them in
shops selling items for mesmerism. I'm not frightened by the sight
of skeletons, uncle!"
Azim also instantly stiffened and said: "What's there to be
frightened about? I've slept night after night in a haunted mosque.
I'm not frightened of the skeletons."
Monai said in a calm tone: "What's there to be frightened about
them, son? These people were frightened of others all their lives.
Poor things, they died only in fright. Azim, I've a desire to bring
salvation to these dead creatures. Till their last moment, they were
useful to others. Now I wish that they become useful even after
their death. I don't know how many boys can educate themselves
with the help of these skeletons; and how many conjugations can
be worked out to mesmerise people. It would mean a meritorious
act in the bargain. Nuru, since you're going to Calcutta, find out
their rules."
Nuruddin and Azim were amazed. Azim said excitedly: "Aha!
You've thought of a wonderful plan, uncle! Such an idea could
have never occurred to us. What do you say, Nuru?"
Nuruddin had become a staunch follower of Monai. He said with
a choked voice: "I tell you, it is after all uncle's brain. He has the
eye of a seasoned man that can discover gold even in the dust.
I'll be going to Calcutta tomorrow itself, uncle. You've thought
with great foresight. But uncle, how shall we transport these skeletons?"
"That's my worry, not yours," said Monai. You don't bother. We
shall make the necessary arrangements. And listen, son. Let's go
on. I was telling you, Nuru, that we should enter into a partnership deal. We should be correct in accounts though we may be
generous while bestowing gifts. Do you understand?"
Nuruddin pretended indifference and, nodding half-willingly,
he said: "Yes, that's right in a way, uncle. But..."
Without paying any heed to what Nuruddin was saying, Monai
observed: "Whatever you save from the five hundred rupees you
got from the nawab saheb is all yours. Azim will have no share in it."

Monai paused for a while under the pretext of scratching his moustache and gave Azim a sidelong glance. Azim remained silent. Monai continued: "Not only that. Whatever money you get even after that, be it five hundred or a thousand, will also be yours." Nuruddin cut him short: "Oh, no, uncle! Azim is also entitled to a share." "Listen, my boy," said Monai. "Don't feel bad. But you can't decide right before me what Azim is entitled to have or not to have. Because you're Azim's friend, it's my duty to think about your interest too. And see, it's nothing to feel bad about; but what I can think about Azim's right and his good, nobody else can. Do you get me? Azim is my friend's son and he's my disciple. God knows that I've made no difference between Nyada and him. That's why listen to what I'm saying. I won't give any right to Azim to have a share in the nawab's money. And, in the business of women, your share will be six annas each and mine four annas in a rupee. The same is the arrangement in the matter of these skeletons. And out of my share of four annas, I shall give one anna to Azim, one anna in charity and keep two annas for myself. Follow me!"

"Alright, uncle," Nuruddin said with satisfaction.

Monai said again: "Well, now about the shop. Azim will have one-fourth share. And when I take the contract to supply food-grains for the army camp, your share will be two annas in a rupee and Azim will have four annas and the remaining ten annas will be for me. Listen, I'm not being unfair, am I? If you've something in your mind, say it right on my face. I won't feel bad. But don't harbour anything in your mind. Do you follow, Nuru?"

Nuruddin was delighted. He smiled broadly and said, folding his hands: "No, uncle. By Allah, I'm very happy. You can never be unfair in your decisions. Really, Azim, I've become uncle's slave from today—I swear!"

"And Azim," Monai observed, "let bygones be bygones. God knows I've no ill-feeling for you in my heart."

Now they were close to Monai's house.

Azim felt ashamed. He lowered his head and said meekly: "I've no grudge in my mind now, uncle. I don't know what possessed me. By God, I'm terribly upset about it."

"You're crazy!" Monai laughed and gently patted Azim's cheek. By this time, they were in front of his house. "Come in and meet aunty. Nuruddin, don't feel bad that I'm taking Azim away with me. After a long time...you understand, son!"

"Yes, yes! I'm very happy. Well, I'm off now. I'll meet you in the morning!"

"Very well. Do come in the morning. We must start the work immediately. May you live long! May God keep you well," Monai said and knocked at his door.

After being thus treated with special love, Azim turned to Nuruddin and said with an air of superiority: "I'll see you in the morning. *Salaam*, brother!"

Monai's wife opened the door. She was a little shocked to see Azim. A faint expression of hatred came over her face. Because of him, she, a daring wife of an old husband, had received a beating from him and had to part with thirty thousand rupees.

Azim faced her for the first time since he had taken the money. He stood before her with downcast eyes.

Monai handled the situation to the satisfaction of both. He started praising her for the affection she had been showing to Azim. He said that she had been remembering him a lot. He had refused to eat sweet rice cooked by her. That was stupid of him. But it wasn't a big crime. Children often do some stupid things. He would certainly give something to Azim before he died. That was Azim's right. Then he said to Azim that after putting Dayal in a fix, he planned to get Chheda Singh on his side and have Dayal's godown looted. Azim would get his share of that loot also. Once the grain bags were stolen, they would have to be loaded immediately on the boats during the night.

Monai also told him that stealing the bags would be no crime. It would be a proper reply to Dayal's acts of dacoity. He warned Azim that Nuruddin should have no inkling of that plan. Monai also reprimanded Azim for befriending Nuruddin. He said: "How could you have anything to do with him? He's a swindler. Whereas, you're respectable, a businessman. It's a different thing to get some advantage out of somebody. But a businessman loses his reputation by keeping company with bad characters. Do you understand?"

Once again, Monai got Azim into a glass bottle. He gave him further encouragement and then sent him off. Monai's wife, however, still did not trust Azim.

Monai pacified his wife: "You're really mad. If I had not befriended them at that time, I would have been dead by now. These fellows let loose *goondas* with nawab saheb's money. They were provoking me also to plan out Hindu-Muslim clashes. What difference does it make to Dayal? He's a big man. But I would have become a pauper. I've taken this fellow into confidence by pettifogging him. And I have played this trick with him so that he will not suspect me at all. Dayal will get his punishment from me. Once he's in deep waters, I shall embroil these fellows separately and wipe them out. I shall make up for all my losses with full interest. Let God be with me always—I shall build mansions in Calcutta. What do you think? And I shall load you with ornaments, my sweet one! I shall take you round Calcutta in a car. Now look at me once, in my name!"

Old Monai's third wife looked at him from the corner of her eyes and smiled. Her curiosity raised so many questions and based on those questions, Monai wove his new dreams. "Yes, once I win my last game, I shall spit on this town and go away to Calcutta. I'll have thriving business there. I'll become a wealthy trader and you'll be my proud wife! We'll have servants. We'll have a car. It'll be my great triumph in Calcutta. God willing, for once I'll have a place of honour among the big, wealthy businessmen of Calcutta. What do you think, my darling queen! I'll load you with gold!"

Outside, the barking of dogs and ominous hoots of jackals were all around. From somewhere came the hysterical shriek of a man. Otherwise, in that little town of dead bodies, only the cries of ferocious animals filled the air.

In his final moments, man wishes to give up life on a note of peace and calm. But the dogs and jackals of the town did not give him a chance even to die in peace. Even before life departed from him, the sharp fangs of dogs tore at the bodies and in no time they turned into corpses and then into skeletons...

Beni was walking with staggering steps, carrying a chopper in his hand. He saw some dogs feasting on a body. He could not bear the sight. He was on his way home, but he turned back. He had no control over his weak legs or his mind. But some power within gave terrific strength to his legs. Beni pounced upon the dogs with the chopper and gave a powerful blow. The head of one dog split and two or three dogs got wounded. The rest fled barking.

The dogs in the town had got used to attacking humans, but they had not been attacked by them. The dogs came rushing at him once more. Beni's blow landed on the neck of a dog, but he slipped and fell headlong on somebody's half-eaten body. The touch of raw flesh was a new experience, the taste absolutely unfamiliar. Beni let out a terrible cry and got up with a jerk. In the process, he pushed one hand right into the corpse. Rotting flesh stuck on his hand as he drew it out. But Beni was not aware of it. Neither did he care. Turning back, he threw the chopper at the dogs. The dogs ran. Beni got up on unsteady legs. His eyes were bloodshot. His hands and face and clothes were smeared with blood and bits of raw flesh.

Somehow, Beni walked towards his home. It had no roof, but that did not matter. The four walls were intact. He had sold the doors and bamboo poles. People had given up living in their houses, but not Beni. He remained there with his newly wed wife.

Beni had married two months before the famine. He was fascinated by her beauty. His wife loved him too. There was none to match Beni in playing the flute and his wife was proud of it. The colour of henna on her hands had not yet faded, but the colour of the world had suddenly changed. The town had become deserted. The horror of death started swallowing the whole town. The physical strength of the people was gradually depleted. But this couple, bound by deep love, got new inspiration for living. Cutting off all relations with the world, they confined themselves to the house. They did not remain apart even for a moment. But since the past four days, Beni's wife had lost her power of speech. Her body throbbed. Beni, seeing his wife's condition, grew more restless. Yesterday, she had not even opened her eyes. Since yesterday, he had kept away from the house. The sight of his wife drifting towards death made him mad with fear. And the world outside appeared even more frightening.

In that harassed state of mind, he had come out of the house. His hands and legs had no strength at all. But a pain more intense than the pang of hunger pushed him on with great force. Monai's temple stood right ahead. In front of it lay a freshly slaughtered cow. The soil beneath was red with blood. The head lay some distance from the body. At a little distance, close to the temple wall, lay a chopper. For a while he stood staring at the chopper that lay by the wall. But Beni's attention was soon distracted. He wished to go home. As he walked, he casually picked up the chopper. He had just started walking when he clashed with the dogs.

Beni reached home. His wife was still breathing. Beni sat near her head and gazed in silence. "She will die," he thought. "She will be freed of me. I'll lose her forever. Then dogs will devour her body. But no—I'll keep her so safe that even dogs will not see her."

Beni's eyes flashed. His excitement turned into frenzy. He

thought, if she gets inside him, she will never be away from him. If she could enter his heart, the dogs would not be able to eat her. But how could she get inside him. The dogs would devour her!

Now Beni worried about saving his wife from death and from being eaten up by dogs. Soon he found a solution. If he could cut her into pieces and hide her in his heart, she would be saved. Death would not find her and dogs would not be able to eat her. Beni got up with alacrity. He picked up the chopper. His wife's heart was beating very slowly. Beni thought he should hurry. He should cut her up and keep her safe before she died. Otherwise, death would take her.

The blow of the chopper fell right on the neck. In a frenzy, Beni chopped and chopped till he dropped down exhausted. Lumps of flesh came into his hands. A little while ago, while beating the dogs, lumps of human flesh had stuck to his lips. It was a new experience. He felt a new excitement as he held his wife's flesh in his hands. He gradually brought his hands to his mouth. His eyes had a lunatic gleam. Beni thrust the pieces into his mouth and started chewing.

Man, driven to frenzy by hunger, still aspired to wander in the labyrinth of life even by killing himself. While fighting against hunger, he was gradually beginning to fight against life which was beyond the awareness of hunger, pain, body, reason and death. This struggle of man was gradually becoming meaningless. Yet, actions inspired by his wild frenzy were continuously on the increase.

The priest had been living in Monai's temple. He had four children, a widowed sister and wife.

After feeding the Brahmins, Monai did not take any interest in making provision for routine food offerings in the temple. He had gone out of town that very night. Three days later, Monai's wife lost thirty thousand rupees, thanks to Azim. When the priest approached her for help after that loss, she hurled abuses at the gods and the priest. She refused to part with even a single paisa. The temple deity was deprived of food offerings. The priest's family starved. He sold the utensils in his house. Then he sold the utensils used for performing *puja*. Later, even the brass images of the deities found their way into the shopkeeper's house. After that, the priest was left with nothing worthwhile to sell. Seven souls of the family, stone images of Radha and Krishna, the temple cow and the calf passed their days and nights writhing with hunger.

Monai came back. But there was still no provision for food offerings to the deities. He was lost in his own dubious activities in partnership with Azim and his attention was concentrated on his "destitute homes". When the priest went to plead with him, he said: "Send the womenfolk to the destitute homes. And what do the deities need food offerings for? In any case, they hunger only for devotion. Their devotees are dying of hunger by lakhs. Do you think the deities would like the food offerings?"

The priest could face everyone else in the family going hungry. But he shuddered to see his children, the cow and the calf starving. Utterly defeated, the priest decided one day to accept Monai's suggestion. He decided to obtain a few handfuls of rice by sending his wife and sister to Monai's destitute home. A violent altercation took place between husband and wife that day. The priest remained firm and went to call Monai's men. But when he returned, he found two naked bodies lying dead. For the fear of being sent away, his wife and sister had strangled themselves with their torn sarees. His innocent children looked on with awe.

The priest was horrified. After losing his wife and sister, the priest burnt in the fire of remorse. The anxiety to save the children plagued him all the more. He could see no solution to the problem, and the children were drifting closer to death with each passing day. He forgot his own hunger in the horror of the hunger of his children.

The priest was in great distress. Then one day he convinced himself that it was no sin to kill for one's survival. His mind was in a whirl. His attention was drawn to the cow and the calf. Hunger provoked the priest to throw overboard his conventional upbringing. He wanted to wipe out his Brahminism and Hindu consciousness. He wanted to sever with the sword of his hunger his learning. He could find relief nowhere. He felt defeated. He wanted to keep himself from falling apart by sitting before the images of Radha and Krishna. He wanted to relieve himself of the feeling that he was about to commit a sin. "Please, tell me, Lord, is it a sin? But what will my children eat?"

The Lord was silent. The smiling face of the image had always remained unchanging.

The priest was irritated: "You're made of stone. You can't even be sold at the price of brass. You serve no purpose. You're of no use to me at all."

The priest who worshipped God, wanted to rebel against God Himself. He needed the support of his own mind in order to slay the cow. He wanted justice at his own hands.

His feeling of revolt grew stronger every moment, because the consciousness of the *samskaras* he had imbibed from birth did not leave him even for a moment. The whole day passed in conflict. One moment he would go to the front of the house where the cow was tied and the next moment he would walk out of the house. One moment he would press the children to his heart and then he would push them away. He would fold his hands and pray, weep and plead before the deities and then suddenly he would start abusing them.

All day long he walked up and down. But the grip of his Brahmin and Hindu *samskaras* did not loosen at all. His anger rose. He went to the *puja* room and banged his head at the feet of the deities. Then, he pulled them out and started beating them with his hands.

That was the moment. With unflinching determination he went to the emaciated, hungry cow. The calf, wailing in hunger, lay still, eyes closed. The chopper lay on the shelf.

The priest went up to the cow. But his mind wavered. Then he came to the calf and as he did so, he was reminded of his own children. The priest's determination slackened again. But he did not want his mind to waver. He did not want his children to die of hunger. Quickly, he took down the chopper.

Still the priest did not have the heart to release the calf. He somehow managed to untie the rope and started pulling the animal. The cow got up mooing and looked at the priest with piteous eyes. Weak body, weak mind and a dogged determination—the priest almost broke under the weight of these. In order to get over the feeling of defeat, he forcibly pulled the cow outside the temple precincts. He did not have the courage to slaughter the cow within the temple precincts.

The priest dragged the cow. The animal shrank with the fear of death that made its legs weaker. After going some ten steps, the cow stubbornly refused to move any further. It collapsed. The priest wanted to drag the cow outside the limits of the town. But even though he was determined to slay the cow and satisfy the hunger of his children with its beef, deep at heart he was still undecided.

When the cow refused to move further, it meant defeat for the priest. He felt enraged. He became hysterical. With all the strength he could command, he struck the chopper at the neck of the cow. The cow shrieked and blood spurted forth like a fountain. The blood, the dying cow writhing in pain, the anguished look in its eyes...the priest stood aghast. Blood flowed on the ground and started gradually drying up. The writhing movements of the cow stopped. The Brahmin *samskaras* of the priest prevailed upon him once again and he felt shattered. The priest abandoned the chopper. He wanted to shriek but could not. His frenzy subsided and his consciousness returned. Tears streamed. "Oh, Mother cow, forgive me. Oh, God, forgive me!"

"No, a sin can't be forgiven. One must expiate for it. I shall expiate for my sin. I shall cut my own throat with this very chopper." And he picked up the instrument. "But what will happen to the children?" he thought. And so, he first decided to kill the children and then himself. After touching the feet of the sacred cow that lay dead, he walked towards the temple, carrying the chopper with him. The sanctifying thought of expiation brought peace to his mind and strengthened his determination.

How would he kill the children with his own hands? But the priest did not let his mind stagger. His determination grew stronger. Even so, he hesitated as he reached the entrance of the temple. His determination slackened again. Chopper in hand, he started walking up and down outside the temple. He thought: "If I don't expiate on my own, then God will punish me and force me to do it."

The idea of punishment was frightening and at the same time insulting to the self-respecting Brahmin. Prompted by hunger, he had proposed to drive his wife and sister to prostitution. That had become the cause of their suicide. The priest was burning in every pore of his body in the terrifying flames of that harsh punishment. It was only proper that he should expiate. But how would he kill his children! The slaughter of the cow had made him a coward and he did not want to be a coward.

The priest suddenly noticed the bush of oleander flowers. There were a few flower plants and bushes outside the temple and the flowers were used for worship in the temple. For want of care for some time, the plants were drying up. He suddenly remembered that the roots of the oleander were poisonous. He felt happy and grateful to God. He experienced a new surge of enthusiasm. He cut the oleander bush with the chopper and dug out the roots. The strength of his hands started failing, but the excitement of the expiation was giving him strength. He collected the roots. He also gathered the dried up branches and went inside the temple.

The *chulha* had not been lit for many days. The priest put the dried up branches in the *chulha* and took the match-box from the shelf. About a dozen match-sticks were left. He lit the *chulha* and kept a pitcher filled with water on it. Then he threw the roots into the pitcher and calmly watched as the brew started boiling. The dry branches in the *chulha* were burning away fast. The priest went on feeding more branches in the *chulha*.

The brew was cooked and ready. The priest was calm. His determination had grown stronger still. He picked up the pitcher and went to the *puja*-room. Keeping the pitcher in front of the idols he said: "Lord, I haven't made any offering to you for many days. Today, the loss of all those days will be made up." So saying, he applied a little poison on the lips of the idols of Radha and Krishna.

Then he woke up the children and brought them to the *puja*-room. He took the youngest child on his lap. The children were getting something to eat after many days. They were happy and impatient.

The father's mind wavered again. But he alerted himself. He poured some brew in the bowl that covered the pitcher and fed the child on his lap. The child drank up with great satisfaction. Tears flowed from the father's eyes. All four children had their stomach's fill of brew. It was almost over. The father wanted some for himself.

Then suddenly, the youngest child started crying, clutching his stomach. Slowly the poison was getting into the systems of all the children. The father looked on in silence. His children were dying right before his eyes. They closed their eyes for good. The priest also wanted to do the same. He broke the mouth of the pitcher so that he could drink the brew more easily. He lifted the broken pitcher. He was about to drink the brew after touching the feet of the idols of Radha and Krishna when suddenly he heard the moo of the calf.

The priest hesitated. He started getting anxious. That poor creature would die wriggling in pain. Very little of the brew remained. Otherwise, he would have given it to the calf also. Then he realized that it was a great sin to torture an innocent animal. He had slain the mother of the calf and was now expiating for the sin he had committed thereby. But did he have the right to leave behind the calf to die? He was worried about his own children. Then, was that calf too not the young one of the cow?

The conflict between selfishness and benevolence perturbed the priest. He wanted to die. He had a strong death wish. Poison was to him like nectar. Life was worse than poison. He had no desire for life. The Brahmin priest, killer of wife and sister and children and cow, had no desire for life.

The calf, as it moved, produced a trembling sound.

The priest was still caught in the conflict. "What right do I have to leave the calf to suffer and die a painful death?" he said to himself. He had committed a sin, and he should live till his life became agony. "Not dying right now, but living in agony would be the best expiation for a killer like me!"

The priest promptly stepped forward to free the calf from life. Then frightened of himself, he shrieked and ran wildly, not knowing where he ran.

8

They had hardly laid Kanak on the pyre when a flock of vultures attacked the corpse. Shibu and Panchu had to run away from there to save their lives.

It was the first day of death in the house. In the morning, Chunni, Shibu's first child, in a desperate fight against hunger had tugged hard at her mother's breast and her teeth had clenched in a lockjaw. From the mother's breast had oozed blood instead of milk and at that moment, Chunni had stopped breathing.

The house had been haunted by hunger for the past fifteen days. Panchu's youngest sister had been laid up with malaria since six days. Seeing Chunni dead, she had cried inconsolably and fallen unconscious.

By the time Shibu and Panchu returned from the ghat, it was time to take Kanak.

Shibu had been very glum since the morning. When Chunni died, everyone had cried. Baba had always been stern and stiff. But Shibu had become speechless for the first time, and his eyes were dry.

Shibu and Panchu were silent all along the way. As Shibu held his daughter's body in his hands, he experienced death at very close quarters.

Right from childhood, Shibu had sustained himself by putting the burden of his inactivity onto others. He had always been stubborn and haughty. He grew in years, but his mind had not matured. He realized that he could not become great on the strength of his status as a Brahmin or on the basis of family prestige or the good reputation of his father and brother. He persisted in his efforts to earn prestige in one go by gambling and becoming a leader. But he did not succeed. His stubbornness changed into indignation. Indignation turned into anger and anger made him impudent. He wanted to hide his sense of inferiority even from himself. He became ruthless...

The famine tore apart the curtain of respectability. His stubbornness, indignation, impudence—nothing helped. He was completely disheartened by his daughter's death. He became more and more ruthless in his efforts to get over the feeling of defeat. He had become insensitive like stone.

Shibu and Panchu returned after burying the child. The two brothers were silent. When they reached home they heard lamentations. As they entered the house, they found Kanak lying dead. Panchu was overcome with grief. Shibu remained stoic.

Parvati Ma'was grieving more than everyone else. Her wailing brought tears to the eyes of the others in the house...

Crying before elders like the in-laws was not considered respectful in good families. While mourning the death of Kanak, Shibu's wife also sought to pour out her grief of her separation from her daughter. But nobody had the strength to cry freely. Physical weakness and the fear of death was forcing down their tears.

Nobody came from the neighbourhood to give condolences. They could not manage to get four bamboos for the bier. Hence, brushing aside their sense of shame in the face of helplessness, they tied Kanak's body in a torn bag and set out for cremation.

They could hardly carry the weight. The two brothers decided to go a little away from the town and cremate the body after getting a couple of bamboos and straw from a deserted house. It was impossible to burn the body with such little fire. But in their effort to do the impossible, they tried to perform the last rites for their sister with stubbornness accompanied by helplessness. They also managed to get a couple of logs and some pieces of wood.

The vultures were hovering in the sky. Shibu stood by the dead body and tried to erect the funeral pyre. They removed the body from the torn wrapping and put it on the pyre. They had no strength in their hands. Their hearts were heavy beyond words. Panchu spread straw over the body. Shibu took out the matchbox and suddenly a flock of hovering vultures swooped down. Panchu was terrified. He was in a hurry to light the fire. He had hardly struck the match-stick when he felt a sweep of flapping wings over his head. The flock of vultures came down with a sudden swoop. Shibu and Panchu stepped back to save themselves from their attack.

Panchu did not even look back after that. He had no heart to do so. Like many other corpses, his sister's corpse too would turn into a skeleton with no identity. He did not even want to think about it.

Shibu turned once to look back. But he could see nothing except the flock of vultures sitting there, big wings outstretched and beaks plucking the body. A few vultures were also hovering in the sky. The sight of his sister's body becoming food for the vultures brought not a single tear in Shibu's eyes. He lowered his head and walked on.

The incident of the slaughter of a cow had become a topic of the talk in whatever was left of that town. A hysterical man who was struggling against death had even been perplexed by it for a moment. So far, people had died in the town in every possible manner. But there had not been a single incident of anyone being killed by a weapon. The slaying of a cow was not an incident of importance. Only Monai was making more than necessary noise about it. A few respected men left in town also gave importance to the incident.

People with reputation were in a bad state. Nothing in the name of prestige was left with them by that time. Their daughters and daughters-in-law too were being openly sent to "charitable homes" and "destitute homes". Everyone knew that such a home was only a euphemism. Yet, everyone constantly talked about saving his reputation. One or two persons had died in every family, but it had become impossible to perform funeral rites. Hence, for anyone who died in the house it was said that he had gone to "another place". Everyone knew what that meant. The quantity of rice they got by selling their wives and daughters was described by them as bought at a hundred rupees a maund. Even if they lost prestige, they were still obsessed with the idea of prestige. At the sight of a slain cow right in front of the temple, the people concerned with reputation started talking in terms of Hinduism. They accompanied Monai to the temple and found all four children of the priest as well as the cow and calf dead. They knew what had happened when they saw blue froth coming out of their mouths. Every respectable man thought it was a good death. They thought it provided a great ideal of saving one's prestige by swallowing poison. They came to regard poison as a symbol of prestige. The controversy about the slaughter of the cow gradually died out. Everyone started longing for poison.

Panchu was very restless and distressed after such a close encounter with death. He felt irritated with death. Would not a single man be left alive in the world? Would the human race be completely wiped out from the face of the earth? Today death reigned in towns and villages. Tomorrow it would spread to the cities. One day, the whole country would be left without human beings.

Gradually, Panchu's imagination came alive. Deserted villages and cities and the deserted world came to be coloured by his imagination. A few people who were known to be wealthy would survive. But how long would they remain safe? When the producer of foodgrains did not survive, with what would the consumer fill his stomach and remain alive? Money, gold, silver, jewellery— would he be able to chew all these with his teeth? Would the insatiable hunger be contained by living in big mansions? No. The rich too would die one day. They too would have to die one day. A small section of society would not remain alive after killing the larger section of society for its own selfish motive. The individual definition of selfishness was wrong by itself. But the fact remained that man did not understand his own interest. Individual interest is, in fact, the interest of society as a whole. When no society was left, how would the individual remain alive?

Panchu imagined the scene of destruction affecting his town and spreading right up to Calcutta, the whole world. All those bombs, guns, tanks, fighter-planes, capital cities, tall, palatial buildings, cars, trains, radios, telephones and all the things of science and technology would ultimately spell the failure of man. And dogs would wallow and welter in those houses. Only animals would survive in the world with the skeletons as reminders of human existence at some time in the past.

Panchu, considering himself the only representative of the human race, indulged in a play of imagination and looked at the world in that light. Two deaths in the family had caused his thoughts to race fast in his mind. He thought with great restraint on his racing mind that he would have to see everybody die one by one. Mother, father, brother, wife, sister-in-law, Tulsi, Dinu, Paresh—he looked at them to his heart's content, as though they would now vanish from his eyes forever.

Panchu was scared by Shibu's gloomy silence of the morning. He knew that his brother's heart was very tender. Despite his high-handedness, Panchu loved him. Shibu always talked too much. He shouted and thundered or quickly burst out laughing or broke into tears. Panchu was used to such reactions in Shibu. He was afraid that his brother had been deeply grieved and wondered if something terrible would happen to him.

Death had taken away two members of the family. Dinu and

Paresh could also die any moment. Both children had swollen hands and feet. Shibu's wife had become thinner than before, a mere frame of bones. And poor Mangala had gone so pale! But her big, captivative eyes were still lustrous. Even now, a smile frequently played about her lips. Actually, she smiled more than before. Panchu had observed that Mangala had been trying to force herself to laugh and make others laugh. But the laughter of Shibu's wife was frightening. When her two rows of teeth parted, she looked really grotesque and horrifying. Tulsi had ceased laughing altogether. She had become listless and absent-minded. Generally she did not move. She either remained seated or stretched out. She was very weak.

Parvati Ma had become irritable, a cover to hide her anxiety. She always went around the house talking and shouting. For no reason, she shouted at everybody in the family, abused everyone and sent them all to hell!

Panchu felt this streak in his mother's behaviour rather unnatural. She had created a terrible scene that morning when Chunni died. When Chunni died, Parvati Ma started abusing everybody. In between, she asked Mangala to get some water. She called Tulsi to hold the child's mother and forced open Chunni's jaw by thrusting her finger and startled everybody throwing the dead body of the child in the threshold as though it were garbage. Panchu knew that Parvati Ma had not gone insane. In that seemingly inhuman behaviour, she had been guided by a deep consideration. By treating that death in the family with contempt and disdain, she had showed a certain ruthlessness so as to shake off the fear of death that had gripped everyone's mind. That action of Parvati Ma saved Shibu's wife from dying at least for the present and prolonged everyone's life by a few days...

When he and Shibu returned home after burying Chunni, there was loud lamentation in the house. Parvati Ma's wailing was the loudest and most pathetic. Before they removed Kanak's body bundled in a bag, Parvati Ma had called Panchu aside and told him gravely: "Look after your brother on the way, my son!"

Panchu was amazed at that instruction from Parvati Ma. But it had given him strength. He had a natural desire to control his own emotions and console his mother. When he started comforting her she said: "Mother Earth maintains its fortitude by itself, son! Even though breaking every moment, the world has survived till today only because of that. Don't you worry about me. I may break, but I won't be defeated!"

After that Panchu had started seeing his mother in a new light. The refulgence of her great self-mortification for the past so many days gave new life to her emaciated body. With that flame of life she had been feeding her children. Panchu regarded his mother in the form of Mother Earth—the earth which man tramples under his feet every moment, but also stand with its support. Panchu wondered how long his mother would be able to sustain herself that way. Panchu wondered how the earth would sustain itself in the face of such atrocities.

Panchu's imagination was kindled again. "The earth, bereft of the human race, will carry on its bosom the memorial of its great sons and lament the loss. But the earth has to worry about its other progeny too. Man's intelligence and all symbols of knowledge and science will mingle with the dust one day and the earth will be covered once more with hills and mountains and greenery. After the signs of human existence are obliterated, the earth will once again become a giver of life and a happy place for its other children—animals and birds."

That thought strengthened Panchu.

After abandoning Kanak to the attacks of the vultures, Shibu and Panchu walked together for a while and then took separate roads. Instead of going home, Shibu had gone north, beyond the Brahmin colony. Shibu's three friends lived there. Panchu did not comment when he started going in that direction. He thought to himself: "It's good. He will feel better."

Panchu went home. When he reached home, he found his mother, surrounded by both daughters-in-law and Tulsi with the fever-stricken Paresh on her lap, narrating her own experiences of the deaths of her five sons. During the narration, she occasionally broke into laughter at the mention of some silly things she had done in panic. Panchu saw that her laugh concealed a terrible exhaustion. Even the glowing lustre of her face could not hide that exhaustion. It was a painful experience for Panchu. But his mother's self-control was a source of strength and he tried to emulate her restraint.

Panchu then went to his father. There was not enough light in the room. The bundles of books kept on the shelves were only dimly visible. A faint light was falling on the cot through the door opposite. His father lay on the bed absolutely still. Feeling somebody's touch on the cot, he stirred. Panchu sat on the cot and started rubbing his father's leg. "When will all this end, Baba?" he asked.

His father remained unmoved. He said in his deep voice: "When the beginning raises its head in this end. We cannot escape the gusts of the changing age, Panchu. If a small section of society is doing penance to awaken the larger society, it may do so. But it cannot be a penance without desire. Let it not be purposeless. When penance is purposeless, it creates hatred in the world, Panchu. You must do your penance with a wish to create a feeling of love in the hearts of men."

Panchu was not satisfied by that answer. He said: "Hatred is not purposeless or meaningless, Baba! It's a natural human reaction."

A smile flickered on Baba's aged face. He said: "Where does hatred lead? Only to destruction, isn't it? And what is this famine of yours? Doesn't it symbolize human hatred? What is this great world war? Truth strikes a compromise with untruth and wages war to destroy another untruth. Man calls it politics and thereby nurtures half-truths. Half-truth is the cause of ignorance. Knowledge is the value of love. And love extends to creation and the creator."

Holding his chin in his palm, Panchu stared at the ceiling of the room. Darkness descended. Gradually, his eyes got used to the darkness and he could see the rafters of the ceiling.

Mangala had gone to sleep, hiding her face in his chest, tired. Even her smile seemed to be struck with terror.

Panchu's right hand supporting her head felt tired. But he did not make the slightest movement lest it wake Mangala. He continued to look at the dim moonlight and stars in the sky. Mangala's touch was more important than his own exhaustion. He realized she had been growing weaker day by day. He feared that the happiness of her touch would become a dream.

Suddenly Panchu heard a scream. Mangala woke with a start. Panchu sat up. Shibu's wife had screamed. The doors of Shibu's room opened with a bang. Shibu called out: "You...*sali!* You threw dust in my eyes and ran away! As though the people in the house will be able to save you! You ill-begotten woman, you're my property! You're my thing, *sali!*"

For the first time Shibu's voice could be heard. Mangala and Panchu stared at each other in panic. Then Panchu came down, Mangala following him. Near the front door, Shibu was stripping his wife and mauling at her.

Even Baba had come out of the room. Parvati Ma, Tulsi, Dinu, Paresh, Panchu and Mangala just stood there, terror-stricken.

Shibu's wife resisted with all her strength. In front of all the family members, a woman was being robbed of her honour and the perpetuator of this crime was none other than her husband who was supposed to be her protector.

Shibu was mad with rage. His logic was simple—a wife was her husband's property and that gave him complete mastery over her. A child could play with his toys any way he liked or even break them. But why should toys complain?

Death had horrified Shibu and he had been restless and agitated all day. There was no escape from that crushing feeling...

Night came. The desperation to conquer fear gradually aroused his sexual desires. He started mauling his wife's hungry and emaciated body so violently that it shattered her. The more he hurt his wife, the greater was his happiness. Shibu's assaults became unbearable for his wife.

Just that morning her daughter had died. Two other children were also on the point of death. She was also grieving Kanak's death. More than anything else, her own physical weakness had made her absolutely helpless. And now Shibu insisted on taxing her body with his violent physical passion. Terrified by his assaults, she screamed and in the face of that danger to her life, she somehow experienced a surge of physical strength.

Shibu was taken aback. He moved a little away from her. Seizing the opportunity, she quickly opened the door and ran down the stairs to save her life.

Shibu trembled with rage. He was not one to accept defeat so easily. He had never been afraid of anyone. He was determined to satisfy his physical desire at any cost. His wife was his property. He could enjoy her as he chose. He rushed behind her downstairs. Disregarding the presence of the members of the family, he insisted on asserting his authority over his wife. Panchu and Mangala turned their faces away. Tulsi quietly stole a look in that direction, evading her mother's attention.

Parvati Ma instantly regained her mental balance. She stepped forward and tried to push back Shibu with all the strength she could summon. Seeing his mother swing into action, Panchu also realized that he should do something. Abandoning all sense of shame, he rushed forward to save his sister-in-law who was almost naked. Parvati Ma pulled Shibu away from his wife and said: "You sinner! Have some sense at least in front of your parents!"

Shibu was boiling. Shibu tried to free himself from Panchu's grip and told his mother: "Go and teach that to Baba! It's time he had some shame too. Leave me alone!"

Parvati Ma felt as though a sharp knife had thrust into her. But she quickly regained her composure. Pushing Shibu away with both hands, she shouted at Panchu: "Throw that wretch out of the house. It's because of my sins that this murderer was born to me!"

Baba suddenly saw clearly the great weakness of his character: his lack of restraint and his impatience in the matter of sex. He had set a wrong example to his children. Darkness had always persisted under the lamp of his learning. He remembered at that moment innumerable occasions when his recklessness had been responsible for the mental perversion of his ignorant children. Defeated by their weakness both parents had become enemies of their children.

As such, Baba had been a man of character. He had never raised his eyes at any other woman in his life. He had regarded his wife as a means to satisfy his physical desires. And, from that point of view, he always considered his wife only his property. Parvati Ma did not lack self-respect. It was a mutual agreement. For the asking, she would surrender her body to him and as price for that surrender, she would have all her whims satisfied.

Baba had been a professor of Sanskrit in a city college. Parvati Ma had not liked living in a city. She lived in their home town. Baba came home every Saturday night. Parvati Ma had given birth to Shibu after her five children had died. She would not let him out of her sight even for a moment. Her attention alone had made Shibu stubborn and irritable. Baba had very painfully realized it and had repeatedly talked about educating Shibu and making him a sensible boy. But it irked Parvati Ma when anyone referred to a weakness in Shibu or criticized him in any way. She would retort with irritation: "All children are stubborn when they are young. As for studying, he will do it by himself when the time comes. What's his age now, any way? And can't one do without studying? If it's for getting money, one gets it even without studying if he's destined to have it. Everybody doesn't build mansions merely by studying and taking up a job."

Baba would warn her: "You're making a great mistake. If you allow the child to remain a child forever, the blame for his irresponsible behaviour will lie squarely on you. Education is not meant merely for getting a job. Learning leads to the building of man's character."

Baba's argument did not impress Parvati Ma at all. She only got irritated. And Baba had no intention of ruining his Saturday night.

Baba was learned and he had a sensitive mind. But he always remained in the dark about this particular weakness. He never considered sexual enjoyment with his married wife anything but a legitimate act. In his foolishness, he made his wife his own prostitute and while indulging in physical pleasure with her, performed dutifully his tasks as a householder.

After he lost his eyesight, his sexual desires became stronger. And Parvati Ma became a toy in her husband's hands. Now Shibu's remark opened their eyes. But what was the point now? Parvati Ma wished she were dead. She went on crying and took out on Shibu her anger against herself: "Throw that wretch out of the house. Take him away from my sight!"

Bakulphul and Tulsi took Parvati Ma to her room and bolted the door from inside.

Scared of Shibu, Mangala also retreated to her room. Shibu, beside himself with rage, shouted at the top of his voice. Enraged by his helplessness, he hurled abuses at everybody and turned to go out of the house. As he walked out, he gave Panchu two resounding slaps.

Panchu remained unmoved. All the incidents that had taken place during the famine seemed to him insignificant compared to what had happened in his house today. When things happening outside filled him with anguish, his mind found peace at home. But now the atmosphere at home was shattered. Today's incident had given him a terrible shock. Now nothing was impossible for Shibu. Beni had murdered his own wife. A cow had been slaughtered. Weapon in hand, Shibu too was capable of murder. He could set the house on fire. There was nothing he was incapable of doing. But would Panchu be able to see all this happening? Would he be able to see his family being destroyed?

Panchu wanted to run away. But he realized that if he did run away, there would be no one to save the family from the atrocities of his elder brother. Still Panchu could not muster up courage to face the situation at home. He said to himself: "I won't be able to see with my own eyes any evil happening here. Let anything happen after I'm gone. If I don't see it, it won't hurt."

Turning away from the path of duty, Panchu took the path of cowardice. "It won't make any difference even if I stay back. Who can stop a blood-thirsty lunatic? I shall go to some other place. I shall go to Calcutta or some such place. I shall look for a job. If I can find a job, the family also will be looked after."

Panchu decided to run away. And with that decision, a terrible conflict raged in his mind. Home, Baba, Ma, Mangala—he was leaving them behind all at once. He was not particularly worried about Shibu, his wife, Tulsi, Ma and the nephews. He thought of his mother with a pang in his heart. With Baba, his relationship was more that of teacher and student rather than father and son. Baba had been intimately connected with every intellectual problem of his. But now he had a feeling deep in his heart that Baba had only a few days left to live...

Inevitably, a day comes in life when a man's relationship with the parents snaps. Ma and Baba would be unhappy at his going away. But his thoughts were particularly concentrated on Mangala. He was very anxious on her account. What would happen to her? Mangala dominated his mind. For a moment he thought of taking Mangala along. The thought buoyed him up. Then a fear gripped his heart that Mangala may stop him from going. She would never go with him leaving Ma and Bakulphul behind. And Panchu was not prepared to live in the house. No longer was home an abode of peace. Panchu's disaffection for home was intense. He was convinced that salvation lay only in that. Even Mangala's attraction was beginning to slacken.

Panchu slowly went towards the door. He wanted to take one last look at everybody before going away. He came back. When he reached the stairs leading to his room, his steps faltered. He wondered if Mangala would be awake.

Panchu came down the stairs stealthily like a thief. The door of Parvati Ma's room was closed. Baba was seated on his cot, hiding his face between his knees. Panchu silently paid his respects to him from a distance. Then he remembered everybody as he bid a silent farewell. Tears streamed from his eyes. He walked towards the front door. As he crossed the threshold, his steps faltered once more. Perhaps he would never return to this house. He stepped out of the house.

Panchu's attention was drawn to his room. Only a little while ago, he had been in that very room, looking at the moonlight and the stars. Mangala had been sleeping, hiding her face in his chest, her arm thrown over him. What happiness that touch had given him! At the thought of that happiness the scream of Shibu's wife and the whole ghastly incident that followed had struck terror in his heart. He hoped Mangala had not been watching him from the window. Panchu was frightened. He moved quickly away and started walking fast, slinking away from the walls of the house...

Gradually, the house receded in the background. In the dim moonlight, it looked hazier and hazier and then was lost to view. He reached the cluster of trees that could hide him. By that time, he was on the outskirts of the town. Panchu halted. He was leaving his place of birth. Before bidding a final goodbye, he looked at everything with affection. He saw before his eyes his own life in that town. He had played and jumped in those fields. He had grown up in that town. He had had happy and unhappy relations with many people. Mohanpur, the place of his birth, was the field of his activities and his struggles. Despite all the uncertainties of the famine, his life had followed a definite tenor. By leaving house and town behind, Panchu was severing his relations with a definite pattern of life. After all his wanderings, he always returned home. But now that centre of attraction was disappearing. In the morning, Ma would come to know...Mangala would feel...the whole house would hear about it.

Panchu walked briskly ahead in order to conquer his weakness. But where would he go? "I'll go anywhere! But I won't go home!" With tears in his eyes, he took the final decision with determination.

Panchu did not even turn to look back. Tears streamed from his eyes and he walked on. He was terribly agitated and perturbed. His head was heavy and his mind was blank. His eyes were full of tears. He was not aware of anything around him. Panchu walked on, without direction, without aim, as though there were no end to his walking...

He heard someone crying in the distance. Panchu's consciousness returned and he was on the hard ground of reality. He raised his head. He felt the sound came but from somewhere quite close.

Panchu noticed someone lying in the dilapidated structure on his left. It was an infant's cry. Panchu followed the sound. A newborn child was crying, frantically moving its hands and feet on one of the legs of the mother.

It was a new experience in Panchu's life. For a moment he stood stupefied. A naked woman lay still before him. The umbilical cord was still connected to the mother's body.

Panchu felt shy. He turned back and tried to walk away. But his legs did not obey him. His conscience nudged him contemptuously for retracing his steps and leaving a newly born child and its mother in that helpless state. But he dared not go near. Deep at heart, he was feeling thoroughly ashamed of himself.

Suddenly, Panchu felt such a strong impulse to save the infant that his fear and hesitation could not hold ground. With firm determination, he turned in that direction. He bent down to have a look at the woman. She seemed to have no sign of life. To dispel his doubt, Panchu held his hand close to the woman's open mouth and nose. The woman was not breathing. Gathering his courage, Panchu placed his hand between the woman's breasts. The heart was not beating either. His own heart was thumping so fast that he felt like getting up and fleeing the scene. But he could not get up. Judging from the warmth in the woman's body, Panchu concluded that she must have died ten or fifteen minutes before his arrival. Instantly, his attention was drawn to the child. It was a boy, weak and soiled, with placenta and the cord still connected.

Panchu felt nervous. He did not know how to save that infant, how to cut the umbilical cord. His eyes surveyed the surroundings, but he could detect nothing that could be of help. It was a broken, deserted house. Panchu's lack of experience made him feel helpless and irritated. He suddenly realized that the child should not be allowed to remain connected with the dead body for long. Steeling his heart, Panchu tugged at the cord with both hands so that it snapped from the middle. The infant was separated from the mother. Panchu picked it up with half the cord dangling from its body. The baby panted as it cried.

Now Panchu had a new problem. How would the child survive? He had no answer. Panchu sat against a broken wall with the child on his lap. He was completely fagged out. He had been starving for days. That very morning, he had carried the weight of two dead bodies. He had also strained himself quite a bit while restraining Shibu. After that, he had walked a distance and now this. Panchu closed his eyes. He felt at peace. The infant on his lap was kicking its legs and throwing up its hands. Even though exhausted in body and mind, Panchu felt happy and calm. And he felt fresh at heart.

Panchu opened his eyes. What would happen to the child? It must be feeling cold. Panchu removed his shirt and covered the child with it. "The child is very weak," he thought. "How will he live? But he may live. He must be saved. He must be given milk. But this unlucky child—where will he find milk? He's been born during the famine. People are dying and this child has taken birth to witness death on the face of this earth. Poor child—his mother is dead!"

Panchu's attention was diverted to the woman. She did not look particularly emaciated. It seemed as though she had had food to eat. She had also some clothes on her body. Her face and general appearance indicated that she was from a good family. To whose house did she belong? How had she come to this place? Her whole history was lost with her death.

Panchu's thoughts wandered and then came back to the present. In the moonlight of the late night he saw that the child's complexion was fair. But he was terribly weak. Panchu hoped that he would not die. The child started crying. Panchu thought that he must be hungry. But hunger—that was the most urgent problem of the present!

Panchu sighed. Having starved for many days, he had got used to hunger. In a way, hunger did not harass him any more. Of course, physical weakness and the thought of hunger harassed him. The thought that the child was hungry caused him great pain. But there was no way he could help. He concentrated all his attention on the child. And the child was crying. Panchu started making slow movements with his legs. The child was quiet after a while. Panchu had a sudden doubt. He took his hand near the child's nose. He felt the child's breath on his palm. Panchu was relieved. "If only this child could somehow survive...suppose I had not come here? Perhaps I sauntered this side only to save the life of this child! Perhaps it was only to save this child that the ghastly incident took place at my house which provoked me to leave the house."

Panchu felt it was absurd to have such thoughts in his mind. At the same time, the incident seemed like a miracle.

Now his mind moved in a different orbit. He started looking at everything afresh: "What course do events in the life of human beings follow? Events follow one another as though they have been predetermined. What does that mean? Do things happen by themselves or by accident? Is life merely a chain of events? Sometimes things happen in life that cannot be logically explained. They seem to have no link anywhere and they happen in such a disorderly manner that they obstruct the straight course of reason or logic...Is it not an accident that the famine has spread all over Bengal? But how is it that this province, characterised by tremendous intellectual qualities, is forever afflicted with disease and suffers pain and torture? As such, the whole country has been passing through a period of great calamity and hardships. But why is it that it is only Bengal that wears the crown of thorns? And then, is the great world war also a mere accident?"

That question was within the purview of Panchu's intellectual capacity. Reason understood the causes of the great war. He felt a certain happiness at thus being able to exercise his intellectual faculty. He looked at the child and felt the pace of his breathing by keeping his palm against his nose. He looked on affectionately at him. He said to himself: "Let the child live!" As he looked longingly at the child, he felt confident he would live. Panchu searched his mind to find out what gave him that confidence. Panchu thought: "This child is born with the roughness to suffer the hardships of famine right from his mother's womb."

Panchu followed the same line of logic: "This child has remained alive even after his mother is dead. Does this not prove the reality of life?"

In the light of such thoughts he viewed like a film the incidents that had taken place during the famine. He asked himself: "Even though millions of people have died, Bengal is still alive. Does this not prove that life is invincible?"

The question itself implied an affirmative answer which was not altogether free from selfish consideration. It had an echo of joy. He saw the life of Bengal reflected in the fact of his own survival. Hence, with that question dominating his mind, his anguish turned into concern and tears welled up in his eyes. One hand was under the child's head and the other rested on the child's legs. The moment he felt tears come to his eyes, his hands jerked. He pulled the child close to his stomach.

The child woke up and started crying. Panchu's attention was distracted. He gave a startled look to the child. He felt peeved. He himself had been crying out of happiness at that moment. But when someone else cried, it irked him.

Anger broke through reason and jumped next to politics. His thoughts came in quick succession: "Bengal has been destroyed right from the start, for fear that Bengal may join Subhash Babu and march with his army. This famine is a political move to keep India in bondage."

In his agitation he felt pity for the child. He felt a surge of affection. Once again he started moving his legs and affectionately patting the child. The child continued to sob and in the process, became quiet: "He's lying with his small eyes closed. How lovely he is! How children inspire love, no matter whose children they are!" Then he immediately reflected: "It's only the child that grows into a man. The moment he becomes a man, he starts behaving in a manner that leads to anger, contempt, violence!"

Panchu was suddenly reminded of what Baba had told him only the previous day: "The penance done without any specific objective will lead to hatred in the world. Don't create hatred, Panchu! Pray that your sacrifice creates love in the hearts of men."

Panchu had not been convinced by Baba's words then. But now that he himself had started thinking along these lines, he was reminded of Baba's words of advice. He was happy to find support for his thoughts. He stared at the child:"Why do I love this child so much? How is it I am so attached to him so soon? Because I saved him? I've saved one life. My love for life has saved this life—yes, that's right!"

Panchu was happy: "Why should I take this as my doing? Life saves itself. It is the same life that is lived in several ways and determined by varied temperaments."

Panchu's mind wandered. He thought: "Life reveals itself as an organized entity by fulfilling itself in every individual body. That alone constitutes society."

Panchu had always heard and read such things, but he pondered over them only today and accepted them as his own. Panchu weighed his words against the words of the scriptures, and both seemed to him to be in perfect balance. He said to himself: "We're only repeating the words of the great."

His consciousness about his own intelligence blew like a balloon: "An illusory feeling of creating a unit led to the belief that man was confined within the limit of one body and one form. But as man's experience widened through his insistence on truth, he freed himself from that illusion and established family and society. The awareness of a unit did not become collective in character. Rather, it still remained divided among the broad sections of society. Hiding the light of truth in ignorance, those big societies marched ahead. Due to innumerable crude and obvious distinctions, man became a stranger to man. That state of unfamiliarity gave rise to fear and fear led to violence. Violence is the product of man's ignorance."

Panchu was aware of being absorbed in his thoughts. He was happy that he had been thinking such lofty thoughts. The sense of happiness filled him with some kind of enthusiasm. The same thoughts continued floating in his mind: "Violence is only a reaction to the good inspiration which is meant to dispel ignorance. The same sharp approach to knowledge for attaining truth through creation turns into violence only by turning against consciousness. Even in the form of violence, its unperceived purpose is to establish itself as an entity. It's alright being conscious about wiping out crude ignorance. What's wrong about it is merely the fact that through violence, it makes an illusory attempt to prove the truth of only its own entity. At the subconscious level, man is certainly aware of this illusion because he feels no joy when a feeling of violence is born in him." Suddenly Panchu became conscious of what he had been thinking and was astonished: "Ah, really! I've been thinking such great thoughts!"

Panchu felt himself one among great men. A messiah who saved the world, the prophet who brought awakening in the world, an incarnation that brought enlightenment. Under the impact of this new experience of mental peace, Panchu looked lovingly at the child. He was so fascinated that he wanted to wake him up and play with him. By showering his love on him, Panchu wanted to enhance the importance of the infant. Suddenly he remembered his hunger. He was afraid the child would cry if he woke him up. He was reminded of his own hunger. He, the messiah, had also been compelled to starve for ten days. He felt angry with the demons who were responsible for the famine. Panchu thought excitedly: "Famine is being thrust on us because we made a legitimate demand for our independence! The repression of India in 1942 was an extremely inhuman attempt to crush and humiliate human feelings in the world. That repression was a demonic act of creating in man's mind lack of faith in truth and non-violence by brutally crushing man's spontaneous urge to attain freedom. Man does not realize the possibility that the very atrocities he is perpetrating on others could bounce back on him as well."

Panchu wondered how man did not understand the simple truth that there was so much ignorance in the world. The list of ignorant people in Panchu's inner consciousness included big names like Hitler, Mussolini, Churchill, Tojo, Roosevelt, Stalin. How stupid these leaders were, that they did not learn a lesson from Panchu Gopal Mukherji! That made him happy. At the same time, he related the atrocities against man to the British and was pleased to imagine them reeling under the impact of the famine.

However, he saw clearly the reality about himself. Only a little while ago, he had accepted for himself the scientific analysis of a tendency to violence. And now he himself was caught in the maze! He felt his ego deflated—it was like a balloon bursting in the process of being blown up. He felt terribly ashamed of himself. The ghost of the messiah vanished into thin air. He felt uncomfortable. "Even though I understood, I still made that mistake." His agitated ego wanted to see the reason for that self-defeat in the irresponsible nature of his intelligence. But what happened was something altogether contrary. He said to himself as though to counter his harassed feeling: "I don't practise what I think and what I consider right..."

The child stirred and started crying. Panchu's attention was diverted. He pressed the child to his heart. "This child must be saved. Saving him is my greatest responsibility at the moment."

Panchu was on his feet. Pressing the crying child to his shoulder, he tried to quieten him, making reassuring sounds.

The warm touch of the child filled Panchu's heart with compassion. His mind, despite its endless limitations, was at peace. Such profound sense of satisfaction, a calm devoid of ego—these feelings rose from some deep recess in his heart and, for a few moments, carried him on the crest of a wave of joy.

Panchu grew conscious of a new type of experience. It was unprecedented. What joy! But as he became conscious about that experience, his joy ceased to be a reality and turned into a mere shadow. Whatever it may have been, Panchu was intoxicated. All exhaustion of the hardships he had suffered since the famine, and the weight of anxieties vanished. He felt himself absolutely pure, calm and light at heart. As he stroked the back of the child, Panchu thought with happiness: "It's through this child that I've had this experience...and like this child, my experience too is like a sprout. Both will grow together. I shall see this child only in that light. I shall concentrate my attention on him—and then there'll be no mistake."

Panchu started walking up and down with the child pressed

to his shoulder. Experiencing a slight tickling sensation, he thought: "What about his name? What shall I call him? What community does he belong to?"

Panchu glanced at the child's mother who lay as still as the earth. Then he thought: "What is his community? His mother lies lifeless. This child is the progeny of man. He's beyond community, religion... That's alright. But now I must think about bringing him up. Where can I take him?"

He thought of Mangala. She would bring up the child. But he hesitated. "How can I go back there?" he thought. "I've now found a larger home. The whole world is my home."

Panchu again made a movement as though to protect himself from feeling like a messiah. "In spite of all that, man must have a home. And are the members of my family separate from this world? Why should I give them up? But things are already bad in that house. How can this child be brought up there? Everyone will wonder and Mangala will say I've brought along a new problem!"

The very idea hurt him. "But then Mangala won't take it that way. Her heart is very tender. A woman's heart is always very tender. She has a spontaneous feeling of mother's love. The mother in Mangala will definitely hug the child."

Panchu thought about Mangala and the thoughts made him happy. He felt a new attraction for Mangala. He desired to return home. He thought to himself: "It was cowardice on my part to have run away from home. I ran away from my duty. What else was it? I didn't try to fight the famine. I simply went on facing hardships. I felt ashamed to beg for myself. Why did I feel ashamed? For fear of losing reputation. There's nothing to be ashamed of feeling hungry. I shall beg for all those who are hungry. My hunger is included in everyone's hunger. It includes my family and also this little human creature I'm carrying."

A new faith surged in Panchu's mind: "Yes, I'll fight. I'll fight against Monai and Dayal, against all those who have appropriated for themselves grains that have brought about this famine."

A wave of mild anger stirred within. But soon a contrary feeling took possession of his mind: "It's not their fault. They perpetrate all those atrocities out of a lack of understanding that has persisted for ages. Don't I have that weakness too? Who doesn't have it? But how can we get over it? Would it be correct to surrender before brute force with which the ruling classes promote this foolishness? Would it not be a crime against truth? Indeed, it would be so. Our duty is to destroy the very roots of this injustice."

"Foodgrains are meant for man to eat. The value of foodgrains is not in terms of money, but in terms of the hunger of people it can satisfy. The selfishness of an individual cannot be allowed to ignore the hunger of society. He cannot be allowed to usurp the rights of man acquired from birth."

Panchu felt a fresh surge of energy. There was new hope and confidence. He resolved to himself: "We shall fight. We shall take over every godown where foodgrains are stocked. We shall live..."

At the same time, he realized that that would lead to more atrocities, and there would be hatred. But would there not be hatred even if there was no fight? It would only be conditional response and would cause self-torture. The result of that inhuman sacrifice at the altar of power was clear as daylight. Hatred on the one hand would take cover of selfishness. Truth would triumph over selfishness. But hatred would remain. The lure of triumph, as a reaction, would turn brutal. Revolution destroyed the brutal tendencies man has traditionally acquired since primordial times. That alone would bring dynamism in new life...

The child stirred in his arms, distracting Panchu's attention. He patted the child affectionately. "Our sacrifice, our hard work, our revolution will make the child's world fit for man to live, a world in which there will be no distinctions of rich and poor, nor of colour and religion, community and nationality. It will be one world— the Society of Man."

He thought: "But this dream must be turned into a reality. It is futile to stand at the crossroads of ideas and just be a witness to this sad spectacle of passivity. The ideals and principles that cannot be put into practice are false. Then what's to be done? What should I do?"

And then the ideas became clear to him one by one: "I must go home. I must save the life of this child. Selfless love and the sense of duty that I've glimpsed through this child have got to be translated into action—I must get food and I must protect my right to live. The class to which Dayal and Monai belong can no longer abridge that right. On what strength does this class tyrannize us? These Dayals and Monais entice some of our own people by baiting them through some share from their wealth. Chheda Singh, Dayal's armed men, the soldiers from the army—who are they?

They're our own people, part of the suffering millions. They cannot remain apart from us. Our organized power, our moral strength, our cry for justice won't keep them away from us for long. The hypnotic charm of the capitalists who occupy the seats of power cannot keep these people under their spell for long. People's power, people's revolution, will raze to the ground their bastions of selfishness. Then alone will this section of human society which is trying to frighten us with the help of our own power be crippled and be warned. Money is the only strength of these people. Once they're unable to buy us, they will realize their position. The aim of their hatred will be the same as ours—money and power!"

It was almost dawn. A red glow brightened the eastern sky. Panchu was walking homewards. The path of Panchu's duty was clear and definite...

Paresh had died during the night. Parvati Ma woke in the early hours of the morning and went up to call Panchu. She found somebody seated on the stairs with a bent head. It was dark and Parvati Ma could not see. She asked: "Who is there?"

"It's me!"

Mangala's voice had never sounded so grave. Parvati Ma was stunned: "You! Where's Panchu?"

Parvati Ma rushed forward. Mangala was on her feet. She desperately tried to keep her big eyes dry. There was dignity even in her anxiety. She said: "He went away without telling me!"

Mangala had come to that conclusion when Panchu did not return till late at night. She was still possessed by thoughts of Bakulphul. She was wondering about her mental state. Her brother-in-law had always been like that. What sins could Bakulphul have committed to deserve him? She had been a miserable woman all her life. Oh, God! How could any man assault a woman's modesty so brazenly? In her place, she wouldn't have got up alive...

Mangala's teeth clenched. The hair on her body stood on ends and a tremor passed through her body as tears filled her eyes. Suddenly she thought about Panchu—why had he not come back yet?

Mangala's heart sank. And after that she could not sit still. She came down the stairs. Parvati Ma's room was closed. Baba lay in his room. Panchu was nowhere to be seen. She looked at the door—it was open. Then she thought he may have gone in search of his brother. But was his brother in his senses at all? However brazen one may be, no sensible man would ever do such a thing.

c   He was insane. He had no control over himself. Suppose something untoward had happened to him?

Mangala sat near the door expecting Panchu to return. As the night advanced, she hardened her heart to prevent her tears. She sat on the stairs sulking: "Why did he go without telling me?"

When it got very late, she had a sudden suspicion in her mind: "He hasn't gone to look for his brother. He has gone away. He has left home and gone away forever. Now he won't come back. He has received a terrible shock. But why didn't he tell me before going? If he didn't want to keep me with him, he was free to do that. But at least he should have told me!"

But when Parvati Ma asked her about Panchu, she could not control herself. Much against her will, her voice choked and tears came. She said: "After his brother left, he has gone away somewhere..."

She could say nothing more. Parvati Ma stood in silence after listening to Mangala, still like stone. But once her tears started flowing, she could not stop them...

Suddenly the latch of the outside door rattled. Parvati Ma looked towards the door. Mangala leaped with great hope and quickly opened the door. Mangala and Parvati Ma froze with fear and stepped back. Shibu had entered the house with Nuruddin.

Mangala shrank behind the door. Shibu and Parvati Ma stared at each other. With a heavy voice Shibu told Nuruddin: "Come right in."

Parvati Ma stared at them as they went inside. Mangala stood terrified near the door.

Shibu went to the front room. Parvati Ma's room was right opposite. Shibu's wife sat there like a statue, the body of Paresh lying close to her. Dinu and Tulsi were sleeping nearby.

Shibu went to Parvati Ma's room. Tulsi sat up in fright. Shibu's wife raised her eyes at her husband. She was bereft of all emotions, all thoughts. When she saw Shibu, she was neither shocked nor terrified. She simply stared. "Get up!" ordered Shibu.

Shibu's wife remained silent, her eyes fixed on Shibu.

Parvati Ma came into the room. She asked Shibu sternly: "Why have you come here?"

Shibu gave no reply. He did not even glance at her. In a frenzy he dragged his wife by the hand and thundered: "Get up!"

While being dragged, Shibu's wife fell on the ground face downward.

Parvati Ma rushed forward to free her daughter-in-law. She turned to Shibu and said sharply: "Leave her! And get out of my house!"

She tried to push Shibu with both her hands. Shibu pushed back his mother with great force and warned her: "Get out of my way!"

Parvati Ma stumbled and was on the point of falling. Dinu lay where he was while Tulsi jumped up with a shriek and held Parvati Ma with both hands. Dinu was saved but Tulsi fell on the ground along with her mother.

Parvati Ma was in panic. She could not immediately get up. Shibu's wife continued to sit still and unmoved. Tulsi, who was crushed under Parvati Ma, struggled to get up. Even Shibu was nervous for a moment. By that time, Nuruddin had come up to the door of Parvati Ma's room. Seeing him at the door, Shibu's consciousness returned. Shaking his wife by her hand he thundered: "Get up, won't you?"

Shibu's wife glanced at him. Then she turned away her face and quietly got up.

Parvati Ma felt herself surrounded on all sides. She could not understand what was happening.

Shibu quickly dragged his wife out of the room.

"Now, give me rice!" Shibu demanded as he pushed his wife towards Nuruddin.

Parvati Ma no longer wondered about Shibu's intention. She had already suspected it when she saw Nuruddin. And now that suspicion was confirmed. The moment Shibu asked Nuruddin to give rice, she flew into rage. Tulsi still stood holding her. Releasing her hand from Tulsi's grip, Parvati Ma stepped forward. She shook with violent rage. She leaped and held Shibu's neck between her two hands: "I'll kill you! I won't spare your life!"

Shibu gasped for breath. Nuruddin rushed forward and freed Shibu from Parvati Ma's hands. Shibu panted and regaining his strength pounced on Parvati Ma: "Sali! You wanted to kill me, eh?"

Promptly Nuruddin held Shibu back. "What childishness is this! Here, take your rice. Eat, drink and enjoy! The lady too will go to the home where she'll eat, drink and enjoy! She'll get ornaments, clothes..."

"No!" Parvati Ma jumped forward and pushed down Tulsi and Shibu's wife. She said to Nuruddin: "Are there no daughters and daughters-in-law in your house? Go, take them to those blasted homes! Go away, go away! Get out!"

Parvati Ma shrieked so loud that her voice sounded hoarse.

Shibu dragged his wife and said: "She's my thing! I'll sell her!"

"No, no! Get out!" Parvati Ma panted as she protested. She was drifting into a swoon. She was on the point of collapse. One hand was on Tulsi's shoulders. She was struggling hard to gather her strength. Tulsi felt the pressure of her hand on her shoulder and she too, staggering, slumped.

Shibu's eyes were bloodshot. He said as he trembled with rage: I'll sell her. I'm hungry...yes, hungry! Give me rice, yes, rice!"

Shibu's wife stood like a stone statue. Tulsi still felt the weight of Parvati Ma's hand on her shoulder. Her face became red with rage. She was battling with herself in her heart.

Nuruddin untied the bundle. At the sight of rice, Shibu leaped with delight. Parvati Ma was still not in possession of herself. She was breathing very fast.

Nuruddin took out two handfuls of rice and kept it on the floor. Shibu was startled. "That's all!"

"What else? Do you think I'll fill your treasure-box. She's a mere frame of bones. But I can give you up to half a seer for this," said Nuruddin looking at Tulsi.

Tulsi was delighted and wanted to get up. But Parvati Ma pressed her down with both her hands, and giving a piteous look to Shibu, begged: "Don't take my life, son. Don't put me to shame, my son. I'm falling at your feet."

Shibu took no notice of his mother's tears. Since his wife had fetched so little rice, he trembled with rage and pounced upon her. "*Sali*! Your price is so low!"

Before he could take a step forward, Shibu felt a resounding slap on his face. Shibu was astounded at being slapped by his wife and trembled with rage. Nuruddin promptly came forward and standing before Shibu's wife held Shibu with both his hands, and said: "Now she belongs to me."

Feeling the grip of two strong hands, Shibu calmed down a bit. Nuruddin held Shibu's wife by her hand and led her away. Like a dumb animal, Shibu's wife went from one master to another.

Shibu's wife had not uttered a single word since last night's incident.

Paresh was dead. She had just briefly glanced at him and then looked away. She had spent the whole night sitting huddled up, holding her knees between her hands. She had spent the night just staring in one direction with her eyes wide open. She had paid no attention to anyone. Having been robbed of her honour, she had become blank emotionally. In her conscious mind there was only the feeling of hatred and all other feelings had merged in that feeling.

Now Shibu's wife was sold. She did not fear the women's home. Since her marriage she had nurtured only this feeling of hatred for Shibu. Shibu had always treated his wife just like a servant maid. Just as the dust gets shaken off the shoes but again sticks to the shoes, Shibu's wife had no other fate except to be at her husband's feet. Shibu's outrage provoked in Shibu's wife a constant hatred for her state of dependency. She was under constant fear of Shibu. She was now completely free after being sold in exchange for two handfuls of rice. Her slapping Shibu was a reaction only to that feeling. His wife, a woman worshipped in the Vedas and the Puranas, had become the most contemptuous slave of man and had got accustomed to daily onslaughts at her husband's hands. After living through the same routine, woman had lost interest in life. And then, new changes were coming, if only in the form of slavery. There was progress, though only for a brief period— woman had the illusion of movement through those changes and she had acquired a new strength. Through her husband, she rebelled against that fear and hatred and the excitement of revolt moved on to another state of stagnation.

Nuruddin and Shibu's wife had crossed the front room and had reached the door. Parvati Ma, with her crushing feeling of help-lessness, was pressing her arms tight around Tulsi.

Nuruddin signalled to Tulsi to go with him. It was a temptation.

Bakulphul's slapping Shibu, and her going away with Nurud-din and then Nuruddin's signal prompted Tulsi to stand up in revolt. In the midst of her tears, Parvati Ma had been humbly pleading her husband: "Are you listening to me? I've lost all my reputation. Your son has robbed me of my honour!"

And then...

"I'm going too!" Tulsi suddenly declared and with all her strength, extricated herself from her mother's grip and ran to Nuruddin.

Parvati Ma's lamentation suddenly stopped. She stared at Tulsi with disbelief. In an effort to reach Tulsi, Parvati Ma collapsed and lay lifeless.

Shibu, seated near that small heap of rice, was about to chuck the first mouthful. He looked at Tulsi with amazement.

Nuruddin stopped as he held the hand of Shibu's wife. With

a smile, he held out the other hand for Tulsi.

Shibu, abandoning eating the rice, sprang to his feet and rushed towards Nuruddin. Nuruddin was on his guard, ready for defence. Shibu came close and pleaded: "Nuruddin? Where's my rice in lieu of Tulsi?"

Nuruddin stiffened: "What rice, pray?"

Pointing his finger at Tulsi, Shibu pleaded for more rice.

Nuruddin advanced towards the door with two women. He said: "How can you have more rice? This one is going with me on her own."

Tulsi was going with Nuruddin with pleasure. She had heard about young women being taken to "destitute homes" where they got food and clothes and lived happily. That was something she had not got so far and of which she had been dreaming for years.

Nuruddin led her forward and led her away.

Shibu insisted like a crying child: "Give me my rice!"

While leaving, Nuruddin stopped for a moment and regarded Shibu from head to foot. Then he laughed: "I say, for whom are you picking up all that row, *sale*! If I give you a single blow, you'll be clean swept from where you're standing! Go and sit in your house—stupid idiot that you are!"

All the time, Mangala had been hiding on the stairs leading to her room. The moment Nuruddin came she had rushed upstairs and bolted the door from inside.

Mangala looked out from the window. Nuruddin was going with Bakulphul and Tulsi.

Mangala stood stunned and amazed.

Nuruddin went away with Shibu's wife and Tulsi. In the face of that humiliation at Nuruddin's hands, Shibu felt helpless and terribly embarrassed. His lips quivered and tears flowed. He continued to cry and eat the raw rice. He looked at Parvati Ma who lay crouched on the floor. He lifted her head. Her mouth was agape and eyes wide open. As a child, Shibu had found support and strength only in his mother. When he could not find any resting place outside, he would come to her. He had taken that support so much for granted that he had ceased caring for it. Now, finding his mother dead, he got into panic. Tears gushed from his eyes. He clung to the corpse of his mother. Then suddenly he laid the corpse on the floor and stared at her open mouth. He wiped his tears and leaping up, picked up all the rice in his hands. Shibu wanted to pacify his offended mother by putting that rice in her open mouth. But suddenly he realized that she was dead. Shibu's hand stopped midway. Like a lost child, he looked around with widened eyes. In the room lay Dinu and Paresh. Father's love surged through his tears. Shibu got up and went into the room. Paresh was dead. Dinu's breath was also very slow. He would be dead any moment. With tearful eyes, Shibu stared at him for a while. Then suddenly, he put a few grains of rice between the slightly parted lips of that child and stood up.

Then Shibu came and stood in front of Baba's room. Shibu looked at his father silently. Only a very little rice was left now. Lowering his hand, he started scattering that rice in front of Baba's room, his eyes fixed on Baba's face. And then he suddenly let out a terrible scream and ran from the house.

Mangala saw from the window Shibu running in a frenzy and screaming aloud. Tears came into Mangala's eyes. Shibu was her husband's brother, after all. While crying for Shibu, she was also crying for her own husband, who had left home.

But Mangala did not want to lose faith. She did not wish to do anything inauspicious by shedding tears. Some voice within her persistently assured her: "He will come. How can he live away from me?"

Mangala wiped her tears and came down.

Baba was walking through the front room with his both hands outstretched, as though groping for something.

Mangala came forward and held Baba's hands. Baba was taken aback. He recognized a feminine hand. "Mangala...!"

Ever since the day of marriage, Mangala had never talked to Baba. Today also she merely said: "Hun..." In spite of trying hard to restrain his emotions, Baba's voice choked. He said with a tearful voice: "Mangala! All will be well with the world so long as you are there!"

Mangala shed silent tears. Stroking Mangala's head Baba said: "No harm would come to you, dear child! He would surely come one day—he would surely come. It's that faith that gives me a feeling of deliverance."

Mangala promptly wound the end of her saree round her neck and touched Baba's feet. Her tears dropped on his feet. He said with a choking voice: "Don't be mad. Now get up. Take me to your Ma."

Mangala supported Baba and led him up to Parvati Ma's dead body. Mangala's heart was bursting with deep anguish. Baba sat down. Passing his hand over his wife's head, Baba sat in contemplation. Tears flowed from his blind eyes. Then in a sudden frenzy of emotion he started reciting in Sanskrit:

Who is your wife and who your son
This world is indeed very, very strange
To whom you belong and whence you come—
Think of that, oh brother,
Worship Govinda, worship Govinda, Gopala, Gopala!

As Baba recited these lines, Mangala felt her heart tearing with grief. Formerly, whenever Baba started his recitation, Mangala and Bakulphul would exchange smiling glances and Parvati Ma, after initial irritation, would ultimately go to Baba's room. That recitation had finally vindicated today the reality of life. His voice became hoarse, faint and then even the trembling of his lips stopped. Although Mangala had become hardened after seeing so many deaths, she felt scared. She would be left all alone in the world. Till Baba was there, she had felt secure. Mangala stared fixedly as Baba's body shook. Then his breathing slowed down and came at intervals. With each breath, Mangala felt it was the end and ultimately the end did come.

Mangala was left all alone. There were four corpses in the house. The house was empty.

She looked all around. Every brick looked like a corpse. She was not thinking about the past life in that house. She wanted to see the future. But she felt utterly helpless at the thought of her future. She felt suffocated.

Mangala found no inspiration from anywhere to live. Yet she did not want to die. Without seeing "him" at least once, she would find no peace even in death. She felt restless and impatient. How long would she have to wait? When would he come? She wanted to be alive when he came—no matter when. However, she had reached a point when she could hardly breathe. She had to struggle to continue breathing. Mangala thought about nothing. She felt nothing.

Then her body moved. She felt consciousness stir within her. Deep in her heart, she remembered his voice so dear to her. She became aware that it was a delusion, and that made her restless. But the voice was now clearer than before.

"Mangala! Mangala!"

Even though her eyes were open, the vision was blurred. The

figure that was dim at first slowly stood in clear focus. "He" was standing in front of her, a child crying in his arms. Tears of extreme happiness welled up in Mangala's eyes. With choked and trembling voice she said: "You've come!"

Panchu saw that Mangala's body was swaying again. He did not know what to do. He quickly put the child on Mangala's lap and sat down, supporting her.

Mangala struggled and was soon fully conscious. She held the child carefully and looked at him closely. Panchu said: "We have to save him, Mangala. I've brought him to you only to save his life."

Mangala hugged the child. Before asking any question about the child, she wanted to tell about what had happened in the house. With tears in her eyes, Mangala stared at the bodies of Baba and Parvati Ma.

Panchu had already taken note of everything as he entered the house. When he saw Mangala sitting immobile, unheeding, unhearing, he had felt scared. Panchu saw that her eyes were open and that she was alive. Then he shook Mangala and called out her name several times. Finally when Mangala awoke to consciousness, tears filled her eyes and she spoke, and Panchu heaved a sigh of relief. Once he put the child on Mangala's lap and she took charge of him, he felt confident and happy. With great patience he said in a calm voice: "Whatever was to happen, has happened. Now take care of this child. Save him. We two shall live only to save him."

In that atmosphere of disbelief, the assertion of faith in life gave the couple extraordinary courage and strength. Panchu felt within himself an ever triumphant, ever growing power. Creation broke through an atmosphere that would not have otherwise inspired any faith.

Panchu said: "Now I'll go and make all the arrangements. Saving the life of the child...yes, and we've also to repay in terms of life our debt to death. Then Panchu asked in a doubting tone: "I hope you aren't frightened?"

Mangala shook her head and reassured her husband: "No. I won't be frightened now." And then, with eyes full of affection, she stared at the child sleeping on her lap.